Eleanora's Diary

Eleanora's Diary

The Journals of a Canadian Pioneer Girl

Caroline Parry

Scholastic Canada Ltd.

Scholastic Canada Ltd.
123 Newkirk Road, Richmond Hill, Ontario, Canada L4C 3G5

Scholastic Inc.
555 Broadway, New York, NY 10012

Ashton Scholastic Limited
Private Bag 1, Penrose, Auckland, New Zealand

Ashton Scholastic Pty Limited
PO Box 579, Gosford, NSW 2250, Australia

Scholastic Publications Ltd.
Villiers House, Clarendon Avenue, Leamington Spa
Warwickshire CV32 5PR, UK

Design and Desktop Publishing: Andrea Casault

Cover photography: Susan Ashukian

Canadian Cataloguing in Publication Data

Parry, Caroline
    Eleanora's diary

ISBN 0-590-74096-2

1. Hallen, Eleanora. 1823-1846 — Juvenile literature
2. Frontier and pioneer life. — Ontario — Simcoe
(County) — Juvenile literature. 3. Pioneer
children — Ontario — Simcoe (County) — Biography
Juvenile literature. I. Title.

FC3095.S6Z49 1994   j971.3'1702'092   C93-094462-3
F1059.S6P3 1994

654321   Printed in Canada   45678/9

*For Camilla Gryski, whose friendship I treasure,
and whose repeatedly brilliant ideas helped Eleanora come to life!*

C. P.

Contents

A Note to the Reader

Journals written more than one hundred and fifty years ago can be very hard to read. To make it easier for you, some words and phrases in the diary passages have been taken out, added in or guessed at. We have tried as much as possible to show what has been done, using the following signals:

. . . means something has been left out;

[this] means something has been added in;

this means something has been guessed at.

Eleanora did not use very much punctuation. Commas, periods and quotation marks have been added where neccessary. But we have preserved Eleanora's own (parentheses) and <u>underlining</u>, and occasional ~~crossed-out words~~.

Eleanora was a creative — and inconsistent — speller. But before you dismiss her spelling as simply awful, you should know that in Eleanora's time, dictionaries weren't widely available, and spelling wasn't regularized the way it is today. Eleanora often spelled by sound, and some words show her accent! Often, she dropped the letter h (ave instead of have) or added it in (has instead of as).

Eleanora also used words in ways that may be unfamiliar to you. For instance, she used the word eat where we would use ate. (In fact, Eleanora pronounced it "et" and this was considered perfectly correct.) Strange usages like this, and some unfamiliar words, are explained in the glossary. What is not there we hope can be found in any dictionary.

Finally, the ⟡ symbol in a box or journal entry highlights something particularly . . . puzzling. We have offered an explanation where we could; sometimes, however, your guess may be as good as ours!

The Editor

Foreword and Acknowledgements

Creation seems to me to be a mixture of inspiration and hard work, and this book came into being with both. It also involved lots of good luck, many people's good will, several new friendships, and more of my time than I ever imagined (yes, and some procrastination, too!).

In June 1988, I was asked to write a book about Canadian pioneers and settlers. I was dismayed, as I knew no Canadian history to speak of (I grew up in Pennsylvania and studied United States History and Literature at university), but I dutifully set off to research the idea. I went to several libraries (favourite places for me), started reading, and talked to lots of people about the whole concept.

Very soon I could see that Canadian young people needed many more truly Canadian history books. I started thinking about a possible approach for mine: to find old journals and letters about real events and feelings, from which I could select the "best bits" and perhaps shape a text which would interest young readers. At that point, I assumed I was looking for material written by adults. I had no idea that children were keeping diaries in the nineteenth century.

However, one of my conversations led me to the Huronia Historical Resource Centre on the site of Sainte-Marie among the Hurons, near

Midland, Ontario. The archivist-librarian there wondered if I would be interested in an unpublished local girl's diary, and sent me a few photocopied pages of a typed transcript made a generation ago by family members. Not only was I interested, I was excited! Imagine, a real young person, whose actual words from long ago could still be read!

I then had to track down the girl's relatives, members of the present-day Hallen and Drinkwater families. This I did through the nearby Simcoe County Archives, and I got permission to first read over and then work on the families' ancestral papers. By January 1989, I was thoroughly involved, and later I even managed to visit the village in England where the diaries began. But the more I learned, the more there was to learn . . . and I grew so absorbed in the particular story of this one girl and her family that they took over, and I was no longer writing a general work of non-fiction. Slowly, the book you are holding in your hands right now evolved.

Creation is also full of surprises and problems. Along the way came missing diaries, found diaries, false transcripts, moving home (and office!) and a change of publisher. Sometimes I've been impatient or discouraged; usually I have truly savoured my work; and always I have been grateful for this friendship across time. Thank you, Eleanora!

And thank you to all the Hallen and Drinkwater family and extended family members through the years who preserved her journals, so that now we can all share them. Of those alive today, I would especially like to thank Norah Bastedo for her gracious hospitality and devotion to her heritage, Catherine Drinkwater for her enthusiasm and humour, David and Willi Bohme, Gretchen Bohme and Anne Orser. And thanks to Joyce Kirkland, of Cheltenham, England, who did invaluable work sorting and transcribing Hallen-Drinkwater family papers during the 1960s and '70s, as she researched her own Williams (Eleanora's mother was a Williams) family history.

In addition, I owe tremendous thanks to many people whose expertise is far greater than my own: Su Murdoch of the East Georgian Bay Historical Foundation; Joyce Lewis and the Ontario Historical Society; Dana Tenny and colleagues at the Osborne Collection of Early Children's Books, Toronto Public Libraries; Rosemary Vyvyan of the Historic Naval and Military Establishments at Penetanguishene, Ontario; Jamie Hunter of the Huronia Museum in Midland, Ontario; Professor Bruce Elliott of

Carleton University; and Jean Bruce of the Canadian Museum of Civilization in Ottawa. Each of them has helped Eleanora come alive in this book.

I am also grateful to Val Wyatt, Ricky Englander and Valerie Hussey of Kids Can Press, for the original idea and keen support (both moral and practical); Jim MacMillan of Mariposa In The Schools (MITS), who initially pointed me towards Sandra Saddy at the Huronia Historical Resource Centre, who, in turn, first showed me the diaries; her staff and Ruth Fowler, a valiant transcriber; Irma Stegner, a more recent valiant transcriber; Kim Walker, my student research assistant in 1989; Gail Cariou of Parks Canada; staff and students at St. Thomas Aquinas School, Toronto and at D. Roy Kennedy School, Ottawa (particularly Angela Borgina and Bonnie Mabee, their respective teacher-librarians); Russ and Win Hewetson and the Medonte Historical Society; Christina MacEwan and her daughter Rebecca Dainard, enthusiastic manuscript readers; Chester Gryski, Sally Beth MacLean, Lyn Sullivan, Lydia Bailey, Philip Martin and folk colleagues Shelley Posen, Vaughn Ward and Anne Lederman.

Invaluable grant support came through the Ontario Arts Council's Writers Reserve and Creative Artists in the Schools programs, and a Municipality of Metropolitan Toronto Incentives Grant, arranged by the director of the Inner City Angels, Joanna Black. Additional opportunities to workshop and perform Eleanora materials in many schools have come through MITS in Toronto, the Writers' Union of Canada and also Multicultural Arts for Schools and Community in Ottawa. The staff at the Ottawa Public Library Main Branch and the National Archives and National Library of Canada were all thorough and helpful in responding to my myriad requests for pictures and information.

In England I thank: Dorothy Yardley (who delights in life in the village of Cakebole, Worcestershire) for her stalwart long-distance assistance; my dear friend Roo Glazebrook (and her sister Sally Thomson) for getting me to Rushock not once, but twice, and for chasing down many loose ends; and Linda Fitzsimmons (with her daughter Megan) for being thoughtful manuscript readers as well as a constant cheering section.

My family gave me all kinds of help — plus a few "hurry-ups!" I salute Richard (the first young reader), Evalyn (another intrepid transcriber) and David (always a patient, sympathetic supporter and provider), with my deepest thanks for allowing Eleanora to intrude into our family life so thoroughly!

Finally, the staff at Scholastic — who all fell in love with Eleanora, too — have been wonderful to work with. Thanks to Diane Kerner for taking on this huge project with such delight! I am particularly grateful for the calm assistance and clear thinking of my editor, Laura Peetoom.

Part I

Eleanora Hallen. 1834
December 23.

Introducing Eleanora

*. . . In Which We Are Introduced to Our Main Character, and
Begin to Know Her, Her Family and Their Story.*

Do you keep a journal, or write a diary? I do, and it's very private!
Perhaps your diary is a record of where you go and what you see or do;
maybe you let other people read it, or maybe not. My journal is where
I write about whatever makes me glad or sad, bad-tempered or
understanding. It is my own, and I don't want anyone else to read it.
However, sometimes I wonder about what will happen to all my
thoughts after I die. Will they stay private? If someone chanced to
read my journal, say, 100 years from now, what would they think of it
— and of me?

Well, recently I made friends — I guess that's the best way to
describe it — with someone who kept her own journals over 150 years
ago. She started when she was ten and lived in England, continued
while emigrating to Canada with her family, and kept writing until
she was twenty-three. All in all, she's quite a character! Of course
she's dead now, and how she died is a sad story, but fortunately her
family saved her journals. Those old pages bring her alive: they are a
mixture of reports on what she and her family were doing, her feelings
about her world, poetry, drawings and just plain doodles.

**Northbrook in 1989,
home of Mrs. Norah Bastedo,
a great-grand-niece of Eleanora's.**

I learned about her diaries through an archivist acquaintance, and I first saw them at the historic family home — a big, central-Ontario farmhouse called Northbrook — where they were carefully stored in a white cardboard box. In addition, I explored an old wooden box of family papers, partially labelled and sorted. Family members through the decades had preserved all kinds of historic memorabilia, from mud bricks in the chimney to portraits of, and drawings by, my friend and her siblings. And, of course, boxes of letters and journals! Two women in particular worked hard on transcribing many of the journals and papers and for some years I have been furthering the work that they began. Today, I feel privileged to be able to tell this tale of Canadian settlers in the first half of the eighteen hundreds, a story which starts in England, with the diary of a little girl.

So, let me present my friend to you — or perhaps I'll let her speak for herself:

This is the journal of me
ELEANORA HALLEN
who was born at Rushock in the county of Worcester
January 19, 1823

April 1st   I began to keep a journal. I am ten years old. I made
Sarah and George, my brother and sister, also Elizabeth, a
cousin, April Fools; it kept me busy all morning. We expected
Miss Holmes our governess all morning, but as it rained she did
not come. I finished today the first drawing on my card.

Many many years have passed since that rainy April Fool's Day
when Eleanora began her journal. (You can think of her as living
around the same time as your great-great-great-great-grandmother!)
Don't you wonder why a girl of ten would happen to start a journal,
one spring morning? I do — but though this book will give you the
opportunity to learn many things about Eleanora, her family and life
five generations or so ago, we'll never know exactly why she started to
write on this day in this year.

Eleanora's journals are full of little unknowns to puzzle over, like
this one, but contain signposts to life in her time as well. You'll find
there are many pieces of the "Eleanora puzzle" that can be put
together to reveal what she and her world were like. And, sometimes,
even what Eleanora does *not* say will be revealing. For now, let's start
right here, with the information in this very first entry, for April 1st,
1833.

For instance, you have already learned she had at least two siblings
— a brother and a sister. Does it sound to you as if her cousin were
living with them as well? On to the next part of the picture: "Miss
Holmes our governess." You might know already that a governess is a
teacher; but you may not realize she is a special kind of private
teacher who works — and usually lives — in the home of the family
that employs her. (Perhaps she had been away to visit her own family
on this occasion.) So guess where Eleanora went to school? At home!
In fact, there was a room in her house that she refers to as the
"schoolroom."

Did you also notice that one of the things Eleanora did on that April
morning was drawing? She and her sisters and brothers — oh dear,
now I'm giving something away! — well, they loved to draw, and you'll
see lots of their work throughout this book.

Finally, did you think it strange when Eleanora noted that Miss

Holmes didn't come because it rained? When has the weather ever prevented you from travelling? Perhaps a blizzard or a hurricane would stop your car or plane, but not plain old rain, right?

If you know something about getting from place to place in the 1830s in the English countryside, you can figure out why rain could keep Miss Holmes away. Rural transportation was pretty limited in Eleanora's day. For most trips, people used their own feet — or an animal's — and for longer journeys, the main form of public transportation was a horse-drawn stagecoach. Country roads weren't paved, so mud, which lasts much longer than rain, was a continual problem.

The Industrial Revolution was bringing many changes to life in England and throughout the British Empire. The invention of macadam, a kind of pressed gravel, made it easier to pave all roads, not just the ones in the cities. And canals and then railways began to spread farther and farther through the countryside. But the roads around Rushock were still just dirt tracks. The Hallens walked or rode, using donkey or horse power, almost everywhere. Every time a message was sent, a visit was made or an errand was done, it took a great deal more arranging and effort than it takes you to

A man with a donkey, from an unsigned Hallen sketchbook dated 1833.

lift the phone, hop on a bus or into your family van, or even pedal off on your own bike. As you read her journals, if you wonder why Eleanora writes about coming and going so much, remember how much energy it took at that time!

Now suppose you assemble the puzzle pieces to be found in Eleanora's next journal entry. You may have to read between the lines sometimes. See what fits together, and try making a list of all the ideas that occur to you as you read:

April 2nd　This day in the evening as we were sitting by the window, we saw Miss Holmes coming up the hill. I finished today a woolen ball for a baby, I put it in my mother's drawer. My father shot at a magpie and broke its leg, he tried hard to shoot it again, but could not. In the evening my father and George, when we had had tea, went to Warsley to see my aunt and uncles; it was very fine, that's why my father went out.

Here are a few connecting pieces and some more gaps to puzzle over for the April 2nd entry: how does your list compare?

— they lived on top of a hill
— some relatives lived near enough to visit — did they walk?
— maybe there was a nearby village called Warsley
— Miss Holmes was a day and a half overdue — didn't it matter? Did she send a message to say she would be late, and if so, how?
— maybe Eleanora had a baby sister or brother
— did her father shoot with a gun, or something else? (He wasn't a very good shot!) Did he hunt or shoot game birds for food?
— why was the wool in the house? For fun, or some other reason? Did they have sheep?

Well, the puzzle is getting bigger, although so are the sections that fit together. However, we still need more "edge pieces," to define the Hallen picture — these will emerge as you read on. The very next day, for instance, Eleanora explains about all her siblings.

April 3rd　Today I made another wool ball for my brother Skeeler Williams; he is only six years old. I think here I had better put down what our family is first; there is:

Sarah, who is 15 years,
Mary, 14 years,
George, 12 years, and a bit,
Eleanora — that's me — ten years,
Edgar, 9 years,
Preston, 7 years and a half,
Skeeler Williams, six years,
Richard, three years,
Agnes, 2 years, and
Edith, 9 months, that makes ten of us.

Here's where you find out that she did have a baby sister. But that's not all — eighteen months later, in 1834, one more girl was born into the Hallen family, making a total of *eleven* children.

To go back to the wool ball I am making for Skeeler Williams, I did not tell him who it was for, but said I would make him one; when I had finished it he was standing beside me, I asked him if he thought it was a pretty one and he said 'yes!' so I gave it to him and he ran and showed it to my Father, Mother and sisters.

With so many brothers and sisters, would you need friends? Young Eleanora certainly doesn't mention any in her journals. Imagine finding all your friends just within your family, from among your brothers and sisters and cousins. And Eleanora's family members were not only her friends, but her classmates, too. Think of it!

April 4th   It was raining when I got up this morning, but it cleared up. I wrote my Aunt Helen and sealed up the letter. We think the pigeons have young ones for we heard them squeak. In the evening we had just finished school, when my Aunt Chellingworth came to fetch Elizabeth home, her brother John also came, he most generally is at school.

Well, there is one little question answered — cousin Elizabeth did live with the Hallens, at least on weekdays. Cousin John must have gone to a "real" school, since he didn't stay at Rushock to study with Miss Holmes. Two other cousins lived with the Hallens most of the time. One cousin, Herbert, was a favourite, and the other, named Bella, was not — she seemed to fight with everybody! These three cousins — Elizabeth, Herbert and Bella — are often arriving or departing in Eleanora's daily entries. So are many other relatives in her large extended family — or letters and parcels to and from them!

April 5th Good Friday   It was a very fine day, we had church in the morning. Richard went to church for the first time and he beaved [behaved] very well. After dinner we went a walk to pick violets, they were so lovely and the trees so new and green. . . . When we came home there was a parcel for me . . . a workbox from Aunt Helen. The baker boy brought some [hot] cross buns that my Grandmama had sent, we always get them from her every year, we sent some of our violets back to her.

In these last two entries you can see the names of two of Eleanora's many aunts (plus you already know she has more than one uncle, if you remember the entry for April 2nd). Actually, she seems to have had at least seven aunts and seven uncles! And that is not counting their husbands or wives, if they were married. In 1833, Eleanora also had three living grandparents and several great-aunts and -uncles, and they all lived fairly nearby. Unfortunately, girls of ten can't always explain how their families fit together very well — whether today or in the last century.

Do you see that you could go on piecing together the Hallen picture for a long time, just with these first few entries from Eleanora's journals to go on? She kept writing for thirteen years and filled many volumes, so there's a lot of material to think about. What's more, I discovered that transcripts of her diaries made during the 1950s, which I used initially, had been shortened or altered in many places. To understand the Hallen story fully, I returned to the originals — and this meant *more* material. Including it all would have made this book three times as long and difficult to read. So I focussed on one particular year, and chose passages from surrounding years that best reveal the character of my friend and best describe her life to modern readers.

Because several volumes of Eleanora's diaries appear to be missing, there are some gaps — even holes — in the whole picture. And because she seldom tells us much about the context for what she writes, even complete diaries leave us curious to know more. I have tried to fill in some of the holes by giving you extra information about the times Eleanora lived in; by quoting from the journals of other Hallen family members; and by including sketches and photographs. These additions appear in boxes throughout the book, to help you read between the lines.

And to help you get the "big picture," the next section is a kind of family portrait, describing Eleanora and her family at home in England: likes and dislikes, what they did during a day, family celebrations and the reasons Eleanora's parents may have had for deciding to emigrate. If you're a puzzler who likes to sort out all the pieces first, or if you're a reader who likes to follow the story from the start, read Part II next!

But if you prefer to start with the big events and puzzle out the rest later, you can skip ahead to Part III, 1835. Eleanora's three original 1835 journals are the only ones surviving today that cover a whole year. From 1833 through 1846, no other single year includes entries for every month.

How fortunate that 1835 *is* complete, because it was probably the most important year in Eleanora's life. This was the year the Hallens moved — the whole big family! Eleanora tells how a great sadness occurred in the spring; how the family crossed the Atlantic Ocean by sailing ship; how it took them about seven weeks to get to New York City; how they used various smaller boats and passenger wagons for different stages of their overland journey; how they stayed in upstate New York for almost four months before finally reaching their new home in late autumn. The entire trip took about six months, but packing up all their things beforehand and getting settled afterwards took several more months.

So you can see that 1835 must have been a busy year, full of changes. If you want to know how these changes affected their lives, turn to Part IV, which looks at the Hallens' first year in their new country. Starting with a long, cold winter, 1836 was a year of contrasts. Using your puzzling skills and sections of Eleanora's incomplete journals, in Part IV you'll discover what was different for the Hallens — and what stayed the same.

It's lucky for us that Eleanora did the kind of record-keeping she did. And, thanks to the generations following her that saved her journals, today we can share in her experience. Do you suppose her story is very different from an emigrant's story today? Will her thoughts seem strange to us? Just how much did life change for the Hallens when they moved to Canada? And what became of Eleanora? Read on . . .

Part II

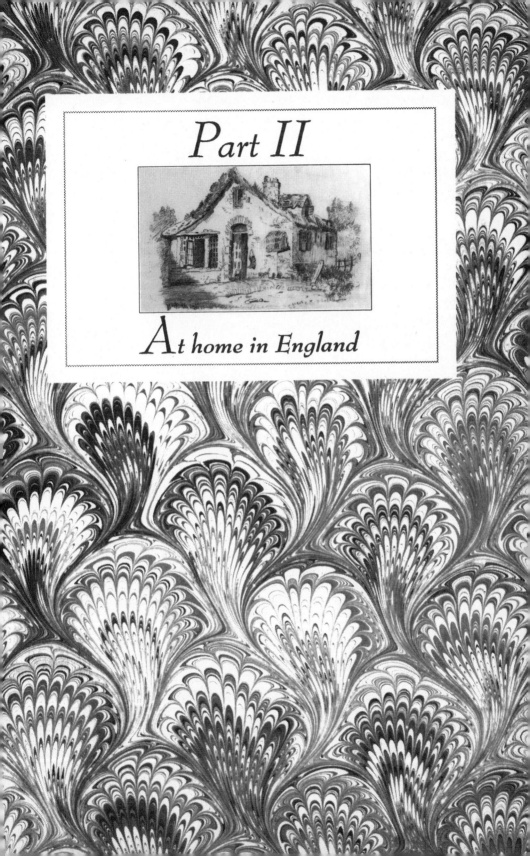

At home in England

. . . In Which We Learn More about Eleanora's Family; What She Looked Like, Thought about, and Did Most Days; and in Which We Consider Why the Hallens Emigrated.

What did Eleanora look like?

We know what Eleanora's parents looked like, but there are few pictures of our main character; which is surprising, for a family that loved to draw. There is the little drawing below that her sister Mary did in 1834, with others of the family; and Eleanora drew a set of tiny profiles of the whole family when they got to Canada. She never says what colour of hair or

Elizabeth Chillingworth
December 2. 1834

Preston Hallen
November 27. 1834

the little Grace.
1834

Eleanora Hallen. 1834
December 23.

Edgar Hallen
November 27.
1834

Richard Hallen. December 5. 1834

A family of the HALLENS MARCH 1836

eyes she had, but here's something interesting: in Eleanora's time, family members and very good friends might give each other small swatches of their hair as keepsakes. Mr. Hallen used to carry some from his children around with him. They have been carefully preserved, and they are all shades of mousy brown, a little darkened with age! Eleanora does say how tall she was around her eleventh birthday, however;

[Jan. 21, 1834]

My Father measured all of us; my Father was 5 ft. 9 in.
My Mother 5', aged 39 years.
George 4' 6", 13 1/2
Eleanora (myself) 4' 3", 11
Edgar 4' 2", 9
Preston 3' 8", 8
Skeeler 3' 5", 7
Richard 3' 4", 5
Agnes 2' 11", 3
Edith 2' 4", 1 1/2
We did not do Mary and Sarah.

As for the clothes Eleanora wore, she seldom mentions them. In the nineteenth century, of course, girls always wore dresses, done up with long rows of buttons down the back. Under their dresses they might wear several layers. One of the few things Eleanora does mention you may have heard of: "We made some bustles for ourselves." (Oct. 17, 1833) They often wore stays underneath, too, which had to be laced up before the dress could be buttoned.

[Dec. 7, 1833]   Bella would not let me do her things up and she broke her stay lace and burst her button holes, so she was to stay [with me] until she let me do it. At last she let me do it, the bad thing . . .

"Pride must be pinched"

This was long before zippers, let alone tee shirts! Girls did wear something like pants, a kind of underwear called drawers (you can tell this entry is taken from an untranscribed original, because of Eleanora's spelling!) :

[July 24, 1834]   After breakfast we went to try to gather mushrooms by the brook. . . it was very wet; I was obliged to change my shoes, stokings and drours drawers . . .

Eleanora sometimes reports on what visitors were wearing or what was in fashion, as you will see. And once her mother and sisters went to a wedding ball, so she describes what they wore:

[Nov. 13, 1833]   Sarah and Mary . . . are wearing book muslin frocks with white satin sashes and white kid gloves; my mother is wearing dark blue silk with broad sleeves and short satin ones under. She has a little cape with some brown fur on it; they all look very well.

Two kinds of bustles.

Above: a "morning dress." Right: sleeve details, by Eleanora.

This fashion plate is from an 1834 issue of The Ladies' Cabinet.
It's likely the Hallens read this fashion magazine because an 1843 issue survives in the family papers, sent by an English cousin.

The next year Eleanora wrote about some dressmakers coming to work at Rushock . . .

> [July 7 & 8, 1834]   . . . to make Sarah and Mary's muslin frocks . . . [which] are going to be made with sleeves full to the wrist, which is now the fashion. . . . Last yere . . . [bonnets] were very large and this yere very small. . . .

While the dressmakers sewed, Sarah read aloud to the group. Eleanora notes that she " . . . began to make . . . pinbefores," so that adds to our understanding of what she wore — big aprons over her frocks.

What did she like to do most?

Eleanora and her siblings loved to play tricks and games, put on disguises and fool people! She writes about those episodes with delight, even though she sometimes got into trouble, just as you might. One day . . .

> [May 7, 1833] Mary put on [Tom the servant's] coat and pretended to turn me out of the room; Tom went past the window and said, "What naughty girls."

They must have giggled, but they weren't punished that time. However, when "the rooms were being whitewashed, we had dinner under the chestnut tree and we were all very naughty so had our tea in our bedrooms." (June 7, 1833)

A code Mary Hallen invented. The top line is her "alph," the next two coded lines are Mary's sentence and the last two are Mr. Hallen's reply. Two clues: Mary has left two letters out of her alphabet, and the first word in the last line is spelled in an old-fashioned way.

**"My father told us owh to make
us look without heads: to put
our cloaks to the top."**
(Nov. 19, 1834)

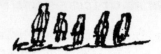

Another day they trick the governess:

[April 28, 1833]   We dressed up a figer [figure] and put it in
my cousin Elizabeth's bed and when Miss H came we asked her
to wake Elizabeth up . . . it was rather fine.

Then there was the day when she and George jumped out and
surprised some elderly neighbours:

[April 8, 1833]   My father taught us a new way to play with
some bowls; I beat 2 times. Mr. & Mrs. Thomas Lett came to tea,
has they were going home George and I hid at the end of the
garden and burst out at them. They did not seem to think it as
funny as we thought they would; George says they are quite old,
perhaps that's why.

And one black day Eleanora . . .

[May 10, 1834]   . . . put tar on [cousin] William's chair at dinner
table. When he moved to get up to get his handkerchief, we heard
a crack and he said he had sat on some tar and he was stuck to
the chair, but he at last managed to get up, but the chair was all
mashed, so he sat on another chair; when he came to get up he
stuck again. He could not go to church in the evening because
he might stick to the seat. We tried to get it off, but it was hard
work and then he was not clean. . . .

She never says if they were scolded or not!
    You'll be glad to know they didn't only play mean tricks. All the
Hallens liked to play games: chess, card games such as "Whist,"
hide-and-seek games like one the children called "I Spy." A favourite
game was a kind of tag called "Prison Bars" — she often mentions it,
and apparently the more who played, the merrier:

[June 12, 1833]   In the evening the Lewis [family], Mrs. & Miss
and all the little ones came; they stayed to tea. . . . While they
were here Miss Holmes played [the piano] and George and Sarah
sang, then we went out of doors and played Prison Bars, but
before we were done they had to leave.

But what about toys — didn't she like to play with them?

Of course the Hallen children liked toys! And mechanical toys — toys that "do" something — were as delightful then as they are nowadays: "Father came home in the evening; to our great joy, he had brought a little cannon for George which made a noise when you let it off." (Jan. 15, 1834)

Do you wonder why the cannon was for George in particular? Perhaps because he was the eldest son, a very important family position. Herbert was the first son in his family, too, and his father (a captain in the army) often gave him toys. Whenever Herbert's father came to visit at the Hallens, Eleanora wrote down what he brought his son: a knife, a ball, whips (with whistles in the handles), a top, a sword and a gun. Incidentally, the sword arrived on a Sunday, and the children had to wait until Monday to play with it.

Eleanora doesn't mention dolls very much. Perhaps the constant succession of new babies in the family was too much of the real thing! Once she does write about Elizabeth buying her a doll from a peddlar and her sisters making it clothes. And one lucky doll ". . . was christened, she had about 40 names," after they had been "playing at romping" with her uncle. (July 18, 1834)

One toy that the Hallens had was a very strange-sounding thing which they "looked in." The first time Eleanora spells this thing "cosemyrayma," the second time "cosmarrama." She probably means "cosmorama," an optical device like today's View Master, which gave a peep show of scenes from many parts of the world (or "cosmos").

A toyshop, c. 1836.

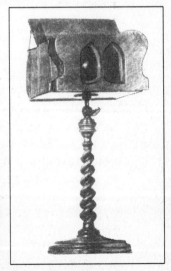

A cosmorama.

The children also liked making things out of natural materials they found around them, weaving hats from rushes and moulding bricks from clay. Their father often helped them, making things like windmills from paper, or a pit for them to work the clay.

> [Jan. 30, 1834]   George and I made 24 bricks today as we intend to build a house in the summer. The little pig [that they were nursing] died, poor dear. We danced a quadrille. My father made a mould for us and we made 100 bricks. . . .

What did Eleanora dislike the most?

Though Eleanora never says she out-and-out hates something, she does describe things she dislikes. For instance, "Miss Holmes tried to teach me some sewing. I didn't like it much; my finger is sore." (May 5, 1833) And if you were to count all the angry entries Eleanora writes about her, you'd have to conclude she almost hated her cousin Bella. Here are some other names for Bella, all from Eleanora's pen: "The great old Bella," "such a cat," "the old thing," "weak-minded," "silly thing." And even though Eleanora resolves that Bella ". . .was very naughty again, but I don't think it worth writing about . . ." (Sept. 11, 1834), she does, again and again!

Isabella Baker
December in
1834.

Bella, by Mary Hallen.

One other thing Eleanora seems to dislike, though she doesn't say such rude things about it, is going to church. "It is Sunday, so we all went to church, as usual we younger ones are all slightly glad when it's over." (June 16, 1833) Rain or shine, the church was part of their lives: "It is still raining, but we had to go to church; it was not so rainy in the evening, so we had to go again, most tiresome." (June 23, 1833) The Hallen children didn't go without protest, however, for later Eleanora says:

> [Dec. 17, 1833]   . . . we wrote a petition that we could stay at home at night, but my father would not let us, the congregation is so small as it is.

So, why did they go to church so much?

There are two answers to this. One is that 150 years ago, religion or church-going was very important, probably more so than for many people today. In a village like Rushock in the 1830s, everyone was

Christian and supposed to go to church. In turn, the church was supposed to take care of them all. Although there was no longer an actual law in England requiring people to attend church, there was still the expectation that "good people" went. So, almost all middle-class families were regular church-goers.

The Christian religion dominated people's thinking then, and everyone believed God was overseeing them and had a purpose in whatever happened. In this way, Christianity was very comforting. It helped people accept many bad or difficult situations — such as the frequent deaths you'll find in Eleanora's diaries — as being "God's will."

Although almost everyone in England was Christian, not everyone attended the same kind of church. They had freedom to choose their manner of worship. There were Roman Catholics and Protestants of many denominations, such as the Methodists, whose chapel Eleanora describes below:

[April 7, 1833]   After church we went a walk . . . and came to the Methodist chapel; it was like a little house by the side of the road; we stood by the window and listened, they first read a verse and then sang, not a bit the way my father takes the service in our church.

"Our church" for the Hallens was the Anglican church. This was (and still is) the official church of England. Anglican clergy christened, married and buried England's kings and queens, and presided over many grand state occasions. Most of England's middle class worshipped in an Anglican church.

So, the Hallens were more or less a typical English family of their time, place and class. They were Anglican, and their church gave them a framework for their beliefs and their behaviour. They were educated, if not wealthy; they said prayers together every day and went to church every Sunday — even though Eleanora and her siblings did not always like it! But reading this entry you may have guessed the second reason the Hallens went to church so often. Eleanora's father, the Reverend George Hallen, was a curate, a kind of Anglican clergyman. He planned and led the church services, wrote and delivered sermons, baptised babies, held weddings and funerals and visited all the members of his church in his parish.

Aside from scheduled church services, Mr. Hallen's job did not have regular, daily hours. His "office" was his study, which, just like the children's schoolroom, was in the big old house where the Hallens

Rushock Church at the turn of the century.

lived, across the lane from the church. So Eleanora's father was at
home a great deal. He taught some of the children's lessons and
helped them with many projects, such as binding their journals. But
he did have to make frequent housecalls to his parishioners — and
work weekends!

What did Eleanora's mother do?

In the nineteenth century — and often still today — a clergyman's
wife supported him in his work by entertaining callers, teaching
Sunday School, and so forth. There was little possibility that she
would have her own employment or separate interests, other than
drawing or sewing, playing the piano or gardening.

> [June 18, 1833]   We took Miss Parker who had come to call to
> see the [new] swing. She is one of those kind of callers who stay
> an over long time, and I think our Mother told us to take her
> outside so that she could lie down for a minute. So we took her
> round the garden for quite a good time. . . .

Besides seeing to visitors, we know what else Mrs. Hallen did —
lots of childbearing! If you look at the age spread of her children, you
can calculate that she was pregnant or nursing a baby for sixteen or

seventeen years. That was a huge amount of work in itself, though few thought it remarkable at the time. Mrs. Hallen got no pay and very little public recognition for what she did. Nor did she get much rest! With such a big family, there was a lot of supervising to be done; the children, cook, servants and governess all needed direction:

[Aug. 1, 1833]   We were sent down to play in the copse; we plaited some rushes. Our cook has left; it's hard to keep one with all us children. Miss Holmes is helping my Mother.

[Aug. 9, 1833]   After tea 9 of us children went to call on Mrs. Lett. . . . While we were there my Mother came. She seemed rather cross when she found so many of us there, but did not say anything until after we had left: which we did at 8 o'clock.

Although the family employed several helpers, Mrs. Hallen did some cooking and sewing and other light housekeeping duties regularly. The children helped, too — they ran errands, plucked duck feathers for a roast or removed seeds from raisins for a pudding. The older girls were learning to cook, and they all gardened. Probably their mother was the instructor.

There were always relatives to visit nearby, as well.

[June 28, 1833]   My mother and I went up to see Miss Eliza Williams [Mrs. Hallen's younger sister]. . . . I got wearied with listening to her description of what was the matter with her, but my Mother stayed to listen. . . .

Finally, Eleanora's mother also had the responsibility of seeing that her children behaved properly and that the family kept up good standards — some of which don't seem important or understandable today. Watch for entries where Eleanora writes about their attempts to be seen as correct, with suitable clothes or dishes or manners — here's an early one (from Mrs. Drinkwater's 1950s transcription. She generally corrected Eleanora's spelling, using "(sic)" in parts she felt had to be transcribed exactly. Sic is Latin for "so"; writers use it when quoting to say that an apparent mistake in the quoted material is not their fault):

[July 28, 1833]   It was very hot when we went to church so I lift[ed] off my tippet and bonnet and put them on the seat. My Mother looked rather cross but could not say anything as she was sitting in a different seat. After tea we all walked down to

the bottom of the lane, except Edith who cannot walk yet. . . .
[later the servant] Maria came to carry Agnes home. While we
were there, Mr. & Mrs. Bo passed; Mrs. Bo spoke, but Mr. Bo
gave his horse a good cut with the whip and they dashed past.
My Mother pretended to be talking to Agnes, but we all stood
and stared at them, the rood (sic) things.

What was a normal day like?

During September, 1833, Eleanora wrote a lot of entries in her journal
about what meals and lessons they had and when, so you don't have to
read between the lines to answer this question. You may conclude she
needed a few grammar lessons, however! Here's the daily pattern
Eleanora describes:

[Sept. 5, 1833] We always have breakfast at 8 o'clock, begin
school at 10 o'clock, went out at one, had dinner at 2 o'clock,
began school at 4 and went out at 6 and had tea. We had sums
and Latin in the morning and singing in the afternoon. . . .

[Sept. 6] We had Latin in the morning and music in the
evening. . . .

[Sept. 9] We had arithmetic in the morning and Latin in the
afternoon and practiced our music and drawing in the
evening. . . .

[Sept. 11] We had geogryfy [geography] and Latin this

Catullus was an ancient Roman
writer of love poetry, but he didn't
write this little verse! It consists of
Latin words put together in a way
that makes no sense — unless read
quickly and with combined
Latin/English pronunciation.
Here's a "translation":

Mollie's a beauty,
Isn't a cutie.
No lass so fine is;
Mollie divine is.
Oh maid our mistress
Hee[d] men of distress:
Can't you discover
Me as a lover?

morning. We ought to have had dancing today, but as Miss Holmes was not here, we did not.

That's as much information as Eleanora gives about weekdays until Miss Holmes departs and the whole pattern is disrupted. On Sundays they went to church — twice, of course — and during August they appear to have had at least a few weeks' holiday from lessons.

Whatever the day or the season, Eleanora frequently mentions relatives or neighbours coming to visit. But it seems as if the Hallens' daily activities were not so much interrupted as enlivened by callers. Overall, a normal day in the Hallen family was probably quite different from one in your family. After all, none of them had to leave home to get to work or to school by a certain time!

One thing that was typical of Eleanora's daily mealtimes might surprise you: the family did not usually all eat together at night. In fact, that was the pattern in most English families that had enough money to hire servants to cook and look after the children for them. Often, the older Hallen children ate dinner (their noontime meal) and drank evening tea with their parents, but they did not all have the evening meal they called supper. Sometimes, Eleanora writes that the older children stayed up for a late supper downstairs — which seems to be because there was extra food. For instance, in 1834 Eleanora records, "This is the first of September, when they begin to [shoot] partridges. We heard a great many guns fired." In a few days she says, "Sarah, Mary, Elizabeth and me stayed up supper; their were 4 partridges for supper; I had a little." (Sept. 6, 1834)

The children also got special treatment when there were guests:

[June 21, 1833] My Uncle and Aunt Thomas came. Sarah and Mary had dinner downstairs; George and I had to have ours in the schoolroom; George, Edgar and I went down for dessert. . . .

September 1 Monday

What did Eleanora think about things?

You have probably already noticed how frank Eleanora can be, at least on paper. Here is another example:

[Dec. 21, 1834] Bella great pig did not go home. She was very naughty because she [was] going home and she noows [knows] we like her going home. . . .

[Dec. 22] Bela is gone home. Hura, hura, huza, huza.

Also, she is often openly critical or sarcastic in her journal:

[May 28, 1833] We went to Mrs. Letts' to see her new house, but as far as I could see it was a very old one; the paper in the parlour looked worse than ours. I forgot to say we had mustles for tea, they may be nurishing, but I think they are unplesent.

Well, there's something else she disliked! Another day she writes, ". . .Tom painted the schoolroom yellow. I don't call it pretty, but some seem to admire it." (June 10, 1833) Or she moans:

[April 6, 1833] My Father, Sarah and Mary went to Warsley to dinner and tea. No one seemed to think of asking me to go, so Miss Holmes and I went a-walking. . . .

Whatever Eleanora's feelings about them, the Letts were generous. They often lent the Hallens their donkey for big family outings.

Too bad we don't know if Eleanora ever was allowed to say out loud the things she thought and wrote down privately.

Eleanora doesn't just complain, however. Sometimes she is philosophic: "It is a raining day, which I expect made the ducks glad more than us." (April 10, 1833) Or, "the poor old hen died this morning; perhaps it was just as well, she was suffering a lot." (Feb. 4, 1834)

And at other times she is a bit of a poet, for she had a sense of beauty as well as fun. "There are primroses and snowdrops out and the crocus are thick on the grass; they look so pretty, especially the yellow ones, like little fairies." (Jan. 14, 1834) And, "the sky looked like a beautiful dress I should like to have for best." (April 13, 1833) Besides having a poetic way of saying things, she also composed poems and silly verse, like this:

[May 12, 1834]

This is my journal and you can see
How very dear it is to me.
Sarah is very homely
And looks very comely
And feed the pigeons dear
While the other people lear.
Mary is very affected
And likes to be in bed
And then she is in her glory
And hates the things she did.
George thinks nothing is so sweet
As when he can get his horn
And then he will the things break
And tread on Mary's corn.
Edgar is always busy
And does his hair which is frizzy
Is very polite
And flies his kite

And of course Eleanora feels romantic and daydreams (or teases others) about who liked whom! Do you imagine she kept these thoughts to herself, or whispered about them with her sisters?

[April 30, 1833] ...We saw a tipsy man.... He staggered about so much I thought he would fall in the ditch; two gentlemen came up, one was rather an old one and the other rather young, they talked to the man until he was past us and then went on. Miss Holmes should take the old one and Sarah, the rather young one. ...

Did she ever get bored or sick or sad?

Yes, indeed! Eleanora was often sick, for several days at a time, though it is not always clear what illness she had. (Headaches, colds and "bilous attacks" are mentioned now and again, and once all the children got measles.) Things sound really boring when she was sick:

[July 11, 1833] In the morning I was ill, so went to bed. The hay is in. . . .

[July 12] I am still in bed.

[July 13] I am still in my bed; I got up but had to go back to bed.

[July 14] Am still here; am being quite ill.

[July 15] I got up. Mrs. Mince came. My mother has gone to Perry to a party, [and] she took Sarah and Mary, so Mrs. Mince did not stop.

In the nineteenth century, before people understood about germs and the importance of cleanliness to prevent the spread of disease, there was a lot of sickness. There were doctors, and different medicines and remedies, but these were often more hindrance than help. Just plain bed rest was one of the safest cures! But it wasn't always enough, and many deaths occurred that could be prevented today.

Most sick or dying people were at home, rather than in a hospital or nursing home where they couldn't be seen. And it was a large part of Mr. Hallen's work to visit the sick, bury the dead and comfort the bereaved. So, in an odd way, death was more a part of Eleanora's life than of yours or mine. In her journals, she often speaks of death quite matter-of-factly; of kittens being drowned, pets dying, boys struck by lightning; of graves being dug up or of neighbours' funerals. At one burial, she even comments, "the poor woman's husband looked as if he wished he hadn't come." (June 7, 1833) So it's not surprising what

Hallen
Hallen

mary

On a cuckoo

Beautious cuckoo on a po bush and gay
Are now as cold as cold as clay
But now you's gone we morn in vain
For that won't bring you back again

2

Ah cuckoo you are gone indeed
And we must follow you with speed
It makes me very malancholy
To think of little Nina's folly

3

She gave you wheat that made you die
And when you died it made her cry
We tolled the bell so solemly
For we shall never again see thee.

By myself
July 30. 1833.

27

happened when the Hallen children's pet cuckoo died:

> [June 26, 1833] Our bird was very ill, it would not even squeak. In the evening it seemed in great pane; we thought the cause was because I had given it some water. It soon died; we all cried a good deal, except Mary who did not want to. We tolled the bell and George opened it and found some cake and water not digested, so we know the poor dear had died of intergestion or do you spell it indegustton. We buried the bird between the rose bushes in our garden. We put a great many flowers by the grave and over it. We had a bell that tolled all the time we were doing the burying and after Skeeler tolled it nearly all dinner.

Not long after that small death of the cuckoo there was a more important one — grandmother Hallen died after a long illness. In her journal, Eleanora describes all the family visits to her Grandmother's deathbed and then the funeral. It's almost as if the Hallen children, in mourning their bird, were practising for what came later.

A cuckoo. Below: Grandmother Hallen, by the grown-up Preston; perhaps he copied it from another painting.

> [May 30, 1834] ... My father intends us to go to the church with the funeral. ... John [the servant] went down to Perry to ask them to lend some of their black things to us, as we had not time to get any. ...

> [May 31, 1834] In the morning we looked through the telescope to see if they were coming; after a great while I saw a person gallop through the turnpike gate, then ... a chariot came, then the hurse with 4 horses and plumes on their heads, then tow mourning coaches, so we got ready, every one of us except the baby and

went into a seat [at the church] so that all of us could see the coffin put in, the little ones stood in a row along the seat. . . . My Uncles staied till the vault was done up and the stone put on. After that we picked some flowers to put in a vause that my Aunt Hooman had sent to put over the vault. . . .

And after that, Eleanora doesn't record anything for a month. There are similar gaps in her journal at other times when the family is saddened by death.

Did the Hallens ever celebrate?

Yes! First of all, in such a big family there were lots of birthdays. But the Hallens didn't always celebrate them — in 1834, Eleanora and her family did not even remember her birthday until two days later, when she writes: "I found out my birthday was last Sunday; I am now 11 years old." (Jan. 21) Imagine forgetting your birthday! Presents don't get much mention, or birthday parties, but they did have music sometimes in the evenings, and the Hallens would have some special food.

[July 31, 1834]   . . . It is my Grandmama Perry's birthday. We drank her health with ginger wine. It was very nice; no one offered me any more.

[Aug. 14, 1834]   It is George's birthday. We always have plum py a frut pie and puding. . . . The piy was very heaped up.

Weddings were another time for special food: wedding cake and wine. It was the custom to pay social calls on newlyweds, to drink their health and eat a slice of cake. More than once, Eleanora notes that the children put pieces of "cake which had been passed through [the]. . . wedding ring . . . under ouher [our] pillow and then ouh [who] we dream of, we are to marry." (Oct. 3, 1834)

Of course they also celebrated the major Christian holidays, Christmas and Easter, and observed Good Friday. Then there were minor Christian holidays and New Year's Day — in 1834, Eleanora noted, "I ate one oyster for the very first time." But the Hallen children's favourite day was November 5 — Guy Fawkes, or Bonfire Night! For that special day gathering wood and making firecrackers began well ahead of time:

[Sept. 19, 1833] We went down to the copse to cut wood for the Fifth of November . . .

[Sept. 29] We axed all the wood to pieces and made a great pile of wood . . .

[Nov. 5] We had our bonfire; it was grand, also some fireworks that my Father had made, but they didn't go off as well as they should.

[Nov. 6] In the morning we lighted our bonfire again, what was left of it; it didn't burn much . . .

By the next year, Eleanora's father had improved his fireworks. The children helped, and they made a lot: Mr. Hallen made "3 dozen of crakers and 1 skib and a roman candle," (Oct. 16, 1834) and Eleanora and George made "a hundred and five [crackers]. The skibs were allso made; their are eighty six. My Father tried six; they were very nice onese." (Oct. 18)
Then the big day came:

[Nov. 5] It was raining when we got up, later it cleared. We put a pole with sticks around it and when it was dark we lighted it; we saw about 14 other fires, but it was the largest. A little boy from Mr. Lett's of The Court . . . was frightened at the crakers and serpents. . . . After we done we had some bread and cheuse [cheese]; it was about 10 o'clock. . . .

And after all that excitement, there was more! Little Grace, the eleventh Hallen child, was born during the night.
Another special time was the evening before All Hallows' Day, which is November 1st. Eleanora calls it "Halloweve," but we know it as Halloween. The Hallen children celebrated with a treat you would not find in a modern-day trick-or-treat bag:

[Oct. 27, 1834] Sarah, Mary and Eliza made some All Hallow Eve Day cakes; I elped to put the names of us on them, every person in the house had their names marked on.

[Nov. 1] In the morning we had the all *hollo* cakes. They were very nice. . . .

The family also played Halloween games. They didn't just try to bob for apples, they aimed to predict their future marriage partners by roasting pairs of nuts or with special dishes of water, "one with clear water in, one with dirty and the third with none":

> [Oct. 31, 1834] . . . [we] blindfolded my uncle and led him to it . . . he was to be maried to a young lady because he put his hand in the clean.

But what about Christmas?

Eleanora doesn't write about Christmas with the excitement many children feel today. In Eleanora's time, Christmas meant lots of visiting and special foods, but there weren't many presents. Christmas trees and Santa Claus were not yet part of English holiday practices.

Here's what Eleanora says about their Christmas celebrations in 1833, two years before they emigrated:

> [Dec. 24] We dressed the windows with ivy and holly.

> [Dec. 25] The Sunday School children came and had dinner of roast beef and mince pie; I went to church, there were 22 people stayed for the Sacrament, it was thought a great number. George and Edgar did not have any pie as they are not quite well.

> [Dec. 26] I forgot to say we had all our books yesterday in the evening. Mr. Mole came to tea, in the evening Sarah sang "So, So, Sir!" We stayed up to supper.

> [Dec. 27] My Mother made me a black apron; Sarah, Mary and I had a pork pie between us.

> [Dec. 28] We went down to see our Grandmama; she has been in bed since last Christmas, over a year; she gave us six shillings between us all. . . .

Pork pies were a traditional Christmas food, which the Hallen children liked to eat but didn't like to prepare. Eleanora's Christmas entries in 1834 give us an idea of the process.

[Dec. 16] . . . My Mother pershauded [persuaded] my Aunt to stay till Saturday because she can help to make pork pies. We are all very glad.

[Dec. 17] The pig was cilled early in the morning. It is a very large one. My Aunt came up with a rod and wipped Sarah and Elizabeth because they were not up. . . .

[Dec. 18] The pig was cut up, we will make pork pys tomorrow.

That very large pig resulted in 33 pies the next day! In 1834, the Hallens' Christmas dinner was similar to that of the year before. Eleanora says, "we got up early and sang a carroll, we had 10 carrol singers." And in 1835 the Hallens had their first Christmas in Canada!

So why did the Hallens emigrate?

Things were sometimes dull, but unless you hate going to church, their life at Rushock sounds pleasant enough, don't you think? Still, the Hallen family left it all behind them. The reason they went to Canada is not to be found in Eleanora's journals, but there are two pieces of evidence in her father's writing. (That's right, her father kept journals, too, as did her siblings.)

First of all, Mr. Hallen took his job as curate very seriously. So, you can understand that he worried when the villagers didn't come to church. Because the congregation at Rushock church was small, the rector, Mr. Thomas Morgan, lived and worked mainly in another nearby village, and delegated his work at Rushock to Mr. Hallen. This meant the Hallen family could live in the rectory, their large but quite run-down house across the lane from the church and called, like the church and the village, "Rushock."

In the 1830s, Mr. Hallen was probably glad to have a job that came with a rent-free home big enough for his whole family. Don't forget, that family included three cousins, a governess and a number of servants, as well as pigeons, pets and other assorted livestock — the cats and kittens, dogs and donkey that Eleanora wrote about. So daily life at Rushock must have been quite crowded and zooey!

Even with free rent, Reverend Hallen apparently did not earn enough money to support his household, for in his own journal, in February 1835, he says that he turned down a dinner invitation because he did "not like to be pitied [for] having resided 22 years on a curacy of £.90 pr.anm. with a family of eleven children." This means he was paid 90 English pounds per year (anm. is short for annum, which means year in Latin) for being the curate at Rushock. It's hard to say exactly what that sum would be worth today, but clearly it was not enough! (Incidentally, we can guess that the Hallens may have earned some welcome extra income from their boarding cousins.)

In another journal entry, Mr. Hallen speaks of "a despair of providing in your native land for . . . beloved ones." During this period of history, thousands of British families were choosing to emigrate to the "new world" in North America. It was a logical choice, considering how hard it was for the parents of large families to give much financial help to their grown-up children. In Canada, land was cheap and there were supposed to be many opportunities to succeed. And a large family would be an asset, not a burden.

> Of all the crops a man can raise
> Or stock that he employs,
> None yields such profit and such praise
> As a crop of Girls and Boys.
>
> *Anonymous*
>
> A large family is in England another term for a large share of poverty — in America the birth of children is hailed as in the patriarchal ages — they are towers of strength. They assist in the agricultural and other duties when young, and when arrived at manhood, the parents feel no solicitude respecting their settlement.
>
> *Observations on Emigration to British America and the U.S.*, Holditch, 1818.

How did they get the money to go?

Of course the Hallens needed money to travel all the way to Canada and relocate there, and they would not travel in steerage class like the poorest emigrants. The family was used to the comforts of their rectory and middle-class way of life. But cabin-class tickets for the ocean voyage were not cheap — and the Hallens needed lots of them!

Eleanora never says much about the family's financial situation, so the picture here is a bit unclear. It is possible that the funds for their huge trip came from Mr. Hallen's parents, who moved out of their big house, Warsley, into a smaller home called Wassall Cottage during January 1834. This move seems puzzling because Grandmama Hallen was very ill at the time. (She died in May.) Moving itself would be hard on a sick old woman, let alone the fact that she was much farther away from her son, who used to visit her almost daily. But maybe the

£ = pound(s)   s = shilling(s)   d = pence

£1 = 20s
1 guinea = 21s   **1s = 12d**

Just what would "£.90 p.anm." buy?

Of course prices differ from city to countryside, and in different
regions, but here are some figures to compare, from a
Manchester Guardian of 1834:

— "keyed organ suitable for a small church," 90 guineas
(£94,10s);

— "handsome horse, six years old . . . , lowest price, 30
guineas" (a third of Mr. Hallen's salary; no wonder the
Hallens only had a donkey!

— a year at a boarding school in Cheshire, 24 guineas
p.anm., extra for children older than ten, or for French
or Greek lessons.

That last figure isn't very different from the governess' salary
of £30 *p.anm.* paid to the heroine of the book *Jane Eyre*,
published in 1848.

A "respectable" funeral — such as the one for Grandmama
Hallen — was a huge expense: in the 1840s, at least, they cost
anything from £40 to £65 for an adult, £20 for a child. On a
much smaller scale, what were daily living expenses? Well, for
example, 7d could buy you:

— a copy of the *Guardian* (all paper goods were very
expensive) ;

— a pound of beef or more than half a pound of butter in
the Bolton market, near Manchester;

— almost a ton of medium grade coal;

— over half a yard (500 cm) of strong black calico, suitable
for children's pinafores.

To wash one of those pinafores, a laundress would charge 1/2d;
for drawers, 1d, and from 4d to 6d for a dress. This information
is all found in the *Workwoman's Guide*, 1838. The *Guide* also
gives the price of a four-poster bed: starting at £2,10s, perhaps
that cost is the reason the Hallens appear to have taken their
beds with them when they emigrated (see Nov.12, 1835).

Again from the *Guardian*, 1834, with 7s you could buy:
- a wagonload of potatoes;
- 20 stone (280 lbs or a little over 127 kg) of wheat flour (enough to keep you in bread for about nine months, at a pound a day);
- or, about three times that amount of oatmeal.

Aboard ship in 1835, Mr. Hallen remarks that the Captain had bought oatmeal for 18d per stone (in Liverpool, only to sell it at the vastly inflated price of half-a-crown (2s, 6d) per stone to the passengers — a captive market once they were at sea.

In Canada, just what is worth how much gets very confusing. There, coins and bills from England, the United States, France and other countries were mixed. As a British sojourner wrote in 1829, "Money matters are of a perplexing nature . . ." (John McTaggart, *Three Years in Canada*).

The costs shown in the tables were compiled by the Rev. Thomas Radcliff in 1833, as an appendix to his book *Authentic Letters from Upper Canada*.

How to arrive at Upper Canada, by New York, and at what cost.

	Steerage.			Cabin.		
From Bristol to New York, -	£5	10	0	£25	0	0
— Liverpool ditto, - -	5	0	0	30	0	0
— Dublin, ditto, - -	4	10	0			
— Cork, ditto, - -	4	10	0	20	0	0
From Limerick, to New York -	£4	10	0			
— Sligo, ditto, - -						
— Londonderry, ditto, - -						
— Belfast, ditto, - -						
— Greenock, dittto, - -	5	10	0	25	0	0
— New York to Albany, - -	0	6	9			
— Albany to Buffalo Point, by Canal Boat, - - -	2	0	0			
— Buffalo Point to any part of the Canadian side, provisions included	0	18	0			

The Rates by Quebec.

	Steerage.			Cabin.		
From Bristol to Quebec. -	£4	10	0	£15	0	0
— Liverpool, to ditto, - -	4	0	0	15	0	0
— Dublin, to ditto, - -	1	10	0	12	0	0
— Cork, to ditto, - -	2	10	0	12	0	0
— New Ross and Waterford, to do.	2	0	0	10	10	0
— Limerick, to ditto. - - £2 to	2	10	0	12	0	0
— Sligo, to ditto, - -	2	10	0	12	0	0
— Londonderry, to ditto, - -	1	10	0	12	0	0
— Belfast, to ditto -	1	10	0	10	10	0
— Greenock, to ditto, - -	3	10	0	15	0	0

Total cost from Liverpool to a settlement in Upper Canada, with comfortable accommodation for nine persons, being at the rate of £15 per each individual. - 135 0 0

Total cost including the above, and also, purchase of 200 acres, clearing 10. Building Frame-house and Offices—some Furniture, Seed, Implements, Tools and some stock. - 421 17 4

Total Expenditure of settling in the Bush 178 0 0

Total Expenditure of settling on a Farm with 10 acres cleared and House &c. built. - 207 0 0

Rushock today. The house has had a facelift since 1835, but the chestnut trees still bloom by the gate.

grandparents' move was a way to get enough cash to finance the ocean voyage and cost of settling Mr. Hallen, his wife and eleven children in a new country. Perhaps all Eleanora's aunts and uncles had decided that this was the thing to do. Still, there is no proof for this idea — it's only an educated guess.

In any case, within two months of the grandmother's death, Eleanora casually notes that her "father is going to Liverpool tomorrow by the coach." She doesn't say why, but you may know that Liverpool was one of the major seaports for emigrant ships to North America at that time. A month or so later she mentions their plans to go to Canada: put this together and you will see that Mr. Hallen must have booked their passage on a ship across the Atlantic. The fact that he got very sick when he returned from his trip might also mean that he was feeling awfully worried about making the big move with that big family.

Whatever the reasons for the move, and however Mr. and Mrs. Hallen managed it, we are ready to begin Eleanora's own account of the voyage to Canada and the first year of their new life. Now that you've had some practice at it, don't forget as you read to watch for, and put together, the pieces and see what kind of picture emerges. Eleanora, you may tell your own story from here. . . .

Part III

*E*leanora's diary

This is the front of one of Eleanora's 1835 journals. It is the third volume for that year, begun in August. Puzzlers will probably guess that the Hallens had a dog named Caesar!

🧩 *"C.PENNY" is the name of the printer of the copybooks that the Hallens used for their journal-keeping. Charles Penny was a "Wholesale Stationer and Sealing Wax Manufacturer" in Cheapside, London, 1826–36. Envelopes were not yet invented — people folded their letters and pressed a blob of special wax down to keep the folded parts together. So sealing wax was an important enough item to be half of Charles Penny's business name!*

Woodblock illustrations like these were becoming more and more common in the 1800s, thanks to the radical new printing methods of a man named Thomas Bewick. Before Bewick, engravings were done on copper plates, which lost detail as they wore down with use. Bewick was a wood engraver who favoured the hardest parts of the hardest woods. His special techniques made it possible to produce pictures in finer detail than ever before. He not only revolutionized book illustration, but is also credited with popularizing vignettes of everyday life and collections of pictures of birds and animals, first published around the turn of the century. Bewick died in 1828, having established wood engraving as an art form in England; it continued as the primary means of book and periodical illustration until about 1880, when photo-engraving began.

Jan 1st Thursday For some years we have always paid my Grandmama and Aunts who live at Perry a visit this time of the year, although on Christmas Day we never leave home. Sarah, Mary, George and I are now staying at the former place. This morning Sarah and Mary drove over to Rushock in my Aunt Ellen's pony gig, but returned to dinner. My Aunt Chellingworth and my cousin Elizabeth came to dinner and afterward John C-th came. After tea played at cards, commerce being our favourite game. Had oysters for supper; they were all much amused at my eating, or rather swallowing, 15 of them, as I had hardly tasted them before.

A playing card, by Eleanora Hallen.

Jan 2nd Fri My Father came over to breakfast. It was a delightfully frosty morning; we afterwards walked with my Father to Kidderminster; before we left My Aunt Hellen gave us each some money to make any little purchase. . . . [We] called at Mill Street on my cousins; my Father stayed to dine there. They begged very much for Sarah and Mary to stay, but they could not. We all dined at Torton.

> *"Commerce" is an ancestor of today's poker, and it was popular throughout Europe in the nineteenth century. Up to twelve people could play, trading cards and bluffing one another, trying to win the "pot" by collecting the highest valued combination of three cards. Once you felt you had the best hand of cards, you hurried to knock on the table. Then everyone had to show their hands.*

Jan 3/4th We walked up to Torton with my Aunt Anne to see if my Father was there. He came in soon after we did and walked back with us. On Sunday they all went to church at Hartlebury, excepting me, who am not well.

> *Not being well prevented Eleanora from accompanying Sarah, Mary and George on a farewell visit to the village of Martin Hussingtree, where several Hallen great-uncles and -aunts lived. From there, they made an excursion to the cathedral (or capital) city of the county, Worcester. We know the trip was exciting because Eleanora included some of Sarah's journal with her own when she copied it out in 1845. In fact, all the entries here, from Jan. 1, 1835, through Mar. 2, are from Eleanora's grown-up copy, with Sarah's bits removed.*

Jan 6th Tues   Much better today. My father came to see me. He said he would come for me tomorrow. I read a great deal. Lucky the dog came up into my room.

Jan 7th Wednesday   . . . My father came for me with the donkey on which I returned home. My Aunt Anne and Grandmama . . . wrapped me up well, it being a frosty morning. When we arrived we went into the study and afterwards I lay down on the sofa by the schoolroom fire.

Jan 8th Thur   I got up to breakfast. Edgar and Preston walked to Perry. They brought a note from my Aunt Hellen saying my Aunt C-th had returned from Martin and has her gig was going for Elizabeth the next day the man would call for me. I was much delighted.

Sarah's day sounds much more interesting!

[Jan. 8] At 10 o'clock my little Aunt Mary, Mary, Elizabeth and I set off to Worcester in my Uncle James' carriage. We went to the Crown Inn where a room had been ordered for us that we may see the members chaired. My Uncles, George, and the two Miss Johnstones came in. It is the first time we have seen the youngest, Jesica. I liked what I saw of her very much. We had a great deal of conversation. She was 15 last October. We saw Bailey the Tory member chaired. My Uncles are all Tories. It was a very gay scene. We afterwards went to Lendal's where my Aunt Mary bought us each a small rosewood work box, lined with blue silk, scissors & thimble. My Great An M had asked her to do so. We also went to a bookseller's and I bought a book "The Mutiny of the Bounty" without hardly looking at it. My Uncle James has not been to Worcester as he does not trouble himself about elections but my U George is very violent.

Jan 10th Saturday   My Father and I set out to Martin about 10 o'clock. They were all glad to see us. My Uncles were all out. . . . George had bought a mask at Worcester. Sarah said she put it on one day and got behind one of the curtains and jumped out on my Uncle George who laughed very much. She then went behind again and only let the mask be seen. My Uncle James coming in and thinking it was only a mask, put the candle he had in his hand under the nose and was rather surprised to see it quickly draw back. Not being well I was to have my dinner when they had their lunch, but my Great Aunt would make me come into dinner. We played at cards. My Aunt Mary won the pool which she gave me. I sleep with my little Aunt Mary.

Jan 11th Sun   I did not go to church although it is very near. . . . It is

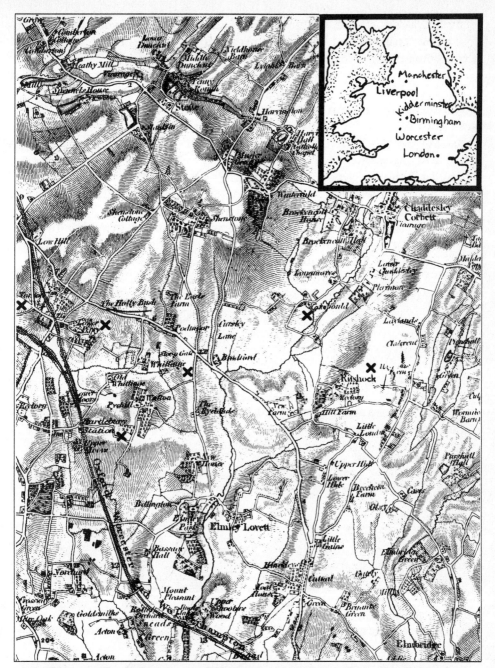

Inset: England. The Hallens' part of Worcestershire, shown above, lies between Kidderminster and Birmingham. Places Eleanora mentions are marked with an X. This ordinance survey map was originally published in 1831.

Rushock is slightly to the right of centre; above and to the left lies Cakebole (called "Cakebould"). Perry, Whitlenge and Hartlebury (Station) are on the left, with Torton on the edge of the map, along the Oxford–Worcester road. Chaddesley (Corbett) is above and to the right of Rushock; Martin is father south, off the map.

my Uncle George['s] church; it is very small, covered with ivy and looks very pretty from the house.

MARTIN HUSSINGTREE CHURCH

Jan 12th Mon   My Aunt Mary and Uncle Thomas gave us each some money. We were all very very sorry to leave. We have been so happy at Martin. My Uncle James is our great favourite. He is the youngest of my Great Uncles; he was a surgeon in the — regiment and was in the East Indies 20 years. He has now been in England about the same time. My Uncle George is the eldest; he is a clergyman. My Uncle Thomas is no profession but lives with them. My little Aunt M returned with us. The little ones were very glad to see us. My Aunt stayed all night. . . . We shall leave Rushock the 10th of March and shall go to Perry until we leave for Canada.

Eleanora's cousin, Mrs. Elizabeth Watkins, probably painted this picture of members of the Williams (Mrs. Hallen's) family assembled in the drawing room at Martin Hussingtree. It was done around 1825 — perhaps that's why there are no children.

Jan 13th Tues   . . . I read one of John's J. books that she lent us through. We 4 eldest stayed up until the servants were all gone to bed.

Jan 15 Thur   . . . My Father had gone to Wassal from where he is going with my Grandpapa and Uncle Simon to Stourport to vote for Winnington.

O f all the birds that e-ver I see, the Owl is the fair-est
For all the day long she sits in a tree, and when the night co-mes

in her degree,
away flies she. Te whit, to whom drinks thou, this song is

well sung. I make you a vow, and he is a knave that drink-eth now. Nose,

nose nose, nose and who gave thee that jo-lly red nose? Cinnamon & ginger,

Nutmegs and cloves, and that gave me my jo-lly red nose. Nose, nose:

A little coloured sketch by Mary of a "jolly red nose" suggests that the song Eleanora refers to as "Of all the Brave Birds" is this one, a three-part "Freemasons" song, published in 1609 by Thomas Ravenscroft, in a collection with other part songs and rounds. "Cinnamon and ginger, nutmegs and cloves" are what go into hot, mulled (alcoholic) cider. It's no wonder all the adults laughed — young Sarah was singing a drinking song!

Jan 16th Fri   After tea my Father returned. Mr Hooper who is going to marry Miss Harward of Hartlebury will very likely live here after we have left.

Jan 17th Sat   Snow on the ground. We heard Miss Eliza Newy died this morning at three o'clock. She was in a consumption. She was 18 years old, a daughter of one of my Father's parishioners. We went into the church to put flowers into the vase above my Grandmama's vault. We have done so ever since she died last summer, as we intend doing it until a tablet is put up.

Jan 18th   All of us went to church excepting who[ever] was not well. There was snow on the ground.

Jan 19th Mon   My mother and Sarah to Kidderminster; there was snow on the ground and frost. It is my birthday. . . . Before they came home Mr. and Mrs. John Lett [called]. . . . I was quite surprised to hear how fluently Mary kept up the conversation. We made the little man rather angry by telling him that Winnington had won as he is not for him. . . . My Mother had bought about 150 yards of calico besides other things to be made up before we leave. About 8 o'clock the little couple departed Mrs L being very anxious that her <u>Johnny</u> should be well wrapped up. Sarah says Mrs. Watkings has given my Aunt Helen all Sir W. Scott's novels which must be delightful. Sarah . . . sang "Of all the Brave Birds" which caused much laughter.

> *More on Sir W. Scott after Feb. 12th! Eleanora and her siblings were teasing the Letts; Winnington lost by seven votes to the Tory (Conservative) candidate. To vote at this time, you had to own property; and to own property, you had to be male and over twenty-one. And to hold public office, you had to be a member of the Church of England.*

Jan 21st Wed   I am busy sewing making myself nightgowns, the first I have attempted. My Mother cut them out; Sarah read aloud. Poor E. Newy was buried today. . . . The baby is very fat, she takes a great deal of notice.

Jan 22nd Thur   My Father came home. . . . My Uncle George had given my father three very large folio books on Divinity and my Uncle Jone on medicine. Sarah and Elizabeth very bad coughs.

Jan 23rd Fri   S and E still not well the latter lay down on the sofa all day. We do not have school very regularly as we are so unsettled and have a good deal of sowing to do previous to leaving for Canada. My

THE

C A N A D A S,

AS THEY AT PRESENT COMMEND THEMSELVES
TO THE ENTERPRIZE OF

EMIGRANTS, COLONISTS,

AND

CAPITALISTS.

COMPREHENDING A

𝕍ariety of 𝕋opographical 𝕉eports

CONCERNING THE QUALITY OF THE LAND, ETC., IN DIFFERENT
DISTRICTS; AND THE FULLEST GENERAL INFORMATION:

COMPILED AND CONDENSED

FROM ORIGINAL DOCUMENTS FURNISHED BY

JOHN GALT, Esq.

Late of the Canada Company, and now of the British American Land Association,

AND OTHER AUTHENTIC SOURCES,

By ANDREW PICKEN.

WITH A MAP.

LONDON:—1832.
PUBLISHED BY EFFINGHAM WILSON,
ROYAL EXCHANGE.

A typical early nineteenth-century book "on America."
What a flowery title! But it is not unusual. During the first half of the nineteenth century, while the tide of British emigration was at its height, there was a flood of books published like this one. Some were about the United States, some about Upper or Lower Canada; all of them contrasted conditions on both sides of the Atlantic and tried to attract and give useful advice to would-be travellers and emigrants. It is interesting that many families who decided to emigrate were reading families, like the Hallens.

Father . . . called on Bishop *Carr*. His son who is in the army had not
long arrived from Quebec. [Father] saw a small bark canoe that
[Carr's son] had brought with him. He lent my father a book on
America. George is a very bad one for telling us news for we once said
to him "now newspaper tell us the news" and I suppose that must be it.

Jan 27th Tues   We are going to give my Aunt Mary at Perry our
oldest pair of pigeons which are great favourites. Their names are
Tom White and Speckled Cooe. The others we give to Lizy [Elizabeth
C.]. After dinner my Uncle Washington came; he is a clergiman; he
had letters from [his children] my two cousins Anne and Mary. Sarah
again dressed up and amused my Uncle a great deal as she talked at a
tremendous rate and sang.

Jan 28th Wed   Sarah did a *drawing* for my cousin Anne. . . . The
clergyman from Chaddesly (a parish adjoining) called to ask my father
to go to a funeral tomorrow evening. I was *taken* ill this evening with
one of my old bilious attacks. Sarah and Mary wrote to my cousins.

[Sarah's journal, Jan. 29, 1835]
My Father and Uncle Washington dined at Perry from whence my
Father went to Chaddesly. I suppose we shall never see my uncle again
without we return to England.

*Sarah sounds sad, thinking about their coming departure. Do you suppose all the
Hallen children were talking about this kind of "last visit," or was Sarah more aware
because she was the eldest? The only similar comment Eleanora makes is in her entry
for Mar. 20th.*

Jan 31st Sat   As usual Sarah and Mary put more
flowers in the vase in the church. Only Sarah went
to church on Sunday. Little Edith often asks when
she will go to church. She says "me go to Perry and
not see Rushock again then go sea."

Feb 2nd Mon   George went over to the Court to ask if it would be
convenient for us to go to tea; as it was, my Mother, we four eldest and
Elizabeth went. When we got there, Mrs. Lett (who has not long been
married) said that as there was a little girl (Miss Row) coming, she
wished Agnes had come. Sarah therefore went for her; she was

delighted to come. They went into another room to play but as Agnes did not want to play at cards with her, George and I did.

Current photo of The Court

🧩 *Look, it's only a farmhouse! Today this farm is called "Rushock Court" and no longer belongs to the Lett family. There are many gravestones in the churchyard, however, with the Lett name on them.*

Feb 3rd Tues   A dull morning. . . . Sarah did a few latin exercises. I wish we could go on with ours, but my Father is too much engaged. . . . My Uncle William (who is a clergiman) came in the evening. He is a great favourite with us all as he lets us play and talk nonsense to him; we always look forward to his coming. Sarah of course dressed up in the mask and came in, which caused much merriment.

Feb 4th Wed   . . . Mrs. and Miss Harward and Mr. Hooper called; they — the former — know my Father and Mother very well. They came to look at the house, as when the latter are married, they are going to live here. We were delighted to see a fly drive up to the door out of which stepped Mr. *Peashell* [Peshall]. It is a very long time since he was here; he had used to come often and as he used to play with us and teach us various tricks we all liked him. He is much stouter than he used to be. He was very amusing at dinner time describing a kind of pudding which made us all laugh as he seemed to know so well how to make one. After dinner I dressed up the cat in the babies cloaths and took it into the room for him to see. . . .

🧩 *Did the children think it was funny that a man could cook a pudding? Or did they laugh because his stoutness showed he made them quite often?*

After the children had had their tea, Sarah dressed herself in the mask & coat &c and Skeeler, Richard, Herbert and Agnes were called down to see a gentleman. They all made her very polite bows and curtsys. She began to talk on politics to my Uncle and pretended to get very angry and at last ended with a pretended fight. All the children looked frightened, but seeing us laugh, it reassured them; but when she set about my Father, Richard could not refrain but began crying,

47

in which he was nearly joined by the others. She then told them all to stand up and make their bows and curtsies directly or that he would bite them. This threat had immediate effect, all of them getting up to do so in a great hurry, Richard in his fright making a curtsey. It seemed to be a great relief when she took her leave as they had no idea who she was.

Richard was about five years old at this time, and undoubtably wearing pants. But, up to now, he had been wearing dresses, as all children under five, boys and girls alike, did in this period. Perhaps Richard would have learned to curtsey before he learned to bow, so Eleanora might mean that he was so frightened he regressed. (By the way, wearing skirts probably lessened the consequences of "accidents" during toilet-training years, and that was important in the days before automatic washers!)

A boy and his baby sister, from a painting, c. 1830.

To Make an Apple Pudding

Take twelve large Pipins, pare them, and take out the Cores, put them into a Sauce-pan, with four or five Spoonfuls of Water, boil them till they are soft and thick; then beat them well, stir in a quarter of a Pound of Butter, a Pound of loaf-sugar, the juice of three lemons, the Peel of two Lemons cut thin, and beat fine in a Mortar, the Yolks of 8 Eggs beat; mix well together, bake it in a slack Oven, when it is near done, throw over a little fine Sugar. You may bake it in Puff-paste, as you do the other puddings.

Hannah Glasse, *The Art of Cookery.*

*Recipes from **The Art of Cookery**, originally published in the eighteenth century, were widely used in other books in the nineteenth, though generally credited to "Anonymous." We would call that plagiarism today!*

Mors Janua Vitae
Entrance to the vault of
George Hallen Esquire
M D C C C X X X V

Feb 10th Tue   In the morning we did not tell little Herbert that his Papa [had arrived the night before], but sent him into his room, pretending we wanted a book. He was delighted to see him. My Aunt Ellen has lent us "The *Monastry*" which is delightful. . . . After dark, my Uncle put on his regimentals. It was very kind of him as we had often asked him to bring them; he looked very handsome in them. As Sarah knew he would be much anoyed for anyone to see him in them excepting his own family, she put on the mask and a coat and came in. It startled him at first, thinking it was a person named Blake whom he did not particularly like.

Walter Scott was aptly named, as he was born in Edinburgh, Scotland, and deeply loved the Scottish "Border Country." He was an early nineteenth-century writer who collected old ballads, composed poems such as "The Lady of the Lake" and wrote over thirty novels. Titles which the Hallens read include Kenilworth, Old Mortality, The Fortunes of Nigel, The Monastery *and its sequel,* The Abbot. He also wrote plays, which were not as successful, and was a partner in a bookselling business which went bankrupt; he was knighted in 1820 and died in 1832, having honoured all his debts.

Scott's historical novels were a new and exciting mix of invention and reality — fictitious people and real events of the past — and readers loved them. Tourists started visiting Scotland just because of Sir Walter Scott's work! His books were so popular that in Britain the Waverley railway station and the "Heart of Midlothian" football team were named after them. And the Hallens, in 1840s' Penetanguishene, Upper Canada, had a sailboat named "The Black Dwarf," presumably after Scott's novel of the same name.

Feb 11th Wed   My Father and my Uncle walked down to look at my Father's nursery at Whitlenck [Whitlenge]. Elizabeth C read "The Monastery" aloud to us as we worked. . . . My Uncle Hooman he brought a note from my Aunt asking us to pay them a visit. My Father read "The Monastery" to us; very interesting. Instead of going to bed, we only put our night gowns over our frocks and then went down into the schoolroom to see how we should look dancing a quadrille. My Father came in and told us to go to bed.

Feb 12th Thur   In the morning pretty little Edith came trotting into the room and said, "Ah Mama, ah Uncle Herbert"; she always says it. My Uncle recommended my Mother to put some Lunar Caustic on a place that has been on her cheek some time. She was much pleased to hear there was something to cure her. . . . My Uncle H went into the church before he left. We all wished my Uncle Herbert goodbye. I suppose it is the last time we shall see him in England; he was always a very great favourite with all of us, playing with us when children &c. We four eldest and Elizabeth went to tea at Mrs. Jackson's; we took the pony and donkey to take it in turns to ride. Sarah and I rode home by moonlight, very delightful.

In Eleanora's time, not only doctors, but also clergymen and ships' captains, kept medicine chests like this one in case someone in their care needed medical attention. Standard remedies were Jalap, a tan-coloured powder made from the sweet potato-like root of the Mexican jalap plant; Calomel, a white, tasteless mineral salt; Senna, the dried leaves of a cassia plant, to be brewed as tea; and Tartar Emetic, a kind of "antimony," or metallic powder. In later journal entries, you will see these names. Nineteenth-century "cures" were generally one of two kinds: those that "drew" sickness out of the body through the skin (leeches and blisters: see Feb. 25th and Aug. 30th) and those that flushed it out ("emetics" and "purgatives"). Tartar Emetic caused the patient to vomit; Calomel, Jalap and Senna tea (all "purgatives") caused frequent visits to the toilet — for one reason or another! "Lunar Caustic," incidentally, is silver nitrate. Unlike many nineteenth-century remedies, it is still used today for much the same purpose, to help heal minor cuts.

Feb 13th Fri   . . . Mrs. G. Watkings (who we all like very much) came in her gig, a man driving her. She asked my Father, Mother and some of us to come to . . . [visit] when we are staying at Perry. . . . The man came with the tablet, but did not put it up as my Father was not at home. We were just going to bed when my Father and my Uncle Thomas Hallen arrived. Maria put a pan of coals into a bed where little Herbert was asleep, not seing anyone was in; it hurt the poor boy a great deal on his ancles. He at first screamed . . . but he soon was quieted, as my Father showed him a number of playthings his Papa had sent him from Kidderminster, whilst he tyed up his feet in cotton wool.

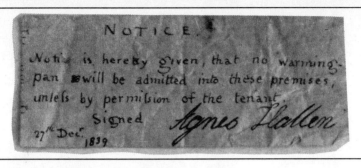

In the days before central heating, bedrooms in winter were cold and damp. A warming pan filled with hot coals made the sheets nice and toasty! And in the days before electricity, if you were a servant going around after dark to warm the beds you might not see someone already tucked up in one.

Feb 14th Sat   Herbert lay in bed all day. My Father has had some blocks of wood brought, that George may try if he can chop, against he goes to Canada. We were surprised to see my cousin William Hallen come in before tea as my Father had not told us he was coming. . . .

Feb 15th Sun   Edith went to church for the first time in the evening. She behaved very well and was very much pleased. She looked very pretty in her little blue silk bonnet. She has had a cough most of the winter and looks very delicate. The baby Grace is very fat.

Feb 16 Mon   . . . The man put up the tablet; it is on the North side of the wall within the communion rails.

Feb 17th Tues   My Uncle William came; we went into the church with him. He was much pleased with the tablet. We took away the vase of flowers.

Feb 18th Wed   . . . We have no school now as Miss Holmes has left and my Father is too busy, but Sarah sometimes attends to her Latin. A carpenter is making some large boxes for the books as my Father as a great many. At dinner time some of us were rather rude as Sarah tryed to persuade Mary to throw a drop of water at my Uncle. Mary having dared Lizzy to do it, she did so when he was looking away. My Father was very angry. . . .

Feb 19th Thur   Saw some lashes of lightning last night. A rainy day. . . . To our joy my Uncle William came into the schoolroom where he stayed about 2 hours and we had a great deal of fun playing at Blind Man's Buff, in which game we ripped my Uncle's sleeve up to the top.

"The Young Folks",
by Ralph Caldecott.

Everybody knows how to play this old game, but did you know that 150 years ago it might also have been called "Hoodman Blind," "Bellie-Mantie," "Bellie-Blind," "Biggly" or "Blind-boc"? One way to start playing was with a chant like this:

Group:	How many horses have you in your father's stable?
"Blind man":	Three — black, white and grey.
Group:	*(someone spins that player around three times)* Turn about and turn about and catch whom you may!

By the way, "buff" is just a short form of "buffeted," so the name of the game means knocked or hit with a blow of the hand.

Feb 20th Fri　My Uncle and Father went into the church to see the man finish putting up the side pieces of carved stone to the tablet. When we were sitting round the fire after tea, John came to the door to say that the man had fallen into the pool at the bottom of the yard. Fortunately it was not deep and he was only wet through.

Feb 21st Sat　My Mother and Mary rode down to Perry on the pony and donkey, from whence they will go to Kidderminster in the gig to make purchases. Directly after dinner, Sarah and George set off to walk to Perry as they will ride back on the pony and donkey. My Aunt Helen was not well. They all came home together; the pony had leaped over the hedge and down the bank about 12 feet but was not hurt. They had bought several dresses &c &c. Just as we were preparing to go to bed, we heard Little Edith scream violently. I ran up directly; she was turning her head from one side to the other and saying, "Look nasty thing" and then screaming. We called my Father and Mother. The former carried her into the study where she got better and quieter. My Mother had a little bedstead moved by the side of hers for little Edith to sleep on.

Feb 22nd Sun　Edith better but stayed in bed until after breakfast. Whenever Maria her nurse comes into the room she says, "Ria me not well."

We all went to church in the morning excepting my Mother who stayed with Edith. It rained so heavily in the evening that my Father did not have service. My Father read to us.

Feb 23rd Mon   Edith about the same; she coughed a great deal in the night. My Mother thinks it is the Hooping cough; we have all had it excepting the baby. Miss Randal the dressmaker came to begin our dresses. Elzabeth began reading "The Abbot" aloud to us.

Feb 24th Tues   A beautiful morning. Edith about the same; her breath is short and pulse fast. My Mother is afraid she has inflamation on her lungs. She was put in a warm bath and went to bed. . . .

Feb 25th   My Father sent for Mr. Watson the medical man: he says Edith has inflamation on her lungs and ordered five leeches to be put on her chest and 20 drops of antimonial wine. I went up to her and sat with her while the leeches were on; she was very good, only crying a very little and saying, "Oh dear dear." A boy came with a note from my Uncle William to my Father: the catalogue of the furniture was taken today at Wassal as my Grandpapa is going to have a sale as he intends travelling. The linen and plate will not be sold.

> *Have you ever seen a leech jar? Doctors, barbers, apothecaries — and sometimes blacksmiths! — kept leeches on hand in ceramic jars with holey lids. Leeches, bloodsucking relatives of the worm, were placed on the skin of a sick person to draw out "bad blood." Like emetics and purgatives, this practice was thought to drain sickness out of the body. Often, patients were simply further weakened by loss of blood. People did not yet understand that the white cells in their blood actively fight infection.*

Feb 26th Thurs   Poor Edith no better. Mr. Watson came; he put a blister on and he wants to know this evening how she is, as he will send some medicine. . . . My Father sat up with Edith.

Feb 27th Fri   Edith about the same. Mr. Watson came; says she is a little better and will get well if she does not renew it. Agnes and the baby are not well. He thinks it is a kind of influenza and that very likely all have it. Elizabeth C was therefore sent home in the evening. The children were put in warm baths. John was sent to Mill Street with a note to tell my cousin Hallens not to come on Sunday.

Feb 28th Sat   My Mother sat up with Edith last night until 5 o'clock, when Mary got up. She is no worse. Mr. W says Grace has inflammation on her lungs. In the evening, Edgar, Preston, Skeeler, Herbert and Richard all took an emetic (as Mr. W had ordered it as they had coughs) as they were not ill otherwise. They all seemed very much amused and had a row of wash hand basins put on a form [bench] all standing by them laughing. I went in to look at them for a short time, but before I went out the tone was very much changed; some saying, "Oh dear, I am so sick" &c &c. They afterwards were all put in a warm bath and went to bed. At night they all had a dose of calomile and jalap which was not much admired. Sarah sat up half the night with little Edith. She seems about the same and asks my Mother to nurse her by the fire.

March 1st Sun   Sarah sat up until three o'clock when my Father got up. The five invalids having senna tea administered in the morning stayed in bed all day, having rice and bread pudding for dinner. Only George went to church. Edith is a little better. She eat a little. She says, "Me go to church when Mama goes." She is a great favourite with us all. My Father read two letters he had received from persons he had written to in America; one was from a Mr. Parry living at a village called Sandy Hill on the Hudson. He gave a very favourable account of the place as being suited for us to stay at whilst my Father goes on to Canada to fix on some land.

> *He was no relation to me, the author! Parry is a Welsh name, as common as Smith in that part of Britain.*

March 2nd Mon   Mary sat up half the night with Edith. I then got up, but as I had a cough, Sarah got up a little after 4 o'clock. I read when she *was* asleep, out of "Kenilworth." We think she is a little better this morning.

Grace is still ill, but the other children almost well. About 5 o'clock this evening Mr. *Watson* came; he says poor Edith cannot remain long in the state she is in. In the evening dear Edith started very much in her sleep; and as Sarah who was sat by her felt her hands were cold, my Mother got her out of bed and nursed her by the fire, which she seemed to like. Before she was put in bed again *her* bed was moved near the fire *place*, but although warmed flannel was put to her feet, she did not seem to get warm. When the others went to tea, I remained with her, sitting close by the side of her bed; she started every now and then very much, and said, "Oh dea dea", as if she was not so well: I therefore went to the head of the stairs and called my Mother who came directly and thinking she did not seem so well I called my Father. They thought she could not live till morning. Sarah,

Mary, George, Edgar and I therefore remained in the room: sitting round her little bed. My Father and Mother on each side her pillow. She went to sleep for a short time; when she was awake she would ask for mink (milk) which she drank. She still continued cold, so that we had a screen drawn round. She seemed to have a difficulty in breathing. She first looked up at my Father and then at my Mother, after which she closed her eyes and appeared to be dozing, breathing quite comfortably. She was quite sensible to the last; after once more opening her eyes, she again seemed to doze, from which she never awoke: her breath stopping so quietly that we hardly perceived it. We were all very very sorry particular-

[*March 3rd Tues*   Our baby Grace] she does not suck, hardly at all. My Mother sent to ask my Aunt Chillingworth to come here.
    Little Edith will be buried tonight. We asked iff we might carry her [coffin]; my Father said we might iff itt was not too heavy. . . . We carried it, all the little ones folowed; the six eldest carried itt. Their was 7 candles in the church. Only John [the servant] and John Jakson and my uncle were their. Their were cross peices of iron on the top of my Grndmama's coffin [in the vault]. . . . John Jakson carried [Edith's] coffin in is harms into the vault; John received it.
    John Jakson tolled the bell for an hour after; my uncle stayed in the church till it had done. When we came home, my Aunt had just arrived; she thinks the baby very ill. Mary slept in a little bed in the room so that if my Aunt wanted anything Mary would tell my Mother.

March 7 Saturday   . . . The mason closed the vault in the church. . . .

March 8 Sunday   The buns came which my mother had sent for to give the Sunday [school] children and servants. We went to church and my father preached; my mother did not go. . . . The baby is very ill indeed. We have put the little vase with flowers in it over the vault; . . . snowdrops and a few primroses and others; their are not many flowers out.

March 9 Monday   Grace is better. . . .

March 10 Tuesday   The baby is about the same. Mr. Watson came; he says she is better. She is very pale and her eies look very blue.

March 11 Wenesday   The baby seems a little better. I sleep in the same room. She opens her hies better. The screen is put all round [her to protect her from drafts]. She is in the cradle, she seems to like it better.

Eleanora's adult, copied journal ends with the Mar. 2nd entry. What a sense of incompleteness lingers after her broken entry about Edith's death. Her final words stop in the middle of the very sentence — in fact the very word! — that might have revealed more of her thoughts about her little sister dying right there in front of them all. Mr. Hallen expressed his sadness very clearly, in his journal, a couple of weeks later, as you will see.

Another English girl, Emily Shore, whose diary was published in 1969, expresses something else. Emily was close to Eleanora's age, also the daughter of a clergyman, and kept a journal from July 1831, when she was eleven and a half, until her death in July 1839. Around 1836, Emily saw the corpse of a young girl and wrote: "The deadly pale of the countenance, the whiteness of the lips, and the unmoving look gives a dead body a very ghastly appearance." Later, when she learned that she had consumption and would soon die, Emily said, "I prayed earnestly for submission to the Divine will, and that I might be prepared for death . . ." So we can guess that Eleanora felt a mixture of Emily's horror, the sort of acceptance she notes here, Mr. Hallen's tearful sadness and his Christian hope. (For a peculiar footnote to Edith's burial, see Part IV.)

Beloved as little Edith was, her death would not have been unusual in the 1830s. At that time in England, for every 1000 babies born, 151 died in their first year alone. Many children suffered and died from food-related problems. Bacteria in milk and parasites in meat were the cause of many illnesses, but often the problem was simply lack of food. Children's chances did not improve significantly until this century, when childbirth became safer, childhood diseases began to be controlled, and more was understood about hygiene and nutrition.

Hearse and mourning coaches, W. F. Freelove., 1873.

Unlike Grandmama Hallen's funeral and the one pictured above, Edith's funeral was very plain; her sisters and brothers carried the coffin, and there was no procession.

March 12 Thursday   A man from Martin came, he brought a parcell with a dozen shirts in. A cart came for the calf, the poor thing was put in it and ran about and was obliged to be tyed. We all went to the nursery window to look out.

March 13 Friday   Att six o'clock we got up, because Herbert must go. . . . Agnes cryed because he went. . . . We are all very sorry to part with the dear little fellow, he is so good.

> *Eleanora's spelling needed practice, and "who" was a common mistake, as this example from an 1834 volume shows! If you think her spelling overall has deteriorated suddenly, you're only partly right — after Mar. 2nd what you see are her original words, not what she copied out — and probably corrected — as an adult.*

March 14 Saturday   The baby is better. . . . It looked so different with the long table [gone], but their was <u>one</u> less at the table that sat by me.

March 15 Sunday   The baby . . . laughed for the first time since her illness. We went to church morning and evening. There was a pretty good number of people their. . . . The vase is still their.

> *Mrs. Drinkwater includes a sentence in her transcription which explains this entry more fully. After Eleanora mentions the good number of people, Mrs. Drinkwater gives: "It was my father's last Sunday." (For more information about Mrs. Drinkwater, turn to the Appendix.) And the Rushock parish register (the record-book of the history of the parish) had this to say about Reverend Hallen:*
>
> All the Parishioners deeply regretted his departure & lamented that he was driven to seek in a foreign land that remuneration for his services which he so well merited, but which his faithful labours have failed to procure for him in this. He left this country followed by the tears of the greater part of his parishioners & the unfeigned regrets of all, & without leaving a single enemy, for all who knew him respected him.

March 16 Monday   Mr. Watson said that . . . [baby Grace] must go down to Perry with my Mother, the sooner the better. My Mother does not want to go at this time, their is such a deal to be done, but my Father thinks itt will be better. . . .

> Eleanora's father was already keeping his journal for this momentous year, though he didn't yet have much time to make entries. On Mar. 14th, he explains the Latin inscription on the wall tablet put up in the church in memory of his mother, and then on the 21st, after his wife and children have moved out of the rectory, he writes:
>
> > I cannot write of [Edith] without tears. . . . O merciful Lord God . . . let me lead the rest of my life as becometh a Christian, so that when I die I may confidently hope to meet my dear Edith again in thy heavenly kingdom. . . .

March 17 Tuesday   Elizabeth and I routed out the bags and sorted them out and made them in little bundles. I got all of my clothes together and my Mother pinned them up. . . . The bags are in a great rumpus and so we had a great heap of old rubbish and stuf. My Mother says perhaps the servants will like to have a few things.

March 18 Wednesday   We got ready and the fly soon came. Their was a good number of parcels to go. The fly jolted very much; it maid the baby cry. When we got [to Perry], we went in the green room. My Mother and I sleep in the same bed, much against my Aunt's wish. Perry is a very pretty place indeed.

March 19 Thursday
. . . My aunts are surprised to see Grace so fat. She very often laughs now and crows . . . . My Aunt Chellingworth as bought a gig; it as a dicky and a seat behind.

March 20 Friday   The baby sleeps very long, so my Mother thought she could go up to Rushock because [today] the aucshanier is going to take the cataloge. . . . When we came there, the auctioneer Mr. Cole was come. He was [listing] the downstairs things. The things were all in a bustle; the study was buried with things which are not going to be sold. . . . When we got [back] to Perry, the baby had been very good. Poor Mary Meloship came; she seemed very sorry indeed [that we are going away]. I remember her since I ever remember any thing. I was very sorry indeed to part with her.

We don't know who Mary Meloship was because Eleanora never again writes of her, but this is the most direct mention of sadness at parting that she makes.

March 21 Saturday   There is a pare tree against the wall; it is coming out. We fed the baby a little, but she is very much against it.

March 22 Sunday   My Aunts wanted me to go to church, but my bonnet and cloak are too shabby. . . . The dafodils are beutiful indeed; they are all about the orchard.

March 23 Monday   The baby's back is always rubed with a linament, morning and evening. The trees are begining to show there bursting buds. . . . We came home to Rushock. George had been making a box so he has painted itt and is varnishing itt; he intends it for my Grandmama.

March 24 Thursday   My Mother is very busy. The beds are to be paked. The buds are coming out upon the trees; I [am] afraid we never shall sea the chesnut tree in its bloom again nor our pretty garden. . . .

March 26 Thurdy   Anne Jakson and Sally scoured all the tin things . . . Sarah, Mary and I washed all the glass. We took itt in turns to nurse the baby. . . . It is very sorowful to sea the things lying about because I now we shall never sea them in order again.

March 27 Friday   We are going to have a wagon from Mr. John Letts of Cake Boll tomorrow. It is a very busy day today.

March 28 Saturday   The beds were all packed up and nearly all the things went except a few in the study. The wagon was heaped up very high. Sarah and Mary walked down to Perry to tell them of the wagon coming; they took the pigeons down with them. The pigeon cubs were

taken down; their were too eggs and a
yougn one [in it]. . . . We set off when it
was dusck to go to Perry; itt was late
when we got their. . . .

the pigon house at Torton

March 29 Sunday   We none of us went
to church. My Aunts did. We did not go
because our things are not unpacked.

Mr. Hallen's parting words were also recorded in the parish register:

[Mar. 28, 1835] I left Rushock with my family with the intention of
proceeding to British America: may it please God to prosper my
undertaking.

   I have lived happily here for more than seventeen years — my two
greatest troubles befell me on the following days, 27th May 1834 and
2nd March 1835; they are both recorded in a monumental inscription in
this church: I have many blessings left for which I trust I am thankful.

George Hallen

   late (this word has a melancholy and strange sound) Curate of this
Parish: I pray God to grant it all spiritual and temporal blessings.

March 30 Monday   All our things are in the apple room and att the
top of the landing. We cleared the landing a little. My Grandpapa
[Hallen] came to dinner. The Sale is at Rushock today. My Aunts' too
servants are out at Torton, so we thought itt would be fun for Sarah to
dress up as a begar wooman and be impertinant. . . . My Grandmama
[Williams] went to the door: Sarah was very pitifull, and so my Grandmama gave her a very large peice of bread and cheese. She was very
thankfull, but wanted money. She went to the
dining room window and teased my Grandpapa [H.] a great deall with begging, which
maid my Grandmama much distressed; she
gave her a penny, but we told my Grandmama
and Grandpapa at last and they laughed; [it
was] a great deal of fun, but I have not time to put it [all down].

---

*An "apple room" might be any spare attic room. You would need one if you lived
in Worcestershire, which is still known as the fruit basket of England. Orchards and
fruit farms abound in that Midlands county: on a map, it's just south and west of
the city of Birmingham.*

March 31 Tuesday   Miss Johns . . . called . . . [and] showed us a small black likeness off herself; itt is a great deal like her [but] it is too tall. . . . She gave it us.

Silhouettes of Great-uncles Thomas and George, made by Preston (as an adult).

Imagine life without abundant snapshots of your friends and family! The Hallens didn't have any. The earliest photographic processes became available to the public around 1840. Before that time, drawn or painted portraits and cut-out silhouettes like these were widely used to remember family members. Silhouettes were relatively quick and cheap to make, and were extremely popular — but there were never enough to fill albums. Usually they were framed and hung.

Oops! Eleanora got the date wrong!

April 1 Wenesday   . . . My Father, Edgar and I went to Rushock; itt looks very desolate. My uncle is going to have a clock my Grandmama at Warsley gave to my father [before she died], and a chess table. . . .

April 2 Thursday   We went to Rhushock to draw the church. The organ was taken to peices and taken in a cart to Perry. . . . My Father dined att The Court; Sarah and Mary att Cakeboll; George and Edgar and I at The Hill.

April 3rd   . . . This morning the cart came with the organ; all the pipes were in a box on the cart, so my Father had to give them to us

Rushock Church, c. 1830, artist unknown.

one by one; we took them up to the top of the house. . . . The wood part was put in the drawing room. My Uncle William came. Sarah dressed up as a beggar and begged of him. He did not no her till she threw the money down and said something that he suspected . . . [Then] he shut the door on her; she rapped at itt till itt maid the house resound. Mary lea, a poor woman [who works] at Perry was much frightened and held the door.

The Hallens sailed for Canada without their organ; it was shipped out later. Eleanora mentions its arrival in her June 1st, 1838 entry and some years later Sarah comments that "the community [was] delighted to hear it." The organ had to be taken apart for every move, and in 1845 Eleanora writes about reassembling it herself:

[Sept 21] Began to put the organ up. J Steele lending us his waggon and Teem to fetch up our remaining baggage. Edgar and I were the organ builders, we at one time began to despair of being able to succeed as two or three notes would [not] sound: but after some time we discovered the fault lay in some dust *rags* [which had] got into the mouths of the parts which open into the wind chest, so that it quite paid us for our trouble.

[Sept 22] Edgar and I were constantly at work on the organ all [day] and had the pleasure of finishing it before night. . . .

Inside a church. 1 altar; 2 communion window; 3 communion rails; 4 pulpit.

April 4 Saturday   We turned our bonnets. Mary took the fur of one of the mantilas that Miss Randall had put on very sillilly and put itt on double.

April 5 Sunday   . . . We went to church, all of us. George went on to call for is jacket at the taylor's, because he had not sent it. . . .

April 6 Monday   My father has taken a sketch of the church, inside, of the tablet part and the communion rails and a little of the pulpit.

> *Here there is a big gap in Eleanora's entries. She left several pages blank in her copybook, so it looks as if she intended to go back and fill them in when she had time. Perhaps everyone was too busy, and none of the grownups had time to supervise journal-writing. It certainly makes sense! In Part IV there is a longer discussion of such gaps, which Eleanora leaves in her journals more and more often as the years pass.*

April 29 Wenesday   We had our breakfast very early and then Mary and I got the children ready. Mrs. Beverley went with us, the children went in a . . . coach [to Liverpool]. We went in aboat to the ship which

Part of a page from *Gore's General Advertiser*, Apr. 16 1835. The Hallens' ship, which Mr. Hallen mentions by name in his journal, is the *Albion* — middle column, fourth down. You can see that indeed, it was "the largest."

is lying in the river. She is a beautifull ship, the largest in Liverpool. She is a Merchantman. There are upwards of three hundered persons on board, including the crew. There is no cow on board; their are too sheep and three pigs. . . . There are 22 cabin passengers, and the Captain, is wife, Cild [child] and Mate. They had not had breakfast when we came on board; their was a great deall of beaf for breakfast. Their is a great deall hanging up in the rigging. My uncle William went on shore and bought a basket for the baby to ly in. . . . My Father and Mother and the boys have the Captain's cabin, and the Girls have some berths close by.

 —Moooo! Some ships did carry a cow on board to provide passengers with milk.

April 30 Thursday   A woman was confined last night. My Grandpapa, uncle William [and some] other clergimen came to take leave of us. . . . Att 12 o'clock a favorable breeze springing up, we weighed anchor. I felt regret has I saw Liverpool gradually fading from sight, but we could not stay out long, being taken very [sea]sick, and very soon I believe all the other people [also]. . . . It was very miserable; we cannot eat atall and [all of us feel] very sick.

May 1 Friday   Edgar is better, [but] we are all very ill. The pilate left us; he is a very fat man. My father went on the poop to sea him go off.

May 2 Saturday   All the cabin passengers dined at table except Mrs. *Haw* and myself. It is very calm; we went on the poop and lay down. The stearidge passengers have a fiddle and flute and they danced. The cabin passengers' names are these: [the Hallens and] George Taylor, Eliza, Charlotte, Margaret, Jane, Andrew, Joseph Neild, Elizabeth, Francis Mollory, Mrs. Mollory, John Doud, Joe Neild, Captain's wife and child, mate.

May 3 Sunday   Misty morning. My Father read service. We are on the poop; the best cabin is on a level with the deck and only the cabin passengers may walk on the top. Saw a sail astern on the larboard side. [There was] a great rush to the side of the ship, [because] a little tin pan with some soup in it went off very nicely.

> [May 3] While at dinner the Captain was alarmed by all the people running to one side of the ship and thought someone was overboard; it proved however to be a small tin vessel belonging to one of the steerage passengers with a cargo of soup on board, which it carried off in fine stile, the sea being quiet and smooth.

May 4 Monday   . . . A fine morning, but nearly becalmed. A sailor called out to George and I to look at a fish; it was about 10 or 12 feet long; its back was a reddish brown. The mate thought it was a grampus and the Captain thought a shark by the discription. Saw porposes rolling over and over. . . .

May 5   The sea rougher than usual, which jolts us very much in our berths. We spoke a vessel, but we were to ill to go out to sea her. Ther name was Jane, bound to Liverpool from New Oleans [Orleans], loaded with cotton. Passed Cape *Clear* this morning; we are now in the Atlantic.

May 6 Wenesday   Wind favorable. My Mother fell down and hurt her back; the Captain, ou was helping her, fell also. . . . The steward said we must have an allowance of water which we feel very much.

May 7 Thursday   The woman owh was confined [is] getting a great deal better. My father goes out but a little sometimes; but he [still] is very sick.

If you had a baby while at sea, would you name your child for the ship? A couple named Porter did! Eleanora mentions the baby's birth, but doesn't record that she witnessed the baptism, which took place June 18th. Obviously, Mr. Hallen carried out his clerical duties on shipboard as well as land, and the baptism became the very first entry in his new parish register.

N.º 1. Baptized 18.th June 1835 Thomas Albion son of George and Sarah Porter, on board the Ship "Albion off. Long Island United States.
                    George Hallen, Off.ᵍ Minister.

May 8 Friday   The Captain caught a
hawk in the rigging; it was soon released.
We saw it; we were in our berths.

May 9   My Mother is a great deal
better; my father is not sick [so] often, but very weak.

May 10   Sunday My father could not read prayers and we are none
of us well.

May 13 Wenesday   Wind more favourable. The stewart said we
must have an allowance of water, which is a great evill.

*Again, Eleanora's father explains her brief comment more fully: "The steward says
some of the water casks leak, so that there must be an allowance, this is sad work for
the children. (May 13th) A few days later he says:*

[May 16]   The daily allowance of water for each adult is one quart, out
of which some is deducted for cooking: the children are a little more
reconciled to their stinted allowance of water.

In The Backwoods of Canada, *Catharine Parr Traill quotes the 1835 American
Passengers' Act, a new law which required:*

Passenger ships are to be provisioned in the following proportion: —
pure water, to the amount of five gallons, to every week of the computed
voyage, for each passenger — the water to be carried in tanks or sweet
casks.... The voyage to North America is to be computed at ten weeks,
by which each passenger will be secured fifty gallons of water.

May 14 Thursday [no entry]

May 15 Friday   I saw a vessell about 12 miles distant on the
larboard side it had lost its *fore* top sail.

May 16 Saturday   As I was lying out at the cabin door, I heard a
great noise and saw a great part of the main
and mizzen mast broken and the fore mast a
little. We went into the cabin directly; the
deck was covered with sales and cords. [The
ship was] driven back a great [way] wile it
was repaired a little. It would not have
happened if the Captain had been up, but he
was lying down.

George Hallen also described the ship a bit more thoroughly than his daughter:

[May 3] Our vessel has three masts: the mainmast has 4 square sails, one above the other: there are now two studding sails one on each side the topmast but one: the foremast has 3 square sails; the two lower ones of each have a studding sail (stansail) on each side: our mizzen mast carries 3 square sails besides a large lower side sail: the best cabin is on a level with the deck: on the top of it is the poop about 8 feet above the deck, where only the cabin passengers go: it is 38f. 5i. by 27f. 2i.

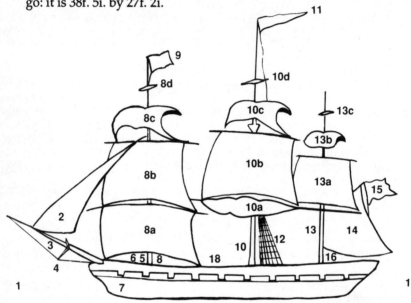

bow **1**	mizzen mast **13**
deck **18**	mizzen topsail **13a**
dolphin-striker (martingale) **4**	mizzen topgallant **13b**
forecastle (fo'c's'le) **5**	mizzen royal **13c**
fore mast **8**	name pennant **11**
fore sail **8a**	poop **16**
fore topsail **8b**	rigging **12**
fore topgallant **8c**	royal **10d**
fore royal **8d**	signal hoist **15**
house flag **9**	spanker (fore-and-aft sail) **14**
hull **7**	starboard side
jib **2**	— facing front, the right side of a ship
jibboom **3**	stern **17**
larboard side	studding sails (not shown)
— facing front, the left	— extra sails attached to each mast
side of a ship	topgallant **10c**
main mast **10**	topsail **10b**
main sail **10a**	wheel **6**

The ship *Albion* was constructed at Saint John, New Brunswick by William and Isaac Olive in 1834. It was owned by John Hammond of Saint John for fourteen years, then was sold and transferred to Liverpool. The view above was painted by Thomas Dove in 1836; the painting below is unsigned, but was done some time in the 1840s, after the ship had been painted with mock gunports — to keep pirates at bay.

May 17 Sunday   My Father canot eat biscuit. The bill of cabin fare is as follows:

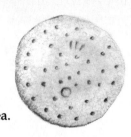

Sunday	Corn beaf and puding
Monday	Corn beef, barley soup
Tuesday	Pork, Pea soup, rice puding
Wenesday	tow Fish, two fowls, boiled ham
Thursday	Corn beaf and pudding
Friday	Pork, pea soup, rice pudding
Saturday	Scouse, water gruel and soup for tea.

Eleanora's father gives the exact same menu that she does, but he adds a note that "The Captain told me that Mrs. Hallen might tell the steward to get anything she liked besides the things mentioned in the bill of fare." (May 16th) He also calls what Eleanora gives as scouse "lobscouse." Lobscouse was one of several ways that sailors ate salt beef — for this dish, it was stewed up with dried peas, any other available vegetables, and powdered ship's biscuit. Sound good? It was still salted meat, and most passengers complained of the lack of fresh meat on long sea journeys.

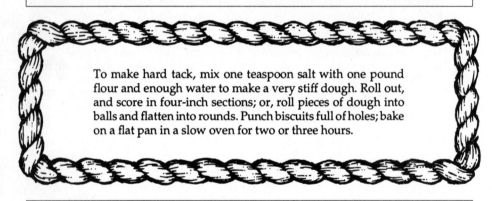

To make hard tack, mix one teaspoon salt with one pound flour and enough water to make a very stiff dough. Roll out, and score in four-inch sections; or, roll pieces of dough into balls and flatten into rounds. Punch biscuits full of holes; bake on a flat pan in a slow oven for two or three hours.

It's a wonder anyone could eat ship's biscuit! The bland combination of flour, water and salt was pretty tasteless. And without even baking powder to leaven the dough, it baked hard as a rock; thus its other name, "hard tack" (bread was "soft tack"). Its only redeeming quality was that it didn't spoil; though toward the end of a voyage it might be home to a weevil or two!

May 18 Monday   We have half a tea cup full of water at dinner. My father sets at table, but I can't.

May 23 Saturday   The sheep [were] killed today, which is a very great treat, as we have lived, on salt meat, all the way. The Captain expects to ketch some fish on the banks of New foundland . . .

May 24 Sunday   A brig in sight; [we] hoysted colours to speak to her [but] she did not seem to want [to] . . . go out of her way but we went out of ours. She was from New foundland, bound to Bristoll, out eight days; her name the Apollo of esciter [Exeter]. Saw four whales; they blew up in the air [spouted]; they have a very sharp fin sticking up which appears above the water.

Flag patterns from Marryat's Universal Code of Signals.

Before radio, it was a challenge to get in touch with passing ships or the shore. During the Napoleonic Wars (1793–1815), Frederick Marryat, an officer in the Royal Navy, developed a system of signals using flags of different colours and patterns, like the ones above. Liverpool, a huge trading city, developed its own flag signals for merchant ships, called the Liverpool Code. Basically, every ship sailing out of Liverpool had a number, and they used fifteen different flags plus a Union Jack to display it. There were also flags to signal a few common messages, such as "let's rendezvous." By the late 1850s, more flags were added, standing for letters of the alphabet, and one to mean "Yes!" The International Code, first established in 1901, combined several signal systems. It was finally revised in 1932, and is still used by today's mariners.

The complexity of the flag system meant you only communicated about essential matters. However, a Mrs. Ellice, in her brief diary, mentions that on the second day at sea they got an amusing message from a passing ship:

Wednesday, 25 April, 1838 The Carybdes made signals, which no-one could understand. Sent down in Alarm for the Capt. who applied to his private signal book & found it was only Mr. Gore wished to know <u>how the ladies were today</u>. Alas for the poor ladies, we were tolerably sea-sick.

Stay tuned for more on Mrs. Ellice!

May 25 Monday   Their is a black boy on board ouh wates on us; his name is *Ianco*. The little Taylors are very fond of him. Just to make him give them water they leave a little pudding, on their plates, for him. I do not like them, at all, Miss Charlotte Taylor, continues, very ill, she does not, come out, of her berth, and Mrs. *Haw*, is the same. Before we came out, Mrs. Mole of Snidge Green gave us a great number of biscuits; they are very nice indeed. The sea biscuits are very disagreeable; my father canot eat them; I am obliged to put a great

". . . they are very nice indeed."

". . . the biscuit in the frying pan."

deal of buter on [them], but [even] then they are very unpalittable. We have beaf and pork for breakfast sometimes; I wish we had provided for ourselfs has we very often envy the Stearidge passengers ouh fry their bacon and put in the biscuit in the frying pan. The allowance of [water] is but a pint for [all of] us and the black boy brings in a jug,

Mʳ STOPS READING TO ROBERT AND HIS SISTER.

"Evʼry lady in this land
"Has twenty nails upon each hand
"Five & twenty on hands & feet
"And this is true without deceit."
But when the stops were placʼd aright,
The real sense was brought to light.

Notice a whole lot of commas in lines six through ten? Usually, Eleanora doesn't use any — we have put them in to make her writing easier to read. But all of these are hers, and they make for strange pauses! So why did she put them in, and so plenteously? Perhaps her parents or older siblings gave her a little lesson on the use of the comma and she got very self-conscious about it. An 1824 text called Punctuation Personified *might have helped her. It includes this rhyme, which only makes sense if you put the right punctuation in the right places.*

which he takes away if their is any left, to keep it for is freinds the talors [Taylors]. But we . . . stop him and make him give it us. They have some barley soup that none of us can eat.

" . . . make him give it us."

Sometimes the sea is very ruff and about twice has washed over the poop. We are very glad to see vessels; first the tops of their mast apear [above the horizon] and then they rise gradually. We over took a very bad sayling vessel, a sweadish one. Her name was the Penelope of Gotenburgh. . . . When we are having our meals, the Captain sits at the top of the table and looks so miserable all the time; he never asks a person to have any more. . . . [There are] no more potatoes and the plum pudding and rice comes very seldom. The Stearidge passengers are some of them very dirty and a few very tidy. Their is a Mrs. Davis in the stearidge, she says she is a Irish woman, but she does not speak atall like [one]; she is quite has much of a lady as Miss Taylor who is

steerage passengers

By Alfred Withers, 1857. The rigging was sailors' territory, and trespassing passengers were punished by being tied up until they promised the sailors a measure of rum!

in the cabin. Mr. Doud got up in the rigging. one day; directly some saylors came and tyed him up till he promised to give them some rum; this he did; they then let him loose. What made him get up was . . . to see [two] large Islands of ice, one was about a mile long.

One day when another sheep was killed . . . there was not half enough for us all . . . only a steak each and one left [over], when there commenced a quarrell between Mrs. Mollory and my Mother . . . at last Mrs. Mollory made my Mother have itt. Mr. Neild one day called for some porter before the cheese came [but] the steward pretended not to hear him and went out of the room. One day a packet ship passed us; [it] came so near we could see the saylors on board. They did not hoist a flag, so the Captain did not. Why the Captain did not we think was because he was ashamed to own his reckoning. I wished to be on board [that ship] very much.

We . . . sit on the poop and used to look what was passing on deck below: this is a sketch of some of us. Several of them went without shoes and stockings which we were not accustomed to atall; there were three very dirty Irish girls that went without. Mr. Neild is rather a fat man, not very, and very light hair; the Taylors play with him a good deal. He sometimes makes Jane Taylor cry, [and then] Miss Taylor reproofs him in these words, "Now Mr. Neild, you do use her too ruffly; you do not no owh to use children. Miss Taylor is very much like an owl; Mr. Doud boasts a great deal of his country. He comes from Ireland; he says it is a great deal better than Ingland. Mr. Taylor says the Inglish do not speak right Inglish but that they

cabin passengers at table

ought to go to Ireland to learn to speak properly. All the Taylors speak very bad grammar; George Taylor is very vulgar indeed.

One night I was awoken by a great noise: a man was saying he was very badly hurt and severall people [were] running; I heard Mr. Molory in a great passion. Presently the Captain was called; Mr. Molory said there was no order kept in the ship and that his door had

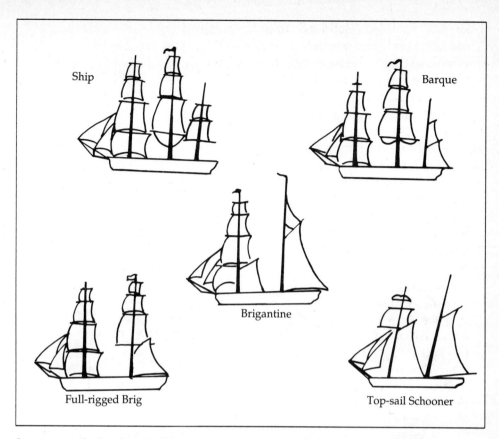

Ship

Barque

Brigantine

Full-rigged Brig

Top-sail Schooner

been nearly broken in by some men quarrelling, and that he was obliged to get out of bed, else it would have been broken. The Captain (great thing) was very angry and told Mr. Molory to get into his berth again. I do not no owh it was ended; thought at first it was a mutiny. It was very fortunate it was not. I always got up early and sat by the cabin door or else on the poop; my father [also]. . . . It is very difficult to dress and wash. The first day I felt better, I com[b]ed out my hair, which was a very long job as having slept without any night cap it was very much intangled. Sometimes the vessel rols so that when I am sat on a bundle, I am made run to one side of the cabin with great violence and then made run to another. One day that I was very thirsty I had a little tea left, so I was eating some biscuit and then going to drink my tea, [but] a role came and settled my nice cup of tea.

The first volume of Eleanora's original 1835 diary looks as if it has had its final page torn out. At this point in her transcription, Mrs. Drinkwater gives, "it was a great dissapointment (sic) to me, as we have so little drink, water is so scarce." Although elsewhere there are lines that she seems to have added herself, puzzlers can tell from the "(sic)" that in the 1950s, at least, the missing page was still there.

[*June 4th* Nothing has happened on board the last two days; we haven't even seen another ship and we find the Taylors so uninteresting and the children are so rough. My Mother does not care to have them play with the little ones.

George Taylor fell down and his nose swelled.
Nose, nose, who gave you that jolly old nose?

June 15th We saw a ship today; we must now be near New York. . . . Everyone on board is very excited; we have been on the boat now for six weeks and are all very tired of it, especially the dull food and the Captain's worried face. George has been fishing, but did not catch anything; the Captain said we should by tomorrow, as we shall be near land.]

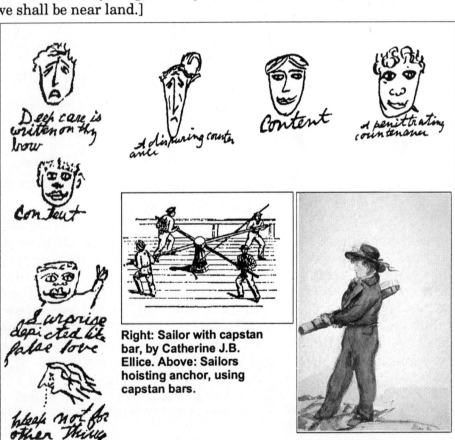

Right: Sailor with capstan bar, by Catherine J.B. Ellice. Above: Sailors hoisting anchor, using capstan bars.

June 4th and 15th are from Mrs. Drinkwater's transcription. At this point she gives several bits of verse, romantic teasing and just plain drivel — the kind of thing you probably write when you're bored — which might have been on the missing page. Perhaps the doodles on these pages, from the covers of Eleanora's second 1835 copybook, were done at this time.

[Mr. Hallen's journal, June 10] . . . When the voyage is long we hardly know what to do for amusement, time hangs very heavily, and there is a feeling of listlessness and inactivity which quite unfits one for serious occupation or anything which requires thought or application. . . . Learnt to tie two or three useful knots .

Mr. Hallen gives a long, detailed and funny description of how they arrange themselves to eat and how they cope with the ship's motion, in an entry that includes potatoes flying through the air and cups of tea dumping on people's laps. Here is a sample:

[June 10] . . . We have seats with carpet bottoms which fold up very like camp stools: these are very inconvenient as in a roll you often slide seat and all from the table, while your plate and tea cup very considerately accompany you; but though they make all the haste they can, they are left behind by the hot tea, meat, vinegar, knives and forks, teaspoon, biscuit and potatoes. . . .

Now might be a good time to discuss a delicate matter. Were there toilets on board, and if so, where were they? (No, not on the poop deck — that name is from the Latin word for the stern, or back, of a ship!) The Hallens had "water closets" in the privacy of their cabins, and chamber pots, which were probably emptied over the side every day. (Later, Eleanora mentions how dirty the ship's hull looks. No wonder!) But the steerage passengers used two "necessary houses," built for them near the forecastle. Mr Hallen describes them as:

[June 6] . . . very slight boarded things. [With the ship's rolling] the doors soon went . . . ; after a few days as fuel was wanted a few of the boards disappeared. In this way they were soon stripped down to the seats; and this morning . . . I could see not a vestige of them remaining. They were a sad eyesore, such miserable dirty ruinous sheds, but I sincerely pity the more respectable class of steerage passenger who must be put to serious inconvenience. Oh, those Liverpool Agents are sad ones, they should certainly have had some more substantial buildings erected but they appear to me from all I can collect to care little for the passengers . . . [once] they get their money to ship them off.

June 17 Wenesday   Saw a ship at a great distance; the Captain thought it would speak. It soon got nearer; it was a very pretty little Sloop. We spoke, [but] the other had no speaking trumpet; he said we were quite in a different Longitude to him. The Captain, thinking he was wiser, said he was sure we were farther off New York. In about an hour after land was seen. Everybody came on deck to see it and general joy was [felt] through the ship. A man named Rece said he saw it first; he said has he was hanging up his trousers he said [to himself] "he was sure that was sunat [something] more than sea." But the Captain would have itt that he [himself] saw it first, (I think Rece saw itt first) . . . [so as] not to give Rece any rum, which he had promised to any one who saw itt first. . . . We . . . saw Long Island with a lighthouse on the end; [no] pilate boat to guide us round Long Island Sound so we went the *East* side of itt.

June 18 Thursday   Got up to see the sun rise; it was a beautiful sight. We could but just see Long Island; I smelt the land very distinkly. Before Breakfast, being a calm . . . [several] passengers fished. . . . A great number [were] caught and I was delighted at having them for dinner. When they had gone down to lunch George put in the line . . . [and] soon felt a bight so he hawled in. A very large fish now appeared and George could haul no longer without calling [for help]. The second mate got . . . it up; it was a shark about 7 feet long; it bit one person [before] it . . . died. It was then cut open; we had some of its skin which is ruff like a fine file. All the stearidge passengers have some. . . .

June 19   After dinner we went on at a great rate, I never remember going so fast. [Then] a fog came on so that we could not see far. . . . My Father afterwards said that he expected the ship to [hit something any] minute. . . . Suddenly the fog cleared a little and they saw land ahead and . . . a buoy close to us: in three minutes we should have struck! We tacked of directly. We saw two light houses and . . . [a] little boat which seemed some times buried in the waves; it soon reached the vessel. The pilate jumped on board. The first words he said was, "Square the main sale." We cast anchor at Sandy Hook; their was beautiful lightning . . . like a firey cord twisted in the scy.

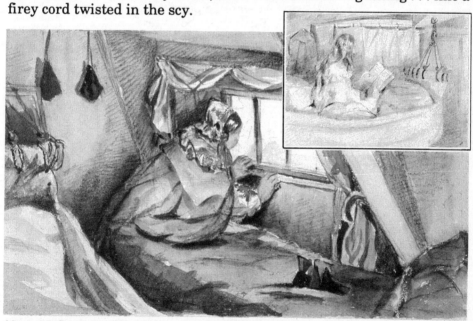

Above: " 'Sentry, will there be a sunrise?' Watercolour of Miss Eglantine Balfour aboard H.M.S. Hastings, 1838." Inset: "Tina in her cot," by Catherine J.B. Ellice.

In the summer and fall of 1838, Catherine Jane Balfour Ellice travelled with a group that included her niece, Tina Balfour, to Montreal. Mr. Ellice was personal secretary to the leader of the group: Lord Durham, Canada's Governor General at the time. Mrs. Ellice's journey progressed in the same way and along more or less the same route as the Hallens'. She painted many of the places, people and activities Eleanora describes — such as reading in one's berth, as Tina is doing here.

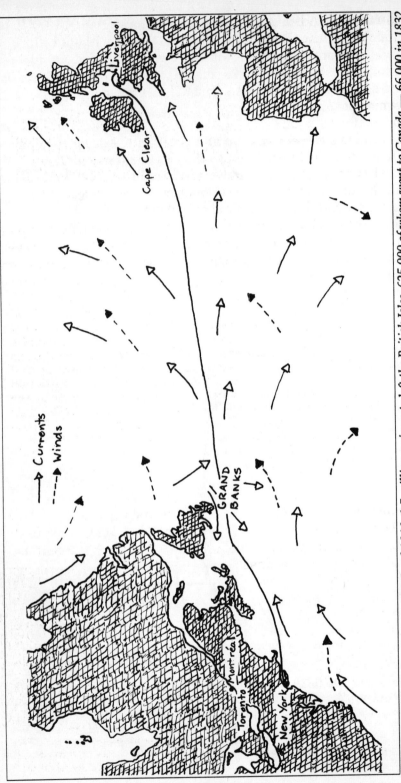

The Hallens' route. Between 1825 and 1846, 1.5 million emigrants left the British Isles, 625,000 of whom went to Canada — 66,000 in 1832 alone. Overpopulation, famine and strife between those who owned the land and those who worked it in Ireland meant that Irish emigrants outnumbered English almost two to one during this period. In turn, there were about twice as many English emigrants as Scots. The top year for emigrants from the British Isles was 1852, with about 360,000 leaving, of whom 33,000 went to Canada. In comparison, the Hallens' year, 1835, was a "slow" one: 44,500 emigrated (of whom 15,500 went to Canada), so conditions were relatively uncrowded.

June 20 Saturday   A beautiful day; we weighed anchor and went up the river opposite Staten Island. The bay was beautiful: the green trees and red and white houses. . . . Soon after a medical man came on board. He says the vessel must be kept in quarantine 2 days, [but] the cabin passengers may go on the shore when they like. . . . My father and

New York from Brooklyn Heights, 1837, by William James Bennett.

some others went on shore who we told particularly to bring us bread and milk. When my father came home he had [also] bought . . . some fresh butter: it was delicious after the hard biscuits. The Captain does not look so miserable.

You probably wonder how effective a quarantine could be when certain, privileged passengers — those of the "better" classes — were allowed off the ship anyway. Ships were small, and cabin and steerage passengers alike would be exposed to any infectious disease on board. (This is another indication of how little was understood in Eleanora's day about the spread of germs.) And how very infectious those diseases were — and still are, sometimes, in some parts of the world. The Hallens were extremely lucky to have missed the very severe cholera epidemics of 1832 in New York and Canadian ports. When Catharine Parr Traill, the now famous English-Canadian author of The Canadian Settlers' Guide, *reached Montreal in August, 1832, she nearly died from the disease. In June of that year over 100 people every day had been struck down, and it was rampant in the States as well.*

June 21 Sunday   . . . My father read prayers and preached. . . . In the evening the boat went to land and my father, Edgar and I went [on shore. From the shore] our ship looked a very bad one: the fore mast was the tallest and the mainmast shortest and . . . [the hull] was very dirty from things being thrown down the outside. It is the largest vessel there. It was delightful to step on tera firma again. Staten Island is a beautiful Island; the houses are chiefly of [painted] wood . . . they look very neatly and very pretty; there are a great many trees up the street. They seem to smoke segars very much [here]. . . .

South Street from Maiden Lane, c. 1834, by W. J. Bennett. In sailing's heyday, the street was known as "Street of Ships."

June 22 Monday   A boat came ... with a man in it who asked if Biddy and Tony were in the ship, they were: they were both very poor children and my Mother had given the little girl a frock. She was a very ugly bold girl: what a daughter for her father to clasp in his harms. ... The Captain distributed cheese and biscuits to the people; iff he had done it sooner, it would have been better. He told the poorest to come forward first. ... The steerage passengers will go tomorow morning.

June 23 Tuesday   Early in the morning the two Sloops came for the steerage passengers; [the] one that went first was quite crowded with them. They were all dressed in their best and looked very well. ... After they were gone the Sailors nocked all the berths down below and washed it well out because [otherwise] the pilot would not come to guide us up to New York: we reached New York very soon. ... The steamboats passed backwards and forwards very often. The deck is nice and clear so that we can run about.

> All this cleaning after the steerage passengers had gone had to do with people's limited — and in this case, correct — understanding of the connection between hygiene and health. But the ship would not be carrying people back across the Atlantic — that traffic was all westward! The usual return cargo for immigrant ships was timber, especially for a ship registered, as the Albion was, in the Maritimes, where logging was an expanding industry.

June 24 Wenesday   We went into the docks with the head of the ship close to land. The custom house officer came on board but did not examine the boxes. ... In the evening has it was getting dusk ... [we went for a walk] in New York. Mrs. Moloy was so kind has to take care of the baby and to insist on My mother going. We went up Broadway and a good number other streets. My mother got tired so my father [hired] a coach and ... we rode by turns .... The baby was aleep when we got home.

Broadway from the Park, c. 1832, by William Barnard and Archibald L. Dick.

June 25 Thursday   ... In the evening Mr. Chester, a gentleman my father had letters of introduction to, came. My father had called on him; he says he will send their carriage for us to come to their house.

June 26 Friday There are a great many ships near us one was named Hallen. The carriage came about 12 o'clock, and My mother, Sarah, Mary and I got in. We rattled over the stone

aved road and sometimes jolted furiously over bricks which aftened [happened] to ly in the street. It made such a noise we could hardly here anything. The servant man talked a great deal about New York. The Americans think it is the finest City in the world. He told us the names of all the places and was very communicative. . . . When we arrived . . . only Mrs. Chester and her sister were at home . . . Mr Chester came at dinner time. It was a delicious dinner after being in the ship. I shall describe it:

Quarter of lamb at top, fish at the bottom, green peas, mashed potatoes and little potatoes and melted butter. The pudding was custard. The desert came on at the same time and cheese; there were some delicious pine aples. There was no beer a[t] table, only water and wine. After dinner Sarah went back to the vessel for the little ones.

Hudson River from Hoboken, c. 1832, by William Barnard and Archibald L. Dick.

They went on the luggage cart . . . to Mr. Chester's store of carpets. . . . [Later] we went . . . [in his carriage] . . . to the steam vessell . . . which is going to take us to Albany. My mother, Sarah [and] Mary had tea first, it was very long table and everything on itt. . . . Not any berths for us. So we slept on a sort of window seat on steps. I slept all night. The others did not sleep hardly atall. They said their was such a great thumping [because] people were getting out all night.

We arrived at Albany about 4 in the morning and then got in another steam boat to go to Troy. Wy we go to Troy is because my father has letters of introduction to two families their.

June 27 Saturday My Father and George when we gotto Troy went to find an hotell for us; . . . it was called the Manshion House. It was a very nice large house at the corner of a Street. The streets are very pretty with trees all up the sides. We can see the . . . Episcopalian church; the top is wood but it looks very nicely. We had breakfast . . .

Hotel dining, 1838, by
Catherine J.B. Ellice.

The Mansion House, Troy, c. 1840.

St. Paul's Church.

fountain

"a very
sticking out
forehead"

Men of Sturbridge Village, a
living museum that recreates
American village life in the
1830s. Straw hats were tall!

in a very long room with a table all down the middle. There were eight windows down on one side. It was all white china. The chairs were put so that the back of the chair touched the table. When we were all seated, a bell rang and 40 or 50 sort of gentlemen came in and seated themselfs. They began to eat immediately and some were not more than three minutes at it. The table was covered with all sorts of things, meat, preserves, fruit, cheese, bread and butter and cakes of all sorts. The landlord told us not to be uncomfortable if we were left last, for they eat very fast. He was very much pleased with such a large English family. . . . There is a very beautiful fountain just before our bedroom window . . . [with] iron palisades round. My father went to call on Mr. Warren who he had introductory letters to.

June 28 Sunday   Our beds have no heads to [them]; there are no blankets on, being so warm. . . . There is a piano in the house; we played on it several times. There is a little girl there that talks a great deal, she has a very sticking out forehead. [People here] seem not to care what mixture they eat such as apple pie, cheese and salad on your plate at the same time. . . .

Straw hats are worn a great deal; my mother bought all the boys one yesterday. Mr Warren called; he got ussome seats at — church. . . . In the evening after church [we all went to call on the Warrens]. . . . I carried the baby. There were two Mr Warrens, Miss Warren and a little boy. I liked being there very much. While we were there the Bishop came in who my father had been introduced to in the morning. They walked home with us.

June 29 Monday   . . . We went . . . to the canal boat . . . [and] crossed the Hudson [River] by running long poles allong the bottom. Two horses drew us. Some parts we pass are very beautiful. The country abounds in wood. . . .
When we arrived at Fort Edward we were nearly all asleep. We went to an hotel where we took up four rooms, none very nice ones.

June 30 Tuesday   The breakfast [was] not so nicely attended nor so nicely laid out as at . . . Troy. My father sett off to walk to Sandy Hill then came back in Mr. Parry's gig. He is a Presbyterian preacher . . . rather short and dark, a turned up nose and turned up mouth and very shaggy black eyebrows; he was dressed in black. He walked about the room humming a psalm tune. My Mother, the little ones and I rode. . . . When we got to his house, his spouse received us; [she was] a very affected wooman indeed. We thought we were to stay dinner, so took off our bonnets and did our hair, but what was our surprise when [they] reminded us it was time to go to the
hottell to dinner. We were glad to go from such an inhospitable roof. . . . This hotel is not such a nice one as at Troy. It has a virando in front. After tea, Mrs. Parry and her daughter came; her daughter is fourteen, a very stupid looking girl. Mrs. Parry advised my mother to have her daughters' hair cut short; she then said "Mary, my dear, take off your bonnet." She asked . . . some of us [to visit, but] . . . the baby, she said, would gett fretful, so did not go.

July 1 Wednesday   The Americans use a great many cant words, such has, "Well, I believe so" or "I presume or calculate so." There is a black servant at the hottell; she dresses like a lady . . . [in] a black silk gown. . . . The servants here are called "helps"; they call nobody Miss or Master; they are a very disagreeable sort of people. They have dinner after us. . . . I have seen a man servant sit down before all the people had all done and begin to help himself.

Almost all immigrants in Canada today have to learn English as a second or third language. There was no significant language barrier for the Hallens, though the accents might have been unfamiliar. Here's a funny thing, however — the American way of saying "I presume so" or "I calculate so," which Eleanora notes, is also mentioned by other observers of life in America. Catharine Parr Traill wrote:

[The Yankees] were, for the most part, quiet, well-behaved people. The only peculiarities I observed in them were a certain nasal twang in speaking, and some few odd phrases; but these were only used by the lower class, who *"guess"* and *"calculate"* a little more than we do.

Mrs Parry informed us that there was no episcopalian church but that a clergyman came 20 miles every other Sunday and had prayers in the Court house. Sandy Hill is on the banks of the Hudson. We have to descend a slanting road to it. The hotell we are at is a very nice one; there is a little park with young trees planted, just laid out in the form of a triangle. . . . From our window we can see . . . the presbeterian meeting house, the top of the Courthouse, a very nice coffe[e] house and some other houses . . . all built of wood neatly painted white. They are very fond of having palisadoes at the top of the houses. The hotell we are at has a virando suported by wooden pillars.

Once again, several blank pages in her journal tell us Eleanora meant to go back and catch up. She never did, so there's a gap of two weeks here. It's likely they were all too busy getting settled to have time to write.

July 15   In the evening Sarah and Mary went down to the brook with the baby. While they were away, a lady came . . . [who] was very fat but looked very good natured. . . . She told my Mother her name was Mrs. Martingdale and that she hoped that we should be very friendly and neighbourly. She said she only just lived across the road at the bottom of the field. . . . We picked a great many currants for a pudding tomorrow. Mr Weston has given us leave to pick as many as we like. . . . They are very beautiful there are so many but while I was stalking them I felt ill so I went to bed.

July 16 Thursday   I am still in bed; I have a headache and feel like I generally do. I like the door open so that I can see in the field. . . . In the evening my Mother and father went with Mr Parry in his waggon to Glens Falls. [Several] people can walk in amongst them and there are two caves. My Mother did not go in both. They saw another presperterian preacher who . . . came to the waggon and said, "Now get right out, walk right along the garden, walk right across the hall and go right into the parlour." His wife was very kind.

July 17 Friday   . . . Madam Parry called; she has a very mincing way of talking; she always says "Yes ommm," and seems to insinuate. . . . I saw [a] gentleman coming to the door where I was sleeping; I could see it was Mr. Charles Weston. . . . I called . . . and Mary came and told him to go to the other door. . . .

> *Sickness seems to have given Eleanora an opportunity to start regular journal-keeping once more. And the tone of her entries has changed. Doesn't the Hallens' Sandy Hill life sound like England all over again?*

July 18 Saturday   . . . I am still in bed. . . . It is the custom here to call in the evening.

July 19 Sunday   We did not no iff there was church, so George went to inquire at Mr. Martingdale's. Their was, so they went. I got up today and feel a great deal better.

Profile by Eleanora Hallen, c. 1833. Pencil.

By Sarah Hallen, c. 1833. Pencil.

By Sarah Hallen, c. 1833. Pencil.

Unknown Hallen, c. 1833. Pencil and watercolour.

By Eleanora Hallen, c. 1833. Pencil and watercolour, after a Bewick woodcut.

By Sarah Hallen, c. 1833. Pencil and watercolour.

July 20 Monday　In the morning my Mother went to the village to buy something to piece the bottom of George's trousers. My Father intends . . . to go off to Canada tomorrow if he can.

> *Mr. Hallen was going on ahead to prepare the way for his family. Initially, he meant to spend his first year getting settled, and then look for work — the first concern of almost all immigrants. But it seems a job found him! It's not surprising. With the influx of settlers, men of his profession were in great demand. According to a report by Bishop John Strachan, in 1801 there were only nine Anglican clergymen in all of Upper Canada. By 1841 there were 150 clergymen plus two bishops — what a growth rate! You'll find Strachan's name in most histories of Ontario. He was Upper Canada's first Anglican bishop, and had a tremendous influence on the development of the Anglican Church and its schools during the mid-nineteenth century.*

July 21 Tuesday　My Father will not go [yet]; he sent to . . . a saddlemaker to make a strap to strap his box. In the evening Mr. and Mrs. Parry called. Mr Ames, a person we have never seen before, called nearly at the same time we were showing them some of our drawings. She — Madam Parry — said, O they were very well done for our age, but [she] did not seem to admire them. Mrs Ames thought they were very well done indeed. We showed them a picture of our house [in England]. Mrs. Parry directly said it seemed a very old fashioned one and the church she made some remark on. . . .

July 22 Wendesday　In the morning my Father set off to go by the Stage [coach], George and Edgar went with him. They [reported] he was obliged to walk, as the stage was full.

July 23　Sarah and Mary take it in turn to go call[ing] with my Mother. . . . The weather is very delightful, it is very hot in the middle of the day.

July 24 Friday　After dinner, Sarah and I went to Practise [piano] at Mrs. Martingdale's; Sarah went first and in about half an hour I went. . . .

> *On or about July 22, Mr. Hallen arrived in Canada, and it seems he was relieved to be on British soil once again.*
>
> I am now in his Britannic Majesty's Dominions . . . may God bless and prosper both him, his Queen and his people, particularly my dear friends and relations. . . . May God bless and defend my dear Sarah and my children during my absence. . . . Bought some milk to drink, received one English penny in change.

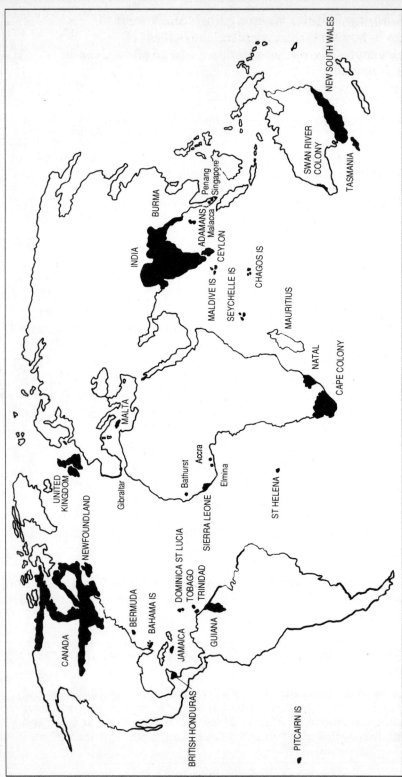

Countries of the British Empire, c. 1830. *The biggest ethnic group among immigrants to arrive in New York in 1835 were the Germans: they were twice as numerous as the Irish, while there were only a few hundred English people and a handful of Scots. Overall, the English middle classes preferred to transplant themselves to lands under British rule. Since the British Empire extended all over the world, they had many lands to choose from. Yet, in the 1830s, wrote Susannah Moodie, "a Canada mania pervaded the middle ranks of British society." The Hallens were only one family among the 15,500 people who travelled from the British Isles to Canada in 1835.*

July 25 Saturday   Miss Weston called. She brought some [very fine] radishes in a jug. Miss Weston is about has tall has George. She has red hair and blue eyes. Mr. Hubert [the Episcopalian clergyman] called; he is going to have service tomorow.

July 26 Sunday   We went to church. . . . There are several people in the same sitting has us. The black girl from the inn comes. She wears [a] black silk gown, white muslin hankerchief, shoes with sandles [saddles] and a bag [made] of beads.

July 27 Monday   Sarah went to practise at Mrs.Martingdale's. In the evening Mrs. Pettit and Miss Pettit called; they said Skeeler and Agnes were very good. . . . The baby began to be naughty, so I had to take her out of doors.

July 28 Tuesday   The children often pull of their shoes and stockings as they like going without. We do not have fresh meat very often. A butcher brings his cart round and so we are ready at the gate when we here his bell.

July 29 Wenesday   Mrs. Martingdale came over when it was quite dusk . . . ; before she had sat long, in came Mr. George Weston and Miss Weston. It got so dark we were obliged to bring in a tin lamp, having no better. . . .

July 30 Thursday   Miss Weston called to ask Sarah and Mary and I to go with her to a tree about a mile off where a young lady of the name of McCrea was killed; she (Miss McCrea) was going with some Indians to her lover who had sent them, but they fell in with another party of Indians which her anxious lover had sent again. They then began to quarrell [over] her and one of them killed her; the tree is a pine. I did not go because I was afraid lest it should do me harm. The housekeeper went with them. When they returned they had brought some moss and an indian pipe which they had found growing.

Miss Jane McCrea was indeed killed by "Indians" in this area, under confusing circumstances, during the American Revolutionary War (1776). Local legend holds she was scalped at the foot of a huge pine tree, which stood beside a spring. Eleanora visits the place on Aug. 21st.

July 31 Friday   Sarah and Mary sleep at Mr. Parry's.

July 32 August 1 Saturday   . . . It was a beautiful evening . . .

August 2 Sunday   Mr Hubert did not come has it is not his Sunday, so we did not go. Several Epsicopalians go to the Presbyterian church when there is no other.

August 3 Monday   In the evening Sarah and Mary went to practise [piano] at Miss Weston's as she has asked us very often. . . .

August 4 Tuesday   . . . Mr. E. Martingdale called to say that Mrs.Clark was going to have a party and she hoped Sarah and Mary would be there. . . . My Mother . . . did not like the idea of them going by themselves, so she would go [too] . . .

Broadway, New York, Aug. 1838, by Catherine J.B. Ellice.

By the mid 1800s, the United States had more than 4 million slaves. Slavery, and people's beliefs about whether it was right or wrong, was one of the causes of the American Civil War. In 1865, with the 13th Amendment to the United States Constitution, slavery was abolished.

Since 1799, slavery had not been allowed in the State of New York. But many people in both Europe and North America still thought black people were inferior human beings. Eleanora's wonder that the black girl from the inn acts and dresses "like a lady" reflects both her experience of English class division and the racism prevalent at the time.

August 5 Wednesday   In the evening . . . Mrs. Parry's impertinent servant . . . [bounced] in; she . . . [had] come for me and Agnes. . . . When we got there, Mrs. Parry asked why the boys had not come; I said that my Mother had thought it would be too much trouble for her. . . . All the evening we played [piano], which I did not like much.

August 6 Thursday   George was ill and lay in bed. In the morning to our great surprise Miss Weston came with a waiter covered over with a handkerchief, and under was some coffee ready made, with sugar and cream, some jelly in a glass, a piece of hot toast and butter and some dryed beef cut in very little slices. She said that perhaps he would like something that was made from home. She did not stay long.

Harriet Pettit House, one of the "Miss Pettits" who ran the school Agnes and Richard went to. She married a missionary and went to live in Bangkok, where she established a school for girls.

Right: Mr. George Weston, 1872.

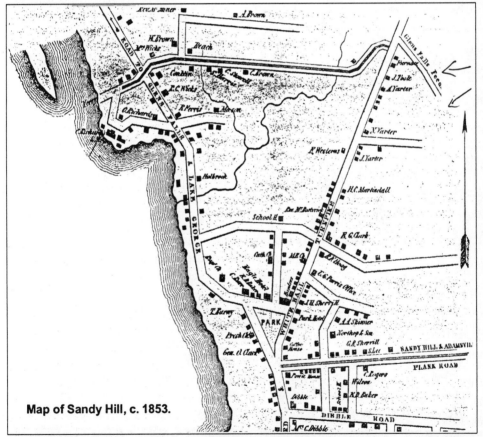

Map of Sandy Hill, c. 1853.

The triangular park is in the middle. If you use a magnifying glass, you can find the homes of the Westons, Martindales and Clarks (names Eleanora mentions) along White Hall Turnpike. A Gazetteer of the State of New York (1824) says that the village of Sandy Hill at that time consisted of about 100 houses and 350 people. That's a pretty big village! The population of settled areas like this was actually falling during this period as many Americans moved further west.

August 7 Friday . . . Madam Parry called . . . ; somehow or other somebody said something about Richard, [and] she said that she had a great deal rather not see him in her situation. . . . He's quite as good looking as any of the rest. . . . We made some little moss baskets which looks very pretty with some ever lasting flowers in them. Sarah and Mary went to Mrs Martingdale's. They danced a great deal. My Mother and Edgar went to fetch them; they had some very nice iced cream.

Who really knows what Eleanora's strange defence of her brother means? "In her situation" sounds like "in her condition," a well-known euphemism for pregnancy. There is an old-fashioned superstition that ugly experiences during pregnancy make an ugly baby. Perhaps Mrs.Parry was expecting a baby. This is my best guess — what do you think?

August 8 [no entry]

Eleanora's original journal entries skip from Aug. 8th to Aug. 16th, as you see. However, she did finish one volume and begin another at this point, so it's possible a page or two are missing. Mrs. Drinkwater's transcription has two additional lines:

15th Tomorrow is Sunday, my Father has not returned yet.
16th My father arrived late last night from Canada.

It's hard not to wonder if Mrs. Drinkwater made these up, although they make good sense. . . .

August 16 [Sunday] It was very rainy in the morning, so that none of us could go [to church], but in the evening Sarah, Mary, George and Preston went. I could not go has I had a cold. . . .

August 17 Monday We thought we could perhaps get some nuts, so George and I set off into some fields near. . . . We saw some nice bushes and . . . [the nuts] were very nice ones . . . not quite so large as cob nuts. We picked . . . great numbers. We took them to the top of a shed with some butternuts [to dry]. The shells of the butternuts got very much shrivelled by the sun. The have not so much kernel in as wallnuts.

August 18 Tuesday Old Mr. Weston called; he brought some boughs of currants for us to eat, which we soon did after his departure.

August 19 Wednesday Sarah and Mary went to call on the Miss Pettits. They live in a very pretty house; one of them keeps a school which Agnes and Skeeler go to. They like going very much; they like Francis Martingdale and *Issill* and Minerva Clark, but they don't like the Parrys nor the other children.

August 20 . . . Miss Cetons [Seatons?] and their brother called. He told my father a very easy way to feather arrows the way the indians do it. He said he liked archery very much. . . .

August 21 Friday   After dinner my Father said he would go to a tree where a young lady Miss Macree was killed by an Indian chief, and then go on to Miss

Nuts .

Small local schools, privately run, were common at this time in the United States and England. Schools for girls like Agnes and small boys like Skeeler were run by women, and referred to as "dame schools." The children were taught the alphabet and some reading from the Bible. Because the classes were held in the teachers' homes, they were also given household chores!

The Jane M'Crea tree, Fort Edward.

This picture is from 1841; by 1853 the "Giant Pine" was chopped down. It was made into canes and curio boxes that were sold at the New York City Crystal Palace Exposition in 1861.

The Jane McCrea tree, Fort Edward.

Cetons. So Mary, George, Edgar, Preston and I went, [too]. We went along the side of the canal. . . . It is a very pretty tree, and very old; the top is off. . . .

August 22 Saturday   . . . We called on Miss Weston; she sang. Her piano is not in good tune; it was Mrs. Martingdale's old one. . . .

August 25 Tuesday   . . . My Mother, Mary and I . . . went to call on Mrs. Nash. She said she liked Mrs. Parry as well as a sister. I do not know how she can; we did not stay long. It is a very uncomfortable day.

4   The Redbreast

Above: the sparrow-sized English robin. Below: American robin, a slightly larger bird

August 26 Wenesday   My Father and George went to Mr. Beaches'; they stayed tea. [He] remembers when [the land] was hardly cleared; he [went on] several bear hunts when he was young. [His house] is very unlike an Inglish farmhouse. They asked George to come and eat plums any day. . . .

August 27 Thursday   There are a great number of robins in the cherry tree; they are not half so pretty as the inglish robins; they are much larger. James Hives, a little boy who goes to

school with Agnes, gave her a great many choakcherries. We picked some off and boiled them; they were very bitter. I went to call on Miss Westons. . . . We walked down to Bakers Falls to a swing in a field not far off; we did not stay long. Miss Weston said the gentlemen of the village had subscribed for it, but I did not think there was much to suscribe for, as their was only four cords [pieces of rope] and a bit of board. When I came home, they showed me some fish, they were rather large. There was a large sun fish. Mrs. Parry and her interesting son John had called and brought them.

This game is dangerous, unless used with discretion. Great care should be taken that the ropes are strong and well secured, and the seat fastened firmly. Little girls should never be ambitious to swing higher than any of their companions. It is, at best, a foolish ambition, and it may lead to dangerous accidents. Any little girl is unpardonable who pushes another violently while she is swinging.

The Girl's Own Book, 1833

August 28 Friday   In the morning the large sunfish was gone; we think the cat that comes about the house as stolen it. It is a wet day. Mary [is] ill . . . inflamation on her lungs.

August 29 Saturday   . . . There was bad thunder and lightning.

August 30 Sunday   In the morning Mr. Martingdale, Squire Hitchcock and his wife [came to service in our house.] George and I went to Mr. Weston's for some horseradish and vinegar . . . to put on Mary's feet. . . . The vinegar was to wash her face with, put in water.

August 31 Monday   I went for lard from Mrs. Weston. Mary has a blister on which is very painful. My Mother to call on Mrs. Doctor Clark and pay her for the butter. . . .

September 1 Tuesday   I was not well; I took an emetic which made me feel a great deal better. Mary is much better. . . .

September 2 Wednesday   I got up. Mary thinks she can get up tomorrow. George caught a bullhead yesterday; it is a very wild sort of fish. . . .

Many nineteenth-century remedies sound absurd today, like washing your face with vinegar to cure a chest cold! A "blister" was another peculiar cure. Just as with leeches, a blister was thought to draw out "poisons" from the body of a sick person. To cause a blister to form, people applied a paste of crushed "blister beetles" (insects whose bodies contain an irritating substance) and water to the patient's skin. Here are some other strange remedies:

☞ For chicken pox, go out to the chicken house after sunset, lie down, and let a black hen fly over you.

☞ To reduce a fever, slice up a lot of onions and bind them onto the soles of your feet.

☞ To stop hiccups, drink water through a folded handkerchief.

Some remedies have a measure of common sense in them, however; for instance, to relieve a cold, pare off the rind of an orange, roll it up inside out, and place a little roll in each nostril. It might look peculiar, but probably the orange oil would help clear your sinuses. And washing your head with whisky might at least drown some head lice!

September 3 Thursday   Mary got up. There was a fire in the sitting room; she is very weak. . . .

September 4 Friday   . . . Mrs. Clark said we may have any vegetables out of her garden. . . . A great number of grasshoppers make a great noise. . . . I see a good number of insects like this [small blot].

September 5 Saturday   Sarah is not well. . . .

September 6 Sunday   We did not think there was church, so we did not go but we had it at home, but while we were at dinner, Mr. John Martingdale called to tell us there was church. They all went but me; I stayed to nurse Grace.

September 7 Monday   My Father shot a bird. John Parry came; he and George were taking hold of the [clothes] line, [and] a great piece of wood fell upon Agnes and I, but did not hurt us.

Sept 10 Thu.   Miss Weston called; we tease her about George, and she likes him.

Sept 11 Fri   . . . Grace is naughtier than usual.

Sept. 12 Sat   [no entry]

Sept. 13 Sun   It was not a sunshine morning. . . .

Sept 14 Mon   Mr. George Weston
was mowing in the field; he told
George to shoot an apple of his head.
George went for his bow and
arrow, — but [then] Mr. Weston
would not lett him do it, but George did it off a rake. . . .

Sept 15 Tues.   Old Mr. Weston came to turn his oats. . . . Mr. Church
. . . asked my father to have anything out of his garden that he likes
and to come every day. They sat on the sill of the door by the cellar,
and Mary was afraid they should hear her washing the dishes.

> 🧩 *Mary is likely feeling self-conscious about washing the dishes because in England that would have been the servant's work. For many people today, it's the dishwashing machine's work.*

Sept 16 Wed   . . . We had some cabbage which was very nice.

Sept 17 Thurs   Miss Tine came to invite my father and
Mother and Sarah and Mary to tea; she then ran off full
of business. . . . They said it was a very pleasant little
party; there was a great deal of silver on the table and a
great many cakes, as usual.

Sept 18 Fri.   In the morning a boy with a little basket
ful of notes came. He gave my mother one; it was to
invite her and my father to tea. . . . Before my Mother
came home we had put the bed in the sitting room. . . .

> 🧩 *The Hallens' accommodations must have had neither enough bedroom space for them all nor a sofa big enough to lie on. Bedtime would have been simpler with that pioneer convenience, the trundle bed; or a modern alternative, the sofa bed.*

Sept 19 Sat   Edgar went to the village for different things. My
father has but two dollars left as the money does not come from
England. . . .

Sept 20 Sun   Dark at night a man came to ask my father to go and
marry him. My father went; he had to go a good way.

101

Sept 21 Mon   Miss Weston and the housekeeper called.... It is Preston's birthday; he is nine.

Sept 22 Tues   The housekeeper and Miss Weston came to tea; before tea we walked into the field and eat some butternuts....

Sept 23 Wed   ...

Sept 24 Thur   ...

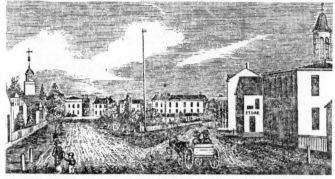

Sept 25 Friday Mrs. Gibson sent a note by a little girl to ask me Mother and Sarah and Mary to tea this evening. George went for some potatoes; he

Sandy Hill, c. 1841. Mr. Hallen's journal says they stayed at the Eagle Hotel (just behind the flagpole) before moving into their small rented cottage.

brought the basket half full, but soon after ... Mrs. Martingdale [and her hired boy] came with another basket full of potatoes and four nice cabbages. In the evening, Sarah and Mary went to Mrs. Gibson's, Miss Gibson showed them some very pretty petrifications.

Sept 26 Sat   ... Miss Weston is going to New york ...

Sept 27 Sun   We had church at home. We read some of our old journals, which reminds us of England.

Sept 28 Mon   George went to the post office, but no letter. The mornings are cold, but not very this morning....

Sep 29 Tues   Sarah and Mary went to Mrs. Parry's to tea; there were some young ladies there.... Mr. Parry plays Backgamon and chess and yet is so against cards and dancings.

Sep 30 Wed   Called on Mrs. Martingdale; she was making very pretty bed quilts of various patterns. The chesnuts [are] nearly ripe. We walked to Baker's Falls.

Oct. 1 Thurs   [When] we went to Baker's Falls, we saw a little brown animal; we got it up into a tree and George shot at it ... but did not kill it.

Oct 2 Frid   . . . Sarah and Mary went to Miss Westons to practice.

Oct 3 Sat   . . . My Mother and I went to the wild beasts show, as neither of us had seen any before. They were very beautiful, some of them. There was a circus . . . [with] a great deal of vulgar witt that I did not care about. . . . They stood on the horses [and] galoped very well. There was an Indian there, which was the best. When we got home, Miss Martingdale was there; she was going to stay tea. I like Miss Martingdale very much.

Oct 4 Sun   We went to church . . .

Oct 5 Mon   Mrs. Martingdale sent some potatoes and cabbages which is very exeptable.

Oct 10 Sat   My father made a great deal . . . [of] boxes; he makes them very strong. . . . [Some are for] Mrs. Gibson and poaching Mrs. Parry.

> *Poor Mr. Hallen! Here in unfamiliar territory he had to rely sometimes on the advice of others. But what if the advice conflicted?*
>
> [Oct. 6, 1835] Received the lg. expected ltr. from Tor. with L69.6s enclosed. Mr. Murray advises me to come immediately, I hardly know what to do. . . .
>
> [Oct. 10] Mr. Dewey advises me to go by waggon with my luggage as far as Schenectady and thence by canal. Mr. Parry advises me to go all the way by canal. Mr. D. talks of hindrances at locks: Mr. P talks of breaking down of waggons.

Oct 11 Sun   We had church at home. The beauty of the country is going; it has been very beautiful lately. . . .

Oct. 12 Mon   In the evening Mrs. *Evening* and her bewitching sister, Sally Stoe, came to drink tea. I no she had a new gown on, I smelt it. . . . I nearly knit one comforter for my wrist. My father finished one box.

Oct 13 Tue   My father had a letter from my uncle William so that he was obliged to go to New York. . . . My mother and I . . . [asked several people] to come this evening. We then went on to the village to by some plates and spoons, . . . as our stock is only three large ones and five little ones. . . . After tea Mr. Martingdale came; he said little Frances was kicked [by a horse], so they all went but Miss Gibson owh gave this description of it . . . "I saw there was something the matter with Mr. Martindill when he comes in, but I asked him to sit by Mrs. Martindill but he did not but [he] looked very sober, so I says 'What's the mater Mr. Martindill?' and he says, 'Frances is kiked, but I hope it is not much.' So there [Mrs. Martingdale] takes on so and wrings her hands and I trys to comfort her, but she would not." Sarah and Mary and Edgar went home with [Miss Gibson] with a lamp all through the village.

Oct 14 Wen   We pick[ed] up the apples to put by for us to eat on our travels. . . . Frances is better.

Oct 15 Thurs   . . . [The housekeeper] is always wanting Mr. George Weston and Sarah to be together; I know she wants to make Sarah in love with him. . . . After tea Mr.

George came (great brute) he looked so silly, trying to be gallant and then he was so particular about his hat.

A restored canal boat at the Erie Canal Village, Rome, New York.

Oct 16 Fri   My father went to Glen Falls to [find out] how the line boats go; they have stopped running. . . .

Oct 17 Sat   . . . Very busy packing. . . .

Oct 23 Wen   Very busy indeed; George and Edgar went to tea at Mrs. Parry's. Sarah and Mary and the little ones went to tea at Mrs. Martindale's; my Mother and father were too busy. . . . Mrs. Martingdale was very good natured. Two of the wagons were loaded tonight. After tea [we] went to Mrs. Church's [where] there was some supper for us.

Oct 24 Thurs   Early in the morning we had breakfast. . . . The wagon soon came and we set out. We were very sorry to leave Sandy Hill. Our driver was the man that my father married; he was very talkative. We stopped at Glen Falls bridge to look at the falls. They are very beautiful, but the scenery is not. It was a very nice ride. We arrived at the grand Saratoga that we heard so much of (by Miss Weston); it did not strike me as anything particular.

Have you ever "taken the waters"? In the 1830s, Saratoga Springs was already famous as a spa, a health resort where people came for rest and restoration. Complex geological conditions has created Saratoga's salty, naturally carbonated springs, and people thought the minerals in the water could cure their ailments. The spa had also become a fashionable social resort, and boasted several big hotels — all with wide verandas supported by wooden pillars, the style that Eleanora commented on back in July.

On the next page is a recent photograph of Olde Bryan Inn, built in 1825, and a picture of High Rock Spring, the first of the many mineral water springs at Saratoga to be frequented by European settlers (who had learned of their curative powers from the native Mohawks). Very likely it is this inn the Hallens stopped at, for several reasons: Eleanora says "inn" and not "hotel," and that they went "down" to the springs. High Rock Spring is directly below the Olde Bryan, and both are at the high end of town. Finally, High Rock Spring is the most renowned.

We went to an inn, but our luggage was not come, so we could not go by the *two o'clock* steam carriage. But before four it was come. . . . We . . . went down to the springs and had some water; I liked it very

Left: the Olde Bryan Inn.

Below: taking the waters at High Rock Spring, c. 1858. In the background are Iodine and Empress Springs.

Bottom: experimental carriage, 1828.

What Eleanora calls the "steam carriage" was the newest form of transportation. For a short time, the railroad was simply a rail road for glorified horse-drawn carriages. The British invention of the steam locomotive was barely thirty years old, and in the State of New York, the first locomotive to draw a train of passenger cars — which still looked like horse coaches — had made its ceremonial run just a few years before the Hallens passed through. Stories of the first trains are full of mishaps, like the burning cinders produced by the engine "DeWitt Clinton," which set passengers' clothes on fire!

much, tho some of them did not. We then set off. We thought we should go by steam and every minuit [minute] expected to go off very fast but it was drawn by horses. It went very steadily and fast.

We arrived at Scenectady when it was dark. There was only one line boat going and the Captain charged a great deal, but at last my father [agreed]. The Captain said we should have every accomodation. When we got in, we went into a little nasty cabin; the kitchen went into it, if kitchen it could be called, for it was only a little closet with a stove in it. It was a great while before they made the beds; . . . they were hung up by cords, 3 above another. All night men were coming in and out which was very disagreable.

Oct 25 Fri   In the morning when we got up we had only a nasty tin bason to use. . . . [An] idly dirty girl was letting the comb ly on the meat and comb[ing] her hair over it in a most disgusting way.

When we were dressed we went into the other cabin, where there was a fine asemblage of Americans. One of them was the most disagreable, inquisitive woman I ever saw. She was asking all day what this cost and what that cost, and "I guess this came from the old country, I guess you brought this with you." She was a thin woman dressed in a purple gown, something like Mrs. Parry; she seemed as if she was smelling into everything.

> ◼—*Yes, it does really say she put the comb on the meat!*

I guess this came from the old country

Left: Bridges over the Erie Canal were very low. Passengers who did not mind the famous call, "Low bridge!" often ended up with a bruised head, or worse, a dunking!

Right: As there was only one tow path, boats passing in opposite directions had to go carefully. The boat in the foreground is a line boat, the one behind a laker.

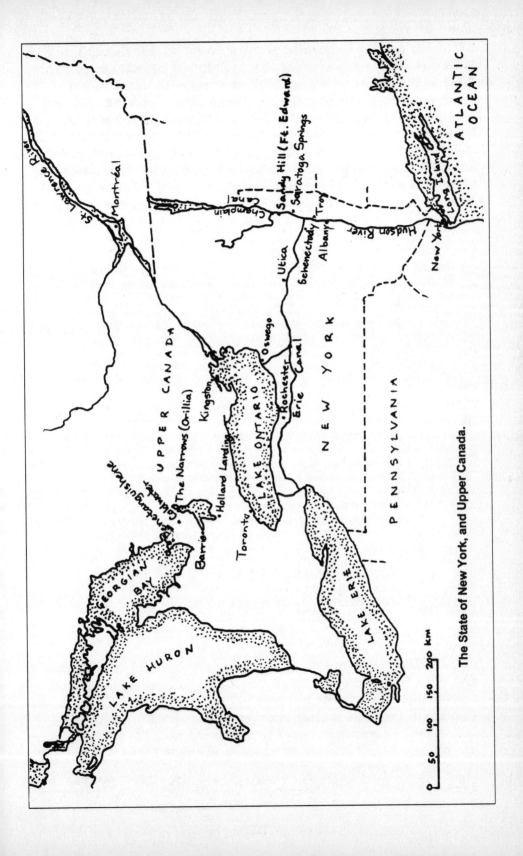

The State of New York, and Upper Canada.

Oct 27 Sun My father had prayers as the people wished him; they were none of them the church of England, but an Irish girl. After prayers my father asked any of them to sing; they sang most out of tune and through their noses. . . . An old man, a presbeterian, was crying, and the people were whispering "It's too much for him" (ridiculous things). Another boat and ours tried [to race] . . . the other boat beat their horses shamefully. . . . I do not know how it ended. The Captain allways said "gentlemen and ladies, come to your dinners;" there was not one gentleman or lady on board. We went into another boat [and] there was a respectable English family on board [named Gamage].

English society in the 1830s was very firmly fixed. Everyone, from the orphaned beggar in the street to the king in the palace, was born to a certain "class," and there was little you as an individual could do to change your standing. Though the class system was rigid, it was complicated, subtle and hard for us to understand. Within certain classes, your standing depended on many factors, such as your church, your political party, where you went to school or whom you married.

It is clear that the new communities forming in the United States and Canada divided themselves less sharply. In the United States, the 1830s were a period of increasing democracy, and people prided themselves on all being equal. (Remember Eleanora's comment that the staff at the hotel in Troy didn't call themselves "servants" but "helps"?) In Canada, society was more organized, but there were lots of ways you could improve your social standing — more so than in England. An ambitious former servant, gifted with good sense and used to hard work, might well become a prosperous farmer and then a pillar of settler society. Understandably, many middle- and upper-class people from the old world felt confused and threatened by this. Mr. Hallen's comment that " . . . the word 'respectable' is rather difficult to define so as to satisfy both parties . . . " (June 4th, 1835) seems a polite understatement!

Regardless of your standing, if you owned a horse, it was not respectable to treat it badly. Here's a little verse, collected by William Freelove, reminding a cab driver not to force his horse too much:

> *Up hill urge me not,*
> *Down hill hurry me not,*
> *Along the level spare me not,*
> *And in the stable forget me not.*

Oct 28 Mon Two of the little children are dreadfuly spoilt, Sammy and Billy. They were continually crying and asking for bread and cheese (they were cheese mongers). They were going to Canada. Mrs. Gamage did not like it atall; she was a fat wooman . . . . She had never been out of London hardly and could not tell barley from wheat. The eldest daughter was thirteen, a great red faced girl, but . . . the most goodhumered. The next was the

ugliest and very winey; the next was rather pretty. . . . Mr Gamage was a very quiet, goodnatured man. We reached Aswego [Oswego] late, so we stopped in the vessel all night. I was rather unwell so I took 12 pills.

Oct 29 Tues   I am a great deal better. There is a steam boat going to Kingston so we went in it. . . . It was very comfortable compaired with the line boats. We were all sick and could not have any dinner, but after I went into my berth and got an intresting book which made me quite well, we could all eat some tea.

Oct 30 Wed   In the morning we saw Kingston. I saw the diference from the United States directly, for we saw the English soldiers exercising. . . . Kingston is a nice little town. We saw several babys being carried about, a thing I never saw at Sandy Hill. We had our breakfast and then went to another steam boat, a great deal better, named The Saint George. The ladies' cabin was a very nice one . . . [with] little rooms containing two berths all round, with a wash hand jug and bason in each. . . . We went on deck a great deal. There are a great many people on board . . . [including] a French Canadian family . . . [with] 12 children — the eldest was about my father's age I should think.

Kingston from Fort Henry, 1828, by J. Gray.

Oct 31 Thurs   The scenery along the lake is very beautiful; their are severall pretty little Islands. [A gentleman on board] asked us some riddles. . . . He called me his little wife, which made me blush (silly thing, because all the rest laughed). We arrived at Toronto in the

The St. George was a unique paddle-wheel steamer, with schooner-rigged sails, built in Kingston in 1834. It and six other lake steamers moved approximately 50,000 immigrants to destinations in Upper Canada during this period.

Left: from *Girl's Book of Diversions*, 1835

The telling of riddles, or enigmas, has always been popular. Here are some others. See if you can puzzle them out!

Either backward or forward
you take me, Ye fair,
I am one way a number,
the other a snare.

'Tis in the church,
but not in the steeple;
'Tis in the parson,
but not in the people;
'Tis in the oyster,
but not in the bell;
'Tis in the clapper,
but not in the bell.

ENIGMAS.

1.

'Tis true I have both face and hands,
And move before your eye;
But when I move, I always stand,
And when I stand I lie.

A CLOCK.

Elizabeth, Elspeth, Betsy and Bess,
They all went together to seek a bird's nest.
They found a bird's nest with five eggs in;
They all took one, and left four in.

evening; we stayed [aboard] all night. A French lady as been in the cabin all the way; she never has come out of her birth. A gentleman has come to see her severall times. She does not drink any thing but milk. The people think she has pretended to be hill [ill]. They think she his a countess [and] has jewells to part with [i.e., she's trying to sell them]. She walked very *nimble* for a sick person.

~~Oct 32~~ *Nov 1 Fri*   We went to an hotel in Toronto [and] to Mr. Murray's to dinner and tea. I like Mrs. Murray and Miss Steel very much; they are very goodnatured. Miss Steele says she likes the woods very much. At night we went back to the hotell . . . the bedrooms are not comfortable.

~~Oct 33~~ *Nov 2 Sat*   After breakfast the Stage [-coach] came to the door; it is a covered wagon. We got in and away we drove with four horses. We laughed and were very much amused at first at the jolting, but we got rather tired of it at last. We stopped at a place to have our dinner where there was a most beautiful fire. . . . We then went on

The Fish Market below Front Street, Toronto, c.1840, artist uncertain.

Stagecoaches arrived and departed in front of the wedge-shaped building in the upper right, affectionately known as "the Coffin Block." In 1835 this burgeoning city had only recently changed its name back to Toronto from York, and its population was about 10,000: there were over 100 stores and 1,000 houses.

Note. During the season of Navigation a Steamer plies on Lake Simcoe, from Holland Landing, Barrie & Narrows.

104	Toronto See No 1.										
170	6	York Mills									
176	12	6	Thornhill. To Vaughan 10.								
181	17	11	5	Richmond Hill							
170	26	20	14	9	Rd to Lloyd Town (distant 12)						
192	28	22	16	11	2	Rd to Newmarket. (To distant market 2)					
197	33	27	21	16	7	5	Holland Landing. Floating Bridge over Holland River 1.x				
202	38	32	26	21	12	10	5	Bradford			
223	59	53	47	42	33	31	26	21	Barrie. See No 27. Kempenfield 1.2.		
238	74	68	62	57	48	46	41	36	15	Flos (Marlow's) Jack's 10.	
257	93	87	81	76	67	65	60	55	34	19	Penitanguishne. To Naval depot 2.

"By Yonge St" road.

Travel by the "Yonge Street" road, c. 1830.

According to Walton's Directory 1833–34, *the thirty-three-mile journey from Toronto (York) to Holland Landing took seven hours: from "12 o'clock, noon" to "7 o'clock the same evening." Furthermore, Yonge Street was still dirt and corduroy in 1835, and the "stagecoach" had only heavy leather straps, not springs, for suspension. No wonder Eleanora complained!*

The Toronto – Holland Landing stagecoach.

and after a terrible ride arrived at *Telposis*. Oh owh delightful, it was a comfortable frame house.

Nov 1 Sun My father took a walk in the morning; there is a miserable pool by Telpsis, full of stumps. It is pretty [here]; there are a good number of log houses about.

Nov 2 Mon We expected to go across the Lake [Simcoe] today, but the Captain came and said he is not going till tomorrow morning. . .

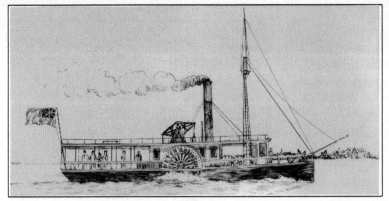

The *Peter Robinson*.

The great surge in immigration during the 1830s promoted the rapid spread of steamships of many sizes and shapes on all the lakes and big rivers of Upper Canada. Groups of investors would buy "shares" to raise the large sums required to build a boat; when it was up and running, each investor got a share of the profits. The steamer the Hallens rode on cost 2,000 pounds to build in 1833. It was named after its principal shareholder, the Honourable Peter Robinson, Surveyor General of Woods and Forests in the Province of Upper Canada, member of the Legislative Council and founder of the town of Peterborough. Peter Robinson built a "commodious tavern" at Holland Landing, which he leased to a Mr. Francis Phelps — Eleanora's "Mr. Felps."

Mr. Felps is going to Newmarket; he is going to get a barrel of butter [and] a barrell of pees; we have a barrell of onions and a barrell of flour [from] him and a barrell of pork at the landing [Holland Landing]. My father, George, Edgar and I went to a tin man's about a mile off . . . [and] bought four little tin cans, a lantern and a coffee pot [to use] as tea pot; we then went to a shop nearer and George bought a fish line and hooks. My father bought a little looking glass and some other things. In the evening we went in a wagon down to the landing; it was very pretty as it was by moonlight. We got in the boat; it was in a river. The country seemed very low.

The Ladies' Cabin aboard a St. Lawrence Steamer, 1838, by Catherine J. B. Ellice.

In contrast to canal boats, lake steamers were famous for their comfortable, even luxurious, accommodations.

Nov 3 Tuesday The river is very narrow [with] dead gras for a great distance of it on both sides. The river winds a great deal. I saw a great many wild ducks. Yesterday Sarah and Mary said [that] while we were out a very respectable man came, but he was so completely ugly his nose seemed as if it had been thrown on, it was so turned up. My father said they ought not to laugh at him so, because if . . . [we] met him again it would be very disagreeable. When we got to Roaches Point [Keswick], the Captain asked my father if he had any objection to marry [a couple]. My father said he had not; he went on shore to marry them. When he returned he said that it was the identical ugly man that Sarah and Mary told him about. There are a few clearings on the side of the lake at Barrie . . . [and] a neat little church, but no clergiman.

The original Trinity Episcopal Church, Barrie, 1872.

Going up into the lake from Barry we passed a very pretty house with a virando in front. We stopped a little in front of it and the person that the house belonged to came down. His name was O'Brian. . . . He said he would be very glad to see my father or any of us at any time. It was dark when

" . . . gentlemen warming their toes at the Narrows . . . , 1836" by H.B. Martin.

we arrived at The Narrows [Orillia]. We slept [on board] all night.

"O'Brian" is Mr. Edward O'Brien, and it was his father who built the "neat little church." It was new and distinguished in 1835 when the Hallens first saw it, but it lost its steeple and was abandoned for a new building sometime before the photograph above was taken.

Edward was a retired ("half pay") army officer, who had taken advantage of the government's offer to pay part of his pension in land. He and his wife Mary built their "very pretty house" at Shanty Bay in the summer of 1832. In her journals (published in 1968) Mary called it "the most tasty house in the country": a two storey, fifty- by twenty-four-foot building of "rough logs hewed smooth on the inside," with verandas (there they are again!) across the front and along both sides. A veritable log mansion!

"The Woods," Shanty Bay, by Mary O'Brien.

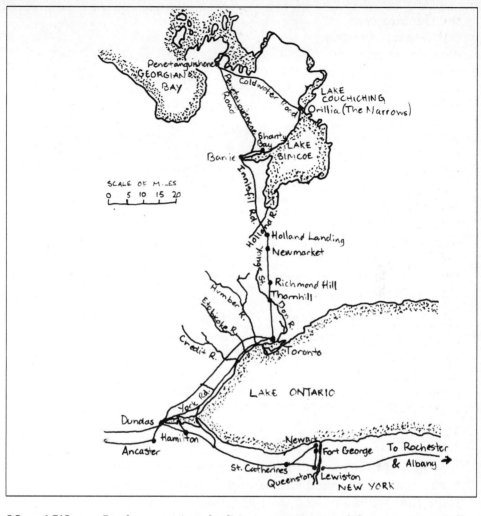

Nov 4 Wen   In the morning, before we went out of the steam vessell, George put his fish [line] in as he saw a good number of fish. He caught nine very soon, but he had not time to ketch more. . . . We stayed on some trunks of trees whilst my father went to . . . [see] about the luggage. We saw three Indian wooman and a man come down to the lakeshore with a canoe. One of them and the man got in and away the woman rowed . . . very fast. The other two filled two bark baskets with water and went up again. A great number of Indian houses are here that [the] Government has built for them, and there is a scool. We went to the inn, a log house. . . . We had the fish done for breakfast; they are perch; they were very nice. My father saw Mr. Drinkwater; he spoke to him.

> *The Drinkwaters!*

After breakfast the wagon was ready with six oxen. My Mother and little ones got in; the others walked. I found several flowers like violets tho they had longer stalks. The road was very bad indeed. Mary and I rode some of the way; we got very hungry and were glad to stop at [Price's Corner] for some bread and butter. It was a neat log house. It seemed a great way; my father thought we had passed the turn into Mr. Steele's but the man said he new the

Indians and Canoe, Coldwater River, 1844, by T. H. Ware.

way. He at last turned in, but before we had proceeded far the oxen refused to proceed. The man went forward; he found that the ground was so soft that the wagon could not go along it.

Settlers often debated whether to invest in oxen, or horses — if they could afford either! Oxen are very strong, of course, and could be left out at night during the warmer months to find their food in the forest. Eventually they could be made into stew, although the meat would be tough! Horses on the other hand needed expensive hay and oats, more care, and were not usually eaten for meat by the British. However, they are much much faster for travelling. The Hallens' yoke (pair) of oxen, which they bought in 1837, cost $90.00; an astronomical sum which they paid over a period of two years.

At last to our great joy we saw a man on horseback; we ran towards him and asked him to stop. He said the road was impassable [and] that we had passed the right road a great while. He advised us to leave the wagon and for us and the oxen to go to Mr. Steele's. The oxen sank up to the top of their legs in the mud and we had to follow the best way we could. It got quite dusk; at last we got to a firm road and went on pretty fast. We were obliged to call to the driver to stop two or three times, he went so fast. At last we saw the clearing and I never felt so delighted . . . seeing a light in the window. We waited down in the fields whilst my father went on to prepare them for such a host of hungry and weary travelers. He soon returned

Coldwater, 1832, by H. B. Martin.

The Cassin-Haugh house, built c. 1830, by Dorothy Clark McClure.

The Hallens' new home was probably much like this one-and-a-half-storey cabin, but without the lean-to at the back; the Hallens' kitchen was part of the main house, according to Eleanora's floorplan (she has marked it "kit"). Settler cabins were constantly being added on to, and no wonder, as they were not very large. This one was only 17 feet, 10 inches by 28 feet (about 5 by 8.5 metres).

with Mr. John Steele for our guide. We soon got to the house where there was Mr. and Mrs. Steele and Laura, a little girl. They received us very kindly and we had a good tea off a very large loaf, which we made a great hole in. . . . Sarah, Mary and I [slept] in one bed in a room, with Skeeler, Richard and Agnes in a bed on the floor . . . My Mother and father in another [room], with Edgar, Preston on the floor. . . . George slept on the sofa in the parlour. I had a most delightful night.

From the Steele diaries (yes, they kept diaries too!) it seems that John Steele is about eighteen years old at this time. When you get into Part IV, you'll suspect that Eleanora developed a crush on him.

> *It would take twenty minutes today to drive the distance the Hallens covered on foot —
> about eighteen kilometres (eleven miles). Here's a poem Mary wrote about their
> experience:*
>
> As we were *driving* so grand
> We were *put* to a stand
> In a mud hole fast we stuck
> As *iff* Canada *wished* us bad luck
> We looked all around as to find us a guid[e]
> But nothing appeared but the great forests wide
> At last very near us we *descried*
> A horseman [unreadable word] taking a ride
> We *flew* to him like a great gale
> And told him the *dolorous* tale.

Nov 5 Thurs   In the morning we made all the beds and swept up the room with a little brush. Mr. Steele is very polite indeed; the house is a very good one; the parlour is a very nice one; Laura is a pretty little girl. After breakfast my father and Mr. Steele, Mary, George, Laura and I walked down to our future house. The Bywaters were still there; they are going today or tomorrow. I suppose it is a nice little log house, all with the bare logs, three rooms downstairs and two up; there is no garden. There is an oat rick in front of the house.

> *How polite Eleanora is being in her comments! Is that what you do when
> everything's strange and you're trying to cope?*

Nov 6 Fri   Mr. Steele advised my father to pull up the turnips before the snow comes, so my father, George, Edgar and Preston went. . . .

Nov 7 Sat   They went to pull turnips again. Laura has a skipping rope; I skipped a little. They have two very large dogs named Fearless and Sneazer; they have also a pretty little dog named *Tiny.*

Nov 8 Sun   My Father is not well. He was obliged to ly down. We had a letter from my Grandpapa . . . [who] is very well. Mr. Steele read service. . . .

Nov 9 Mon   Laura and I walked down to the Bywaters. We went in the little parlour; all the furniture is out but the sofa. They have nearly pulled all the turnips and are topping them.

Nov 10 Tues   Laura and I walked with my father . . . through the

Lay the cloth,
Knife and fork,
Bring me up a leg of pork.
Don't forget the salt, mustard, vinegar,
pepper!

— *nineteenth-century skipping rhyme*

This play . . . is a healthy exercise, and tends to make the form graceful; but it should be used with moderation. I have known instances of blood vessels burst by young ladies, who . . . have persevered in jumping after their strength was exhausted.

from The Girl's Own Book, 1833

wood down some very pretty *country* where the brook ran. I read very often. . . . The wagon is at the Bywaters to take them. They asked my father to lett them stay a week or two longer, but my father said he could not and Mr. Steele is afraid if they can get us to the house whilst [the Bywaters] are in they will stay till sleighing time which would be very uncomfortable.

Nov 11 Wed   My Father walked down to Rushock (we have named it that name). He came back with the agreeable news that [the Bywaters] were gone. My Mother and the boys went down; the boys stayed. . . . Laura is much disturbed lest George is not comfortable. It snowed a little [but] did not stay on the ground.

Nov 12 Thur   It was very miserable when we got to Rushock. My father was very much tired, for he had cut down a tree and it had lodged. The things were all in confusion and hardly [any] seats to sit upon. The beds were all on one side of the room, for they had all slept downstairs before the fire. The first thing to be done was to get dinner . . . beef stewed with potatoes and turnips. Mary washed up the plates. We then had to get the beds up in the large comfortless bedrooms and air sheets to put on them. It was

"A Bush Road, Upper Canada" by P.J. Bainbrigge, 1842.

121

Mother, Grace, George, Edgar and Preston sleep in the room over the parlour; and Sarah, Mary and Agnes, Skeeler, Richard and I sleep in the other.

Nov 13 Friday   Edgar and Preston went up [to the Steeles'] for my father's box. They brought down a quarter of lamb. We have 20 fowls that I feed. We have also two pigs. We are a little more comfortable.

Nov 15 Sun   Mr. Steele and Mr. John Steele came to church. We had a nice fire; it is very cold.

Nov 16 Mon   To our great joy a wagon load of luggage came. We had to put something for the man to eat in the parlour: some fried pork and potatoes. We have only the sofa, 3 rickety stools and two chairs to sit on.

Nov 17 Tues   The man went very early in the morning and took the two chairs. Mrs. Steele and Laura came; we had time to put the room rather tidy. A man named *Pope* brought 12 chickens; my Father bought them. Four cocks were killed.

Nov 18 Wed   My Father and George are chopping in the wood; I went and cut down a little tree.

Nov 19 Thur   Another waggon load of luggage. The man went the same night because the time before the oxen had done a great deal of damage. The chimney set on fire, but my father put it out. It is only built of lathe and plaster; the plaster is nearly all come off and it is very dangerous.

> "Fire! Fire!" cried Mrs. Maguire.
> "Where? Where?" cried Mrs. Blair.
> "Down the town," said Mrs. Brown.
> "Oh, Lord save us!" cried Mrs. Davis.
>
> — *old nursery rhyme*
>
> *Chimney fires were almost commonplace in the days of log cabins and open fires. Naturally, their frequency increased in homes where chimney builders saved time and effort by using materials like lathe (criss-crossed strips of wood) under mud plaster, instead of stone.*

Nov 20 Friday   We have it a little more comfortable. My Father's hands chop very badly.

Of course Mr. Hallen's hands chop badly! After all, he's a minister, and did not spend his time in England chopping wood. Provident settlers laid in approximately twenty cords of wood for each winter's heating and cooking needs. Not only were the Hallens late in starting their winter's woodpile, their wood was not seasoned, so it would not burn well. (A cord, by the way, is a stack roughly one metre deep, one metre high and three metres long; or, two logs deep, as high as your shoulder, and as long as three giant steps.)

Speaking of provident settlers, many emigrant guidebooks had lists of the supplies and furnishings settlers would need. We don't know the details of the Hallens' belongings, but Mr. Hallen noted they had "36 cwt. [cubic hundred-weight] of luggage." One cwt. equals 112 pounds, or just under 51 kilograms. So they brought a lot, that much is certain!

This advice-filled letter was written by Edward O'Brien of Shanty Bay to his future minister, Reverend Ardagh, telling him what to bring with him in 1842. Presumably conditions were not too different seven years earlier.

As to what you should bring with you, don't bring a servant; unless it is someone long known and trustworthy, have nothing to do with them. In the way of furniture, chests of drawers are the only thing that you should attempt to bring, and that because they make good packing cases. If you can pack well, all odds and ends that won't sell, such as fenders, fire irons, etc. may be brought. Bring all your bedding, carpeting (old carpets, and besides, ones [that] make the best packing wrappers). All your delph and cutlery — get a proper packer from an earthenware establishment and stow the delph in barrels — good water-tight casks are the best of all packing cases, and will be very useful here; don't bring an extra boot or shoe, except the ladies, who may judge for themselves as here the material and make are coarser — bring your own saddle (. . . the best are made in Cork) also a side saddle as the horse is at times the only means of conveyance. Mrs. O'Brien does not recommend Mrs. Ardagh to lay in any store of clothing, further than may be required for the coming season, but she advises a  substantially large supply of threads, needles, etc. Being myself very fond of a certain degree of refinement, I would recommend if to be had conveniently and fresh any choice kitchen flower or garden seeds or roots of the common hardy kinds. They cost little and take up no room.

Incidentally, if you were thinking, "Ugh, turnips! Who would want so many?" you should know that they weren't all for the Hallens to eat. Because turnips were very easy to grow, even in half-cleared fields, they were used as winter cattle feed. As the Hallens had no livestock yet, Mr. Hallen might have sold some of this particular crop for much-needed cash.

Nov 21 Sat   The black wood is very disagreeable for my Father to cut; it blacks him and George very much.

Nov 22 Sun   Mr. Steele, [his son] John . . . and Mr. Josheph Willson came to service; there are not seats enough, so a board was taken up. Fox and his daughter were here; Fox kept his seat by the fire and did not offer it to anybody.

> ■▶ *It's hard to know exactly what Eleanora means, but presumably they simply lifted up a floorboard (which must not have been nailed down) and laid it between two chairs to make a temporary bench. Makes you wonder about walking on those floors. . . .*

[Nov 23   Grace has not been very well today; we are all busy with her.

Dec 1   Grace cries a good deal and keeps us awake at night.]

> *Once more, mysterious missing entries! Neither Nov. 23rd nor Dec. 1st are in Eleanora's original. In fact, there are two blank pages between Nov. 22 and Christmas; we can guess again that she meant to go back and fill them in. So it looks as if Mrs. Drinkwater supplied these entries herself, perhaps using information from another Hallen's diary. And next, she obviously thought Christmas 1835 was more than "different." She added the word "very" to her description.*

Dec 25 Frid   I got up early and put some hemlock in the parlour and hall; it is a diferent Christmas day to last year. In the morning . . . [the Steeles] came in the cutter; it is a very nice sleigh. . . . Mrs. Steel is better. While Mr. & Mrs. Steele were receiving the sacrament, John Steele, Laura, George and I walked up . . . to ride down in the sleigh. [It] was very delightful . . . like been [being] in a boat. We had roast beef and mince py for dinner. George had a bad pain in his face, so he went to bed.

Dec 26 Sat   George is not well; he lies in bed.

Dec 27 Sunday   [The Steeles] came in about the middle of service. . . . After service, Laura, Mary Wilson and I went into the parlour; they *told* each other about people.

Dec 28 [no entry]

Jan 3 Sun   . . . [The Steeles] came in the ox sleigh with seats in it [for a church service]. Mr. Steele thinks my Father has made a nice clearing.

Purbrook, 1854 — home of the Steele family, by Eleanora Hallen.

Jan 4 Mon   Sarah walked with my Father to Mr. Steele's. She is going to stay there till Wednesday. George and Edgar walked up with their axes to grind.

Jan 5 Tues   We manage very well without Sarah.

Jan 6 Wed   Edgar went up for Sarah. When she came down she said the night after she went Mrs. Steele had been taken very ill with a violent pain in her back and that she is very ill now. . . . [Sarah] knew . . . she would be wanted so after dinner Edgar and Mary walked up with her. One of the hens flew into the wood and we could not get her out but the

[next copybook] other I got home. Some body nocked at the door whilst I had my stocking off so they nocked a second time before I went to the door; it was Mr. Joshep Willson. He brought back an auger my father had lent him; he did not stop. Mary & Edgar soon came back.

Eleanora's diary for 1836 begins at the end of her last 1835 copybook. This is the only time she does not start a new volume with a new date and the sense of a new beginning.

Opposite: a cross-written letter.

When you think of how difficult it was for the Hallen family to get to — and then find — their new home, that letters from England found them may seem miraculous! The British postal service had actually been functioning for many years in North America. Halifax and Lower Canada had post offices before the American Revolution; we have that famous American, Benjamin Franklin, to thank for opening them (based in Philadelphia, he became deputy postmaster of England in 1753). But after the United States became independent from Britain, postal service fragmented. The military carried much of the mail, and often private individuals, stopping at a town to check for their own mail, were were asked to bring letters to their neighbours deep in the bush.

By 1800 there was a postmaster at York (Toronto-to-be). However, despite the best efforts of the postal service to cope, by the 1830s rapidly expanding settlement throughout Upper Canada meant that even new post offices could not keep up with demand. Private carriers were often much faster and cheaper than official ones and there were lots of complaints.During this period, there was also a lot of heated political argument about where post offices would be located and who would benefit from the money collected through the system: local administration or far away London.

The cost of postage came to be based on weight only, not distance, after reforms in England in 1840 (these included the innovative postage stamp) and in Canada in 1851. The cost was high, and paper was very expensive. This led to the diabolical — for the eyes! — practice of "cross-writing." By writing widthwise, and then again lengthwise, thrifty letter-writers could get a two-page letter onto a single piece of paper. One preserved Hallen letter has one section written diagonally, as well!

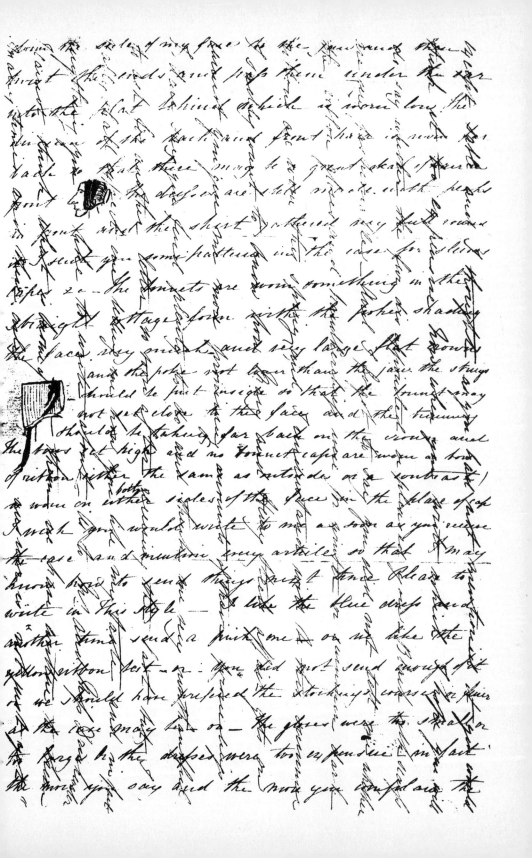

down the sides of my face to the jaw and then
thrust the ends and pass them under the ...
into the ... behind which is worn low the
... at the back and front there is never ...
back ... that there may be a great deal of ...
front ... the dresses are still made with peaks
in front and the skirt gathered very full round
... I send you some patterns in the case for sleeves
... &c — the bonnets are worn something in the
straight cottage form with the ... shading
the face very much and very large flat crowns
and the poke not lower than the jaw the strings
should be put inside so that the bonnet may
not set close to the face and the trimmings
should be taking far back on the crown and
the bows set high and no bonnet caps are worn ... bows
of ribbon either the same as outside or a contrast
worn on either both sides of the face in the place of cap
I wish you would write to me as soon as you receive
the case and mention every article so that I may
know how to send things next time Please to
write in this style — I like the blue dress and
another time send a pink one or not like the
yellow ribbon best — You did not send enough of it
or we should have preferred the stockings coarser or finer
as the case may be — The gloves were too small or
too large but the dresses were too expensive in fact
the more you say and the more you ...

Part IV

Canadian Rusticity

. . . In Which We Learn about the Weather, Stories, Struggles, Visits, Fun and Family Life of the Hallens at the New Rushock.

And so, 1835, that eventful year for the Hallens, has passed, and Eleanora starts a new journal volume. If you want to know what Eleanora thinks about either the year that has finished or the new one that is beginning, too bad — she's not reflecting on very much, at least not in writing.

However, her short comment about Christmas is tantalizing: " . . . it is a different Christmas Day to last year." Perhaps the Hallens' Canadian Christmas was different, but not very significantly so, since she gives no details. Yet it feels as if that sentence is a careful understatement, loaded with feelings that are too much to write about. The very fact that Eleanora says little about Christmas 1835, and appears to say nothing about the new year in the new world, may tell us that life was not just different, but difficult, maybe too difficult — even overwhelming — to acknowledge after less than two months in residence.

To begin to understand what the Hallens experienced, it is useful to know something about Upper Canada in the 1830s. Except for a sixty-kilometre-wide strip along the St. Lawrence and the shores of Lake Ontario, and a narrower strip along Lake Erie, Upper Canada was almost entirely forest, dotted with meadows and lakes, criss-crossed by rivers. A few roads had been cut through the forest to service the scattered settler clearings, but water was the key means of long-distance transportation.

Short-distance travel was worse than in England — the Hallens didn't even have a family donkey, let alone an aunt's gig to borrow! Not only was the wilderness vast and physically difficult to traverse, but there was a real danger of getting lost in it, and there were fearsome wild animals, as well:

[Jan. 17, 1836]   . . . I forgot to say my father and George thought they heard a wolf but they did not kno, so they hasked Mr. Josep Willson. He said it seems to be a fox, but I no it was a wolf because he said he had heard one [and] that it gives a bark and then a <u>turuble</u> long howl.

The Hallens settled in Medonte Township, in an area that is known to tourists and cottagers today as "Huronia" (referring to the original inhabitants, the Huron Nation), which lies on the western shore of Lake Simcoe and the eastern part of Lake Huron, or Georgian Bay. The new "Rushock" was a small log house in a clearing in the backwoods, about twenty kilometres west of the Narrows between Lakes Couchiching and Simcoe — the present-day city of Orillia, Ontario. Their cabin had housed the Bywaters, tenants of Captain (or Mr.) Steele, a retired naval officer. Mr. Steele wanted to establish a church on his land, and welcomed Reverend Hallen and his family for that purpose, probably helping to support them for the first few years.

In contrast to the well-settled State of New York, in the 1830s Medonte had only recently begun to be settled by European people. A few, like Mr. Steele, were British retired (or "half-pay") officers, "gentlemen" with more or less money. Some of the immigrants were very poor; and some, like the Hallens, were somewhere in the middle. The area was also inhabited by the Ojibwa people. Eleanora mentions them only occasionally; however, the status and territory of this nation were big issues during her time. Their traditional hunting grounds were getting smaller, and the boundaries of Native reserve

At the time of the census that Eleanora mentions in 1837, there were 140 households in Medonte Township. A household might be a family like the Hallens, with a husband and wife and many children, so it is hard to say how many people there were. In 1842, another count was taken, and this time it showed a total of 548 people in Medonte. In the Simcoe district, the total number of people was 12,592 that same year.

lands kept shrinking as more and more settlers arrived to clear the land and create more farms.

The government allotted the Ojibwa areas for farming, and paid them for building cabins, a school and mills for wood and flour in Coldwater, the nearest settlement to the Hallens. The Ojibwa, traditionally hunters, did not take to this new, agricultural way of life, and slowly abandoned it.

But where there are mills, there are settlers. Within twenty years of the Hallens' arrival, the European population in Medonte would increase dramatically. Most of the Native people would move to Manitoulin Island, though a number would stay, establishing three reserves in the area. The County of Simcoe would be formally designated (1843), postal services "nationalized" (1851), and the Ontario, Simcoe and Huron Railway well underway. So, in less than one generation, the Hallens would no longer be "in the bush," as settlers called it.

Still, in 1836, in the middle of their first long, cold Canadian winter, life for Eleanora Hallen and her family was strange and challenging. And perhaps that January came too soon to take stock and was too difficult to allow them to pause in the daily business of keeping a family of twelve warm and fed.

So, just how cold was it?

You will recall Eleanora saying it was very cold back in November; it seemed to just get colder as the weeks passed.

[Jan. 18, 1836] The weather is cold. My father and George chop evey day.

[Jan. 29] In the morning My Mother and I went to call on Mrs Willson. It is a long walk; the road is pretty well beaten. It is not so cold. . . .

[Feb. 1] It is dreadfully cold. We can hardly keep ourselfs warm. George Wilson called to warm his hands. . . .

[Feb. 2] It is still very cold. The buckets are frozen *very* thick and it is difecult to thaw them. Mr John Steele called to ask if we wanted any thing from Cold water, as he is going, but we did not. I called my father to dinner: I make the woods resound! I heard the bells on the horse has John Steele was passing.

[Feb. 3] I put some curtains up in the little parlour round the stove which make it very warm. My father made a table to go round the stove which is very comfortable.

[Feb. 4]   It is very cold. We are in great want for a broom. My father made us one of hemlock. We had some salt pork which has been boiled & roasted; we liked it very well. I am glad to get to bed.

[Feb. 5]   This morning when I came down my father told me that a pot with water standing in it had frozen has thick has a crown piece. The oil is frozen in the lamps. We had rice and apples for dinner. The little ones have dinner in the parlour, has the table can't hold all of us. The cat has burn[ed] her back quite brown. Sarah shivers and does not feel well.

[Feb. 6]   I don't no what to put.

This last, very short entry may reflect what a hard time the Hallens were having in frigid Medonte. For a week after this, Eleanora makes no regular entries. Perhaps she was simply too cold to write!

What about snow? Was there a lot of it?

There is no entry announcing when it began, but at Christmas 1835, Eleanora spoke of sleighs, so we can be sure the scenery in December was already much whiter than in the old country. Fortunately, the Wilson family helps fill in the picture: Mr. Wilson's diary, which also exists in local archives, states that the first snow of the autumn fell on November 8th; the ground was covered on the 20th, and on the 28th he wrote it snowed " . . . every day all week . . . mill stopped for want of water. Snow bitter; 1 1/2 to 2 foot drifts." During February's cold snap, we read there has been more snow — and the cold continues, as well:

[Feb. 22, 1836] . . . My father got some of the snow of the roof that is the flatest [part], for Mr Josheph rather alarmed him [referring to its weight].

[Feb. 25]   . . . My father went to Coldwater — a cold walk. . . .

[Feb. 27]   I forgot to say that yesterday I went out into the wood and walked about a great deal. When I came in I thought I could not feel my great toe, and it was frozen. I rubbed itt with snow and itt soon came to ittself.

[Mar. 2]   My father did not call us quite so early. It is very difecult to get up these cold mornings. . . .

[Mar. 4] Quite a thaw the wind was high but quite warm. . . .

[Mar. 5]   . . . In the night the wind had changed, and it was a cold frost, to our sorrow. . . .

[Mar. 6] When I came down this morning, my father had just lighted the fire. It is a cold morning, but not so cold has it has been. . . . My father had filled the bake kettle full of ashes and put it under the table, which made it warmer for him. The fire was nice & warm in the stove. . . .

[Mar. 10] It was very snowy, indeed it snowed continually. . . .

[Mar. 11] This morning Preston found a little three legged iron pot full of ice and [it had] splitt. I dare say we shall have that Mr Joseph Willson for a drink of water. The snow is very deep indeed — the ckiken pen door was quite stopped up. . . .

[Mar. 17] . . . Sarah was pursuing a thing that had fallen of the [clothes] line. She got nearly up to [her] middle [in the] snow and was obliged to role as [well as] she could. There is a thin coat of ice on the top of the snow . . . [and] pools of water about. Agnes fell into a tin of water she had to undress and ly in the cradle. My father went to see Butcher as he is very ill, but as it was such bad walking he stayed tea at Mr Steeles. . . .

[Mar. 22] Sarah & I make my father's and mother's bed. I do not like it much as it is so cold [upstairs and the bed] is nearly broken down. Mr Josheph Willson called; he had been after a deer. He had snow shoes on. I tryed them on — I walked pretty well in them. . . . My father tied the snow shoes on; he liked them.

What did the Hallens do?

At home, indoors, family life had its routines, like chores:

[Jan. 22, 1836] In the morning I gett up before the rest generally and put breakfast. After breakfast Mary washes the tea things. Sarah generally puts dinner, and then Sarah and Mary wash it up. Mary and I make the beds. Either of us put tea [things out], and I wash them up.

Plus, there seem to have been regular lessons, though we don't hear much about them. An entry in January reveals the only mention Eleanora makes of them in 1836: ". . . I teach the little ones generally every morning." She also makes a couple of references to her father

The inside back cover of Eleanora's only surviving original copybook from 1836 and beyond.

Eleanora often used the margins of a copybook page to illustrate specific journal entries. But many of the doodles you have seen came from crowded pages like this one.

attending a meeting about building a school — but never writes any further news of it.

Of course, home life for the Hallens was always enlivened by their pets (they get a puppy from the Steeles) and their pranks:

[Feb. 22, 1836] . . . Noble makes a great howling at night & nearly all night. He is a very nice little dog. . . .

[Feb. 26] . . . Sarah dressed up in my father's coat and gaiters, with his hat, and went to the wood to [meet him]. . . . She said she was the governor. My father did not know her at a distance; he thought it was young Mr Drinkwater, but she looked so very large about her legs, as her frocke was pinned between her legs, by that I should have known her. *Sarah dressed up as the governor*

[Feb. 29, 1836] . . . The cat & Noble eat of the same tin; they are better friends now. He runs about with is tail cocked up. Grace is frightened when he comes near her, because he jumps on her. Grace is cutting some teeth which makes her cumersome. George began to build a house of the snow which had been taken of the roof in lumps. We have broken so many basons that their was not one for me to have soup in. George took the plaster off his leg; it was well. . . .

30 days hath September April June and November Feb days are 28 alone and all the rest are thirty one except in leap year I opine Feb days are 29

Whether during lesson time or not, Eleanora continued to make up silly poetry about her siblings. And they always shared letter and journal writing, as well as that special treat: reading.

[Mar. 1]
Mary a very long dream has had
Sarah if I explain it may drive her mad
Sarah sat on a sofa so cheep
By the side of her *Jona* [John?] so *peep*
He drew up to her with a speech so fine
He says Sarah will you be mine
Sarah then in a great fashion fled
and called him all names she had in her head

138

[Mar. 2]   ... We tryed to have tea early; my father read a novell called Hellen which came from Mrs Steele. It was very intresting. ...

[Mar. 12]   Our most comfortable time is night because all the little ones go to bed, and my father reads. Saturday is a busy day as we have to make it tidy for Sunday. The pot with the potatoes slipped into the fire and we could not get them out till they were done and then got it up with a cord.

[Mar. 14]   Little Grace this morning took up a copy book and pretended to read. My father put down the letters that were received and sent. I began to make a pair of mokasins for myself has I have no shoes to fit me. ...

[Mar. 17]   ... We nearly finished the *tale*; it is very intresting. We wanted my father to read more, but as it was so late he could not. A man called to leave his flour, as he was tired; we were glad he did not stay.

[Mar. 18]   Wailand's daughter came for the flour. I should think it was very heavy. My father just before dinner went to Butcher's. Sarah & Mary ironed. . . . Hellen (the tale) was so intresting we were very sorry to leave off. There is not a great deal till the end; [so] we said we wanted to finish a hole in a stocking or something.

[Mar. 30]   ... John Steele my dear, too dear John Steele — you shall be mine — I never will forget or slight thee my John, oh, dear John I am your dear ~~Eleanora~~ Sarah dearest faithful ~~Eleanora~~ Sarah.

Did they still go to church as often?

Well, yes and no. There was church every Sunday, just as there had
always been — but only a morning service. And the Hallens didn't go
to it, it came to them, at least for the first year or so. Lots of entries
give details of their Sunday visitors. This was only a temporary
arrangement, however, as Captain Steele's goal was to build a church
in Medonte.

By July 1837 Eleanora writes of walking with the Steeles to see
"the place where they have been under brushing," in preparation for
cutting down the logs for the new church. By that time the Hallens'
parlour was no longer adequate for the new congregation:

> [June 18, 1837] We had to dress in a great hurry because my
> father was waiting for us to go to Livingstons', where he has
> service. The Willsons and Steeles went; there was more than
> forty people there. In the evening Mr and Mrs [and] Jhon Steele
> and Laura came to tea. Mr Steele and my father taulked about
> a church that they are going to put up about the autumn.

But all of this is getting ahead of the winter of 1836. . . .

Did they ever get out?

Getting out of their cramped cabin as much as the weather permitted
must have been a relief. In March, Eleanora writes often of their
excursions:

> [Mar. 4, 1836] . . . I took Grace in the sleigh into the wood. . . .

"delightful
return from
*a delightful
picnic near*
Drinkwaters
neighbors
going through
bush 1838"

Unsigned —
but drawn
in Eleanora's
style!

[Mar. 8] In the morning I went into the wood with the sleigh and made a slide up & down a hill. When I came in there were too haunches of venison — the Indian had come again. . . .

[Mar. 9] Preston, Sceelar, Richard & Agnes all went down into the road and went all round. It is the first time they have done it. I climed up the corner of the house nearly to the window where Mary and Grace were. . . . My father read.

[Mar. 20] . . . After dinner George, the littles & I went in the wood with the sleigh.

[Mar. 24] I take Grace a ride in the hand sleigh in a box. She is very healthy; her hands and face are quite red. Sarah's frock is a complete compact of patches thrown on each other.

Despite the weather and the challenging walking, the Hallens visited many people, especially the Steeles and the Willsons, their nearest neighbours (twenty and thirty minutes away by foot on a good day!). There were the usual neighbourhood favours to fulfill, lending and borrowing and advice-giving, plus Mr. Hallen was beginning to gather his new congregation.

[Mar. 18, 1836] . . . My father had called on a great many poor people, English, Scotch & Irish. He was going to Mr Rutherford's, [but] it was such a way, such bad walking and narrow path that he did not go.

Judging by Eleanora's enthusiastic descriptions, the best visits of all were long ones, like going to the Willsons' overnight or the Steeles' for the evening:

[Jan. 11, 1836] In the morning Mr. Joseph Willson came. . .to take us to dinner. . . . When we got there we were welcomed by Laura [Steele] and Miss Willson. Laura had been staying there all the week. They had not had their dinner but had it when we came. [As we had had our dinner] we did not eat any meat, only some puding.

The room is a nice large one: the walls are the bare logs with pictures hung round; their [is] a piano that they brought from Scotland and all their furniture, . . . [and] a stove . . .which gives out a great deal of heat. In the evening Mr Josheph put on his kilt, it is a Highland dress. It is of plaid with a scarf and bow of the same. It comes above his knees, and his legs are not covered, which looked very disagreeably. He had short stokings with very low shoes.

After tea we played at cards, the old maid and bachelor, and "Tom come kittle me," a vulgar game. We then played at "the traveller." We all sat in a round and Miss March stood ap. She began to tell a tale about a traveler, and when ever she said "house" or "inn" we were to jump up and turn round. She named us all: I was called "cook," Mary "house keeper," and so on, and whenever she mentioned either of our names we jumped up and turned round. Mr Josep wanted a dance, but none of the others [did], so we played at blindman's buff.

After [that], we had some supper and then went to bed. It was a small room, but very comfortable. Laura & I lay in a bed on the floor, and Miss Marsh, Mary and Mary Willson [lay] in a bed with curtains. There was only a deal partition between us and the boys and they made a great noise singing and laughing.

[Jan. 12] In the morning the boys made as much noise. . . . Laura is very ridiculous with George: she told us up-stairs that she . . . loves George Hallen and allways would love him. Miss March said . . . [that] when [she goes] to Toronto [she] would forget George and fall in love with the first person she mett with. But [Laura] said she <u>would</u> not. . . .

[Mar. 21] In the morning Sarah & I went up to Mrs Steele's to practise. . . . By the house we mett Mrs Steele & John Steele coming to fetch us. . . . Sarah went on to practise but I got in the sleigh and went down to our house to ask if we may stay dinner; we may stay.

Soon after we came home [to the Steeles'] Mr Drinkwater came. My feet were wet and so Miss Steele took me into her room to change my shoes. I had holes in my stocking, so that I did not like to change them, but Miss Steele went out of the room and Sarah came in, so we pinned the holes up at the heeles.

Before tea My father and George came. Mrs Steele sang & Sarah, George & my father. Mr Steele and Mr Drinkwater [were] saying that when they came here . . . they [the Steeles] had to go in a boat, Mr Drinkwater in a canoe.

"Gentlemen on their travels, Lake Simcoe, 25th Sept., 1832," by H. B. Martin.

When Miss Steele was playing a quadrille, Mr Steele said it seemed so much like dancing that we must dance. So Mr Drinkwater, John Steele, Sarah & I stood up to dance. My [borrowed] shoes were very large, but I managed. Mr Drinkwater nearly forgot itt; he said it was 6 years since he danced. Mr Steele said the gentlemen did not exert themselves enough, so he stood up and danced a figure to show them. He cocked up his chin and looked so funy that it made all of us laugh a great deal. About nine we went; they had expected us home before has it was late by our watch.

The Hallens had callers, as well: people coming to church service, on errands or just to be sociable, like young Mr. Joseph Willson. Once Eleanora describes exactly how he sounds at their door:

[Feb. 16, 1836]   . . . About dusk we heard the disagreeable inteligence that too men and oxen with a sleigh were at the bottom of the laine. I looked through the window where I was putting Agnes to bed. They seemed to be trying to get up here. After a little while when I had lighted the lamps, a nock at the door came. My Mother went to the door when I never was so glad has to here, "How do, Mrs. Aln?" It was Mr Josheph Willson and a man. He said he had a bit of a . . . *scab* on his cheek; he put some spirrits on. . . .

Given the conditions of life in the bush (or in "the howling wilderness," as many settlers called it), it may surprise you to know how much visiting went on. In spite of the cold, winter was the best season for travelling. Frozen rivers and lakes made smooth byways, and deep snow on the roads evened out potholes and bumpy corduroy. In her journal entries for January through mid-May 1836, Eleanora mentions no less than seventeen different names of individuals or families. They all came and went every Sunday, of course, but also during the week, averaging out at least one every two days during the coldest months, and increasing in frequency in the spring. In April and May, the Hallens received or made visits on at least three out of every four days, if we use Eleanora's diaries to gather our statistics — and there might have been more than she mentions!

The variety of callers was great as well. Besides the Steele and Willson families, and other settlers with letters to deliver or foodstuffs to sell, there is the washer-woman Mrs. Butcher, her husband (who, appropriately, did some butchering for the Hallens!) and "Cavina" (probably Cavenagh) the man who helps with farming chores; a surveyor, a census taker, another clergyman, Captain Anderson (the Indian Agent and new postmaster at Coldwater), and various Ojibwa visitors.

By Anna Jameson, 1837.

What did people do on all those visits?

You can tell a lot about peoples' activities from the descriptions of Eleanora's long visits, above — they did everything from dining to dancing. But probably the most important part of any visit was the news and stories everyone shared. Some stories were minor gossip, others were real attention-getters:

[Jan. 25, 1836] In the morning my father cut down a large maple tree. My Mother and I walked up to Mr Steele's. Mrs Steele is better. I went and saw the pupies; they are very pretty.

A woman and child came to sleep here. Her name was Wailand — she was Irish. They had come over three or four years since. She said they (her husband and herself) had to find there shanty, for their was no road cut and they had to carry everything on their backs from the Narrows. . . .

[Feb. 25] . . . My father came home about four — he had had dinner at Mr Willson's. He said Mr Willson told him [stories] of several people that were lost. He said that a girl was once sent from one house to another, [and] she was lost. People were [searching] after her for tow or three days till they quite gave her up. [Then] a farmer was walking in his clearing [and] thought he saw some thing moving behind the trees. He went towards it and discovered that it was a female. She ran off has if afraid. He called some people and they caught her. She seemed quite wild, [but] in a few days she recovered; she said she had heard the people after her, but could not get towards them. She had lived on roots and buds.

Another man was lost and he was so near to here (this house) that he heard the Bywaters' little child crying, but could not get near the house [because] it was a storm at the time. A[nother] woman was going along the Cold Water rode with a pig, and a large bear came out of the wood. She did not know what to do, but she did not like to leave the pig, so she shook her stick at itt and it went into the wood again.

[Mar. 25] . . . Miss March and Miss Mary Willson came. The room was very untidy, but we swept it up. Mrs & Miss Steele called [too]; they brought our basket and a book named The Spy. They did not stay long; Miss March stayed tea, & Miss Willson had a tooth ack, so she had some wiskey to put in her mouth — it made it better.

They said that about three years ago that a vessell went upon the island of Anty Costy at the mouth of the Saint Laurence.

145

They [the people from the vessel] saw a sort of tent erected, [and] they went to it. A great many human bones lay about, and in a hamock they found a dead man. Their was a paper saying that they were so famished that they eat each other. So very shocking!

Cannibalism was not a common problem! But, sometimes, callers were because the Hallens tried to be sure things were tidy, that they were properly dressed, or had their better utensils on the table. All of it seems extremely important, but sometimes hard to manage:

[Jan. 14]   While we were at dinner we heard a dog bark. We thought it was Tiney [Steeles' dog] so we took the very bad knives off the table, that the little ones *used*. It was Sarah & Laura; they went into the parlour. . . . In the evening — rather, [at] dusk — a boy came. He asked if he might sleep here all night. He said he had some oxen but has we had no place to put them . . . they stood in the hall.

[Jan. 31]   In the morning Miss March, Mary Willson, Mr Joseph William & George Willson came. They all walked [here], but Miss March would not stay dinner which made Mr Josheph Willson frown, but I was rather glad for we have but three dishes [and] one of them very much cracked. . . .

[Feb. 7]   Whilst we we were at breakfast a nock at the door came. We were in a consternation — we sat in mute dispare, all except my father. It was the Willsons; they had brought some brooms that a squaw had made. They were ironwood except one, which was birch. . . . I don't like Mr Josheph Willson.

[Feb. 14]   Mr Steel, the Rutherfords & Willsons came. I know that the Willsons had had a scolding for *staying* last Sunday, for they went very soon and were not quite [so] familiar. We took Grace out in the sleigh; it was very cold.

[Feb. 22]   We expected Miss *Steele* to call so we were in all prim order. Mrs Steele, Miss Steele & Miss Drinkwater came; they did not stay a great while. They brought some milk, which is very acceptable. . . .

[Mar. 14]   . . . In the evening we espied Sneezer, which caused Sarah to take of her druggate apron and put on a black cotton one and Mary to put on a cloth cape. My Mother also put on another cap, because we saw Mr Steele in the wood. He is very considerate indeed because he did not come in till he had passed the window. . . .

Were the Hallens glad or sorry they emigrated?

Funny thing — it's hard to tell what they thought of living in Canada, because Eleanora doesn't really say, one way or another. It's another case of reading between the lines or piecing together a partial picture. When the Hallens moved into the Bywater house, Eleanora described the bedrooms as "comfortless." That word probably describes much of their life for the first few years. In fact, ten years later, Eleanora makes a revealing entry in her grown-up diary:

> [Dec. 2, 1845] . . . . I found a volume of Sarah's old journals written the first year we were in Canada and describing accurately the miseries we endured. It is really most interesting and I fully intend copying it out. . . .

But, Eleanora's journals themselves are not markedly miserable or comfortless. Generally she sounds cheery and finds much more than the weather to report on. Sometimes the peculiar necessities of Canadian living even offer an opportunity for laughter:

> [Mar. 13, 1836] We thought we should be very late, so we made haste. Bed was very comfortable — we made a great heap of clothes on me. . . . Mr, Mrs & Miss Steele came down in the ox sleigh — Canadian rusticity. . . .

She occasionally notes that her father has made some improvements to their little log house, or built some new item of furniture — especially seats for those attending church service in their parlour:

> [Jan. 8, 1836] My father has made Grace a little chair. . . .

> [Mar. 6] . . . My father is thinking of building a chimney; Mr Tomson hadvises [him] to have it of stone, has that is more durable.

Gradually, the cold is waning and the days lengthen . . .

> [Mar. 18, 1836] . . . In the evening when we had just begun

tea (we had it by daylight), my father came, so
we put up the curtain and lighted the lamps. . . .

[Mar. 25] . . . It is a beautiful day; it is so
mild. . . .

[Mar. 26] It is a beutiful morning. I went
out of the back door and lay down on some
straw with Grace. The sun felt nice and
hot. . . .

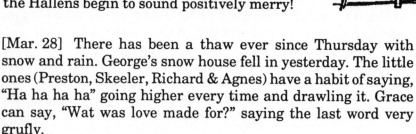

and the Hallens begin to sound positively merry!

[Mar. 28] There has been a thaw ever since Thursday with
snow and rain. George's snow house fell in yesterday. The little
ones (Preston, Skeeler, Richard & Agnes) have a habit of saying,
"Ha ha ha ha" going higher every time and drawling it. Grace
can say, "Wat was love made for?" saying the last word very
grufly.

[Mar. 30] It is a beautiful morning; there has been a slight frost
in the night. It thaws thow. Sarah, Mary, baby and me went into
the wood — it is very pretty where they are clearing. . . .

Finally, the sap begins to run. Canadian spring has arrived —
although the Hallens don't yet recognize it.

[Mar. 31] The snow bore [our weight], so Mary, George,
Edgar and I went into the wood opposite our house: it is very
pretty. Their are so many little hills. We sank in some times.
I went into the wood to my father. I saw some sap running out
of some maple treese, so I told my father. He got an auger and
tapped a few trees I think and we put some tins under them.
We caught a buckett full. . . .

It is interesting to note that, overall, Eleanora's journal entries
get significantly longer as the days do. When the cold is not so
bitter and the Hallens can feel spring coming, and they see that
they have indeed managed to survive their first winter, Eleanora's
diary comes alive, like the earth and the trees. Here is her journal
for April and half of May 1836, when she mysteriously stopped
writing until December.

I can now esclaim oh I think the sow will go

April 1 Frid When I came down in the morning George made me an April fooll two or three times. He called out to the little ones that Mr Josheph Will was going along the road in his cilt. It made them all jump out of bed and run to the window; then George called out, "Ah you April fools!" We caught another bucket full of sap. One of the hens are ill, her name is Dido, I hope she will gett well.

April 2 Sat Saturday is a day of clearing out and cleaning. I took Grace into the wood whilst they were doing itt. . . .

April 3 Sunday . . . Mr Rutherford always says, "Good morning, your Reverense" to my father. Mr Steele says that two Moreen [Marine] officers that have lately settled in Tharo (the next township) have had all their luggage burnt in the fire at New York. George went with the Willsons; Mary and I went and read our journals. My Mother rode on the little sleigh with the baby. My father and George drew itt — it looked very funny. . . . I forgot to say yesterday we boiled the sap. We had about the great pot full, and a half, and boiled it down to a very little; but Miss March said it must be boiled more to make molasses.

April 4 Mon I locked the chickens in their pen for them to lay, because we wanted to sea if they do lay. I lett them out about 12 and watched them, but did not find any eggs. . . . My Mother melted down the bad fat for soap: it smelt badly. . . . I had to mend my pen with the great carving knife. . . . Mr Steele thinks we shall have no more cold.

April 5 Tue The snow bears very well. This morning we ran about a great deal; it freezes harder a great deal today. . . . We have seven acres of land cleared, I think 5 under cultivation. The house is log, with three rooms downstairs and two up. One of the rooms downstairs are very large — the kitchen — but, has we have done a small part off with curtains round the stove, it is

149

"For Mr. William Perry. This sketch was taken in the year 1838, it represents the boys making sugar in the wood near the house at Rushock. The one standing up is watching the last proofs over the fire, it is now turning from a thick maple syrup into sugar imperfectly grained: the one kneeling on one knee stirs it till it is cool to prevent it forming into a hard cake. The other kettles contain the maple sap boiling down."

Unsigned; probably by Mary.

more comfortable. There are a great many little holes or cracks about [in the walls]. We have four rouf bedsteads, one downstairs; 2 tables, one of my father's making which goes round the stove; 2 forms of my father's making which holds, rather crowded, 3 persons; three of the Bywaters' that hold only one person; a *rough crasy* sofa to old about three people; we have a cradle for the baby made out of an old narrow box of the Bywaters. We have very little earthen ware: 12 wine glasses, 12 tumblers, two deccanters, very small, mustard, pepper, and salt things. We have also some pots and kettles. I think that is a general discription. Their is a pot that we always call the little man in black.

April 6 Wednes   It is cold this morning but *thaws* very well. We went in the sleigh up and down the hills before the house. . . . we went into a very pretty valley (even now it is winter), with a brook running on one side of it. I saw a parrtridge — it was about the size of a hen; it was very pretty; it seemed very tame. Sarah and Mary ironed. . . .

April 7 Thurs   Early in the morning before breakfast My father, George, Edgar, Preston and I sallyed [sallied] out to show my father the pretty valley. . . . In several places [the brook] falls from one place to another. We went a little way up it and then got up a little hill and went along rather gradually sloping ground. I saw a partridge fly up near us. . . . George with his axe

shaved a little barck off the trees that grew round [a pool]. Very soon after we found the sight trees and other trees with blazes. We folowed them till we came to the road — their was a blaze and three notches on a sight tree. . . . We then passed were they are clearing and passed by Ella's grove (a grove named after me) and went till we came to the other trees that were blazed. We saw another partridge. Breakfast was ready when we got home.

We slided down a very steep hill in the clearing; it rather wett us. After dinner My Mother & father went to Mr Steele's; they took some butter and the books. Mr Josheph Willson came with some lumber on the sleigh with two pair of oxen. He says the road is very bad in some places where the snow is gone. We had to entertain him ourselfes. We asked him to stay to tea, so he did. He says he has seen a stufed murmaid; he has seen 5 or six wolfes at Barry town were he was before he cam here, and he has seen a rattle snake in the "Cauld water rod" (has he calls it) about 3 feet long. He gave us long histories of the Bywaters getting tipsy. He said there had been several shiprecks, and that some poor mens' fingers were frozen. Something about him telling it made Mary and I laugh, so Sarah said, "Whatever is their to laugh at?" So we said we were laughing at Grace in her cradle (but the little thing was sleeping quietly). He went at half past seven. [When] My father, Mother, George & Edgar came home they had a book named The Pilate; we had not time to begin it. Miss Steele had a bad headacke. My Mother said that Cap Anderson is not going to the Manantuling Ieslands [Manitoulin Islands] now. Their are caniballs in the Islands.

Both The Spy *(1821) and* The Pilot *(1824) are by the American novelist James Fenimore Cooper (1789–1851). Often called "the American Scott," Cooper carried the historical romance into the American frontier.* Jacob Faithful, *referred to below, was by none other than Frederick Marryatt, the Royal Navy officer who invented the Universal Code! It is a sea story, like* The Pilot; *perhaps that's why Joseph Wilson recommended it.*

April 8 Frid We went out in the morning to try to go to the other end of the lot, but we could not go on has the snow would not bear [us]. My father floundered up to his kneese in snow and we very often got in. So my father told George to cut down a young bass tree for us to peel and then . . . cut the branches off for us to make some snow shoes. Edgar, Preston and I made some — they did not do very nicely. It rained today. Mr Joseph & Will Willson came with some lumber. Mr Jos brought "Alice Grey." It is sung in Ingland, quite comon about the Streets. He asked us owh [how] we liked Jacob Fathful. He tinks it is a beutifull tale: it does very well for him, but we think it is very vulgar. It rained when I went up to bed; it tabered on the roof. My father read The Pilate.

April 9 Satur Mrs Barr called with 14 doozen of eggs, has she calls them. My Mother bought 4 dozen for aff a dollar. She had some nice little peices of butter quite fresh. When we went upstairs to make the beds, Grace cryed such a deal after Mary that she was obliged to go down. I looked through the boards that are open; an Indian came in without any cerdomay [ceremony] and sat down. My father asked him what he wanted, [and] he said he had shugar. It was maple shugar, very nicely made nearly white; my Mother asked him the price. He said pork, so my mother gave him two peices.

My father was able to chop today, but his hand is not quite well. It is now a fortnight since he strained it . . . . Grace is very heavy to walk about with; she trots about to the door to sea the chickes. My father read.

April 10 Sund . . . Mr. Joshe gave us some inglish newspapers to look at. Their have been 7 or 8 shiprecks betwen [ink blot] and Ing land. Whilst we were writting our journalls, Sarah nocked down one of our precious inkstands. Grace is now crying, but she has been this evening a very good girl. Sarah and George *had* a grand scuffle about Sarah's journal, has George ran away with it. Sarah was asking for her writing case; little Grace trotted outside the curtains and brought it in, angelick creature.

April 11 Mon In the morning John Steele called with the things Lob had brought from Toronto, but their were no brooms. Noble was very naughty, for has I was hitting him Mary took hold of him to take is [his] part, and he scratched her *nale* all up. It was obliged to be plastered up well. After dinner Edgar and the little ones were clearing out under the house and three boards up and the curtain down, [when] Mrs & Miss Steele came (direfull to behold)! My Mother was in a very bad gown with holes in, so that she had to fly to other regeons [regions], but oh! she had no other gown upstairs so that Mary with great injeniousness got it by degrees. Mrs Steele says that in the shantees that sometimes their are so many bugs that they are obliged in the sumer to sleep out of doors. Their are also a great number of flease every were.

April 12 Tues . . . Mary made Preston a birch cap. I finished a drawing of a child's head. . . .

Preston's birch barch cap

April 13 Wednes . . . It snowed very fast, oh *infilicum me*. We had a nice long day. We had mashed potatoes and bun for our dinner. . . .

April 14 Thurs Their is a high top of snow to all the stumps. . . . It thaws at the front of the house. It snowed all day. In the evening after dinner we heard a nock at the door. Mary toor off her apron and my Mother ran out of the room: it was Mr William Willson. In about alf an hour he gave his father's compliments to my father and [said] that he had sent is account. My father said that he had not received his money, so could not pay him; he seemed rather

Child's head, by Eleanora Hallen, 1836.

bashfull. We did not want him much to stay because we wanted to read. He stayed tea. I had to rock Grace to sleep; I had to sing to her; I bauled very loud — it made us all laugh. Mr Wil Willson pinched Noble's ear and nose, which teased him and made him make a noise. I dare say they allways tease their dog. Mary said that Mr Will Willson would fall in love with her, if she went in. He departed after tea, and I washed up the tea things directly, and then my father read. Richard staid up and roced the cradle has Grace was naughty.

April 15 Fri In the morning old Mr Willson called. He said their never had been such a hard winter since he has been here. He has been 3 years I think, or four. He thinks that it has been worse every winter. He said that last winter they had planted their potatoes [by this time]. My father made a bury for the potatoes and buried them. . . . George got some birch bark and put it on the [end] of a long stick and did it about. Grace was very much pleased. My Mother told us about when she was young. . . .

April 16 Sat My father, George & Edgar went to try to explore, but they could not get out. A beutfull thawing day; it reminds us of summer, if the detestable snow was not their. In Ellas Grove their is a patch of ground; their are paticas and other plants I can sea the flower of it coming. I took Grace into the wood (she is very heavy); she was very much pleased to sit on the Ground and play with the dead leaves.

In the morning an indian came; he brought some shugar that was made yesterday. It was very nice, but not quite so good has that the other indian brought . . . my father gave him two peices [of pork]. He said, "This is bad, I want fatter," so my Mother gave him a fatter peice. He had a blancet-coat on and markasins. Richard fell into the brook whilst he was getting some water in a can; he went to bed has he was so wet.

April 17 Sun . . . There are Scotch, Irish & English come to church. Has Mr Steele was not here, is chair was vacant, so my Mother asked Mr Rutherford if he would take it. This made the foolish Mr Josheph Willson begin to titter to himself. We did not have the long table but had a barrell with the pasteboard at the top and then put the green baize all down and it made a very respectable appearance.

After church my Mother asked Miss March if she would stay [for dinner], has she had walked. . . . She went into the parlour to sit, has it is so warm today. . . . We had pork fryed in bater, mashed potatoes, plum puding & mince roll. We had but just dishes enough, and we were obliged to put the potatoes in a pey [pie] dish.

It is a very hot day; there are several butter flys flying about. The Willsons after service shot at Sneezer; it made him illtempered, and when George told him to go home, he bit his harm [arm], but not badly. Miss Marsh stayed tea; . . . [she] wishes to be thought young, but I think nobody would think she was. . . .

April 18 Mon It is very mild. They were going to boil shugar, but it came on violent rain and continued to rain all the morning and a great part of the evening. Round the potatoe bury their is a pool of water, and so George dug a drain from it. Mr Josheph called in the evening with is plaid cloack on. He has *lanky* red hair and two bullets for ies that he stretches up and draws is brow up in creeces. Is under lip is allso drawn down; alltogether he looks very wise. I think he called for a a drink of water. My father made a most enchanting little table out of the old one that went round the stove.

April 19 Tues It was a nice day. In the morning Reed Mr Steeles servant called to ask my father to marry is sister. They will come at 12 o'clock. . . . They did not come all the morning but whilst we were at dinner George went to [the door?]. He called out for us to come and sea the proceshion: a man carried a red flag and all the people went after in couples.

We were obliged to pack all the dinner things up in a great hurry and put the little table and prayer books. Then Mary, Edgar & I ran up stairs to look through the cracks; we could sea very distinctly the bride was dressed in a black silk gown with white sleeves and lase collar. The bridegroom had white trousers and a blew hat with yellow gloves. After the service was over, they fired tow guns.

Mr Josheph Willson came so after they had come [left?]. He said they were all Scotch and that in Scotland they always go like that when they are been married. He boasted that he new every body that were there and that a great number talked Gaelic. He said they wanted him to go very badly because to daunce tonight they have to go 7 miles. He wanted us to go very badly, so my Mother said we may! He said that we should see the mackich [magic] lantern; we new [knew] they had no oil so we took the oil can.

When we came to the bottom of the lain, there was the ox sleigh, but the oxen could not move because they had got down in a brook [unseen beneath the snow]. They were obliged to be taken out and he then turned the sleigh; he said that he could drive the oxen in Gaellic if they could understand him. The oxen went very fast down the hill after Queenses clearing, and we were nearly upsett. We mett Wailand and her eldest daughter. Mr Jo Will seemed very well acquainted with them and talkad a great deal. When we got there, there was only Mrs Willson, but Mary Willson soon came down. Miss March is not well. They have had the roof on fire; their was a large hole round the stove. . . .

The magic lantern was an early slide projector.

After tea they had the machic lantern; there [were] a great number of pictures. They wanted us to stay all night, but we did not. Coming home we got some birch bark off the trees and lighted it; it gave a great deal of light.

April 20 Wed We boiled the sap for we are going to make some shugar. Mr William Willson came. . .[and] stayed dinner; he has dark hair grey ies [eyes], little screwed up mouth and his mouth turned up at the end. . . . My father and I went down to the bottom of the lain and went along a peice of terra-firma. Mr Josheph J Willson came; he only called for nothing. We finished The Pilate. It was a nice day.

April 21 Thurs Sarah and Mary went to Mr Steele's. . . . when they came home they had no news exept that the mason was gone to gale [jail] for fighting. We tease Sarah about Mr Josheph Willson, but I don't think she does like him perticularly. Grace as a very curly head and grey ies. Her hair is light. . . .

April 22 Fri In the morning Sarah & Mary set off to go to Mr Steele's, has Mrs Steele had asked them to stay all day. . . . My Mother finished my frock after dinner and then I got ready. Grace was very naughty all the time. My father made a thing of some peices of wood to carry our birch bark at night, and George rapped some up in his cloack and took it up. It was very slippery; we left the birch bark and thing under a bush and then went on.

There was a great deal of the clearing bare and in little patches all about. Mr Steele has a barn, cow house, pigsty, hen house, wash house and dairy all down from the house, but not joining each other. The heap of chips before the barn door is a great deal higher now the snow is all away. Miss Steele took me into her room to change my shoes and stockings; . . . [her room] is papered and has a stove and *every* thing very comfortable.

Aftere tea we danced a quadrille twice; one time I did not

dance and and another Sarah did not. Miss Steele played so she could not dance. After tea Miss Steele sang and Sarah; she played "The Old Inglish Gentleman." Mr Steel says that the mason is not gone to jail. He said that Reed came to himto ask him to marry is sisters & that Mr S told him that he would not, has there was [now] a clergiman. So Read said, "I am afraid they will never be fixed and they have been stumped three weeks" (that is the bans been put on a stump). We went after nine. It as been a nice day; got to bed about 11 o'clock.

April 23 Sat In the morning I heard my Mother call out that the buds were coming on the trees beutifuly. George looked out of the wendow and there was all snow — two inches of it! It melted tho before evening. There was a regular cleaning of every think and we moved the bed the other way, which made the curtains go straight. My father made a very nice long bench with a back and sides, a great imbelishment to our furniture.

April 24 Sun A nice day but cold. Our usual congregation came: all the Rutherfords sat on the new sort of sofa.

April 25 Mon In the night I was awacken by a very loud noise and was much freightened when I discovered it was thunder acompanyed with violent rain. It sounded on the shingles drearleful, has their is no ceiling. I was comforted to find that they were all awake; they said the most violent had gon over. It went away but soon returned.

April 26 Tuesday It was fine but windy. I don't no what aftened, for I was a naughty girl and did not keep up my journal. good naughty good naughty good naughty . . .

April 28 Thur My father said that the roads were so bad that he could not go on to [see] Cavina, so he went today; he took his gun. Whilst he was away, as I was in the logging I heard Sceeler. I went to sea what was the matter. Richard had chopped the top of his head, but fortunatly not much. He was crying very much when Cavina came in, which stopped his crying very soon. Cavina had not seen my father; he brought some onions and some pumpkins sead. Sarah does not like him so we all walked round the feild; he is disagreeable in smoking and sitting. He sat about an hour and a half. My father came home before tea; he said that he should have stayed, only that Cavina had told him of Sceeler. It is a nice day; the snow is going.

April 29 Fri   It was hard rain in the morning before we were up and wrained rather after breakfast. It was fine in the evening a little. My Mother and father and us went down to the brook. George pushed Sarah in; she walked about a little, but [it] being rather deeper than she thought, she came out.

April 30 Sat   Nothing aftened [happened]; oh dear, oh dear, oh dear.

May 1 Sun

It was very nice and hot. Mr Steele came quite *smartly* for he had a large straw hat. Mr Josheph came and he had the top of his kilt on but we took no notice of it. Mr Steel says, has we took notice of the cold [days], we must mark down the fine ones. . . . [We] all went a walk in the wood. There are some some flowers coming which the Willsons call Johne quils. We did not go far. . . . The snow is nearly gone.

May 2 Mon

My Mother began to boil the birch sap out in the wood to make beer. In the evening John Steele called with his gun to ask my father to go shooting; my father went. They got no game. . . .

May 3 Tues

Mr Willian Willson called to ask for some body to go with him to get curant trees; Edgar went. We worked in the garden and got it rather better done. In the evening George & my father went to meet him; . . . he had some currant trees which my father set [out]. . . .

May 4 Wen   It was a nice day rather cold. My father has made

159

a ring for the flower [bed] and then there is flower borders round, we raked it as well as we could and [planted] most of the Rushock seeds. My father set some mustard and cress and some spinach.

The snow is all gone which is delightfull. There is a great many paticas [hepaticas] in the wood; they are single; there is dark blew up to white, and diferent shades of pink; they are very pretty.

May 5 Thur My Mother has continued boiling the sap ever since Monday, she did not know were to put it, so my father began to dig a place in the bank fronting the north. He dug it out today; there [is] room for more things than the barrell. Whilst we were in the wood my father called out to tell us that Mrs and Miss Steele were come; we went in. Mrs Steele had brought some carrots and leeks; she said that vegetable soup was very nice and that she had brought these carrots for it. When they had come my Mother was a sad figure, so she had made her escape up stairs. We gave Miss Steele a small quantity of several of our seeds.

May 6 Fri . . . Cavina brought a beutiful large fish . . . and he gave Agnes a little bull head, but which he called a cut fish. We wrapped it in a cloth and boiled it, has we have no place to put it in. This morning George and I had an egg because we have each found 12 eggs each yesterday. . . .

May 7 Sat My father covered the top of the root house with dirt. Sarah, Mary, George, Edgar, Preston & I went in the wood to fetch some logs. We named them has we brought  them: the first was Martha and the next Susana, & [then] Dorothy. We dressed Dorothy in Mary's nightcap and my pinbefare [pinafore]. In the evening we put the barrell in the root house and filled it with beer; my father filled the *door* up with a draggate and straw. . . .

May 9 Mon Sarah . . . washed I think that's all. Let me sea, why I don't like a washing day — but I don't no what for. "I do not love thee, Doctor Fell; The reason wy, I cannot tell."

May 10 Tuse . . . Cavina came to sow the wheat. The way he sows it is, he walks over the feild and throws it before him; when he has done it all, he gets the oxen and fastens a [h]arrow behind them. It is like this. * He finished in the evening.

May 11 Wed In the morning, dire dismay, Miss Steele came up to the doore, just as Sarah without her frock (which I think was better) emptied some slops. She was obliged to fly, calling out, "Oh, Miss Steele!" Miss Steele brought an old tea pot full of milk, which was very acceptable. She asked if it would be quite convenient for Mr an Mrs Steele to come to tea this evening. . . .

I am so lazy. It is a hot day; as I am writing Minerva is looking for a nest. The window and door is open; a little fire in the stove; and the room quite tidy. In the evening they came. Mr Steele liked the rake that my mother had made. They went away before it was quite dark.

May 12 Thurs We went to the brook and Sarah and Mary put their feet in, but I pulled off my things exept my shift and got in and lay down — it was very comfortable.

May 13 Frid . . . Mrs Steele came to show my Mother owh to make the soap; they made it. Mr. Steele came with her; he showed us owh to do the sides of our gardens, as we were doing them [anyway]. It looked very neatly indead. Mr Steele said that Mrs Steele could not go a way that my father as cut in the wood, because, he said, "You are not so active has Mr Hallen." But Mr[s] Steele, when she heard him say it, said that she would go — for that reason!

I think it was today that I counted 83 musquito bites on Grace's face, but she would not let me count any more. There are some very pretty yellow dwarf ~~perry winkly~~ turn again gentleman and also some very pretty 3 leafed flower[s], some white and some red.

May 14 Sat In the evening my father, Sarah, Mary and I went up to Mr Steele's to tea. We went along a path that he has only scufled with his feet; it was a shorter way, and we crossed the road twice. The snow is all gone. I will just discribe a canadian road: perhaps there is cordoroy for a long way; then when you are off that, you have to jump from stone to stone, and if you slip wo be to your shoe and stocking for you will be plunged above your ancle.

Mr Steele has a very large clearing; it his a great deal enlarged by what he has done this winter. Miss Steele took us into the garden, which she has made very neat. The grass looked beutifuly green. Mrs Steele took us into her dairy: there was a great deal of milk which looked very comfortable. Mr Steele and my father were very busy studying a speech for the govenour. I should think the govenour would be very much honoured. Miss Steele and Sary [Sarah] sang.

A corduroy road, by T.H. Ware.

May 5 [15?] Sun
I forgot to say that yesterday, whilst we were out, a man came with some pork which my Mother bought, but this morning she found [it] was not good. The man is going to call for his money so that we can return it if he likes. In the evening the man came; to our great joy he brougt three letters frome my uncle Herbert and William and the other frome my Aunt Mary and Lewes. We all went into a very beutifull valley by the side of a brook to read it. My Aunts said our Aunt Hellen was very happy when she died, and sent her love to us. . . .

May 6 [16] Mon . . . . [Eleanora's marks]

May 7 [17] Tues   In the evening Mr Steele and Mr Bruff called he is an epescopall clergiman. Mr Steele came to the window and told us not to bustle for that he was an old woodsman. When they came in I got beind [behind] the curtains because I was such a figure. Mr Bruf is rather bald but not Grey hair. We looked over our seeds and put them to their diferent sticks. They did not stay long. Their is a very pretty three leaved flower out, some red, some white, some pink. There were also some very pretty heartsease.

This is the last entry in Eleanora's journal for 1836. One more entry for this year was written on a separate sheet of folded paper. Perhaps this was also the last of the copy books the Hallens brought from England, for (so far) no other complete volumes have turned up. All that we have are mixed-up fragments from other years, some pages loose and some stitched together.

Did Eleanora keep her journal all her life?

From what survives, it looks like Eleanora did not make many more regular entries over the

"The Backwoodsman" by Anne Langton.

next few years. She skips from May to December 1836 — then to June 1837. Often, her writing is a sort of catch-up report.

[Dec. 18, 1836]   I am now going to begin to write for all the sumer. The trees looked very nicely when they all came out. The paticus were a very pretty yellow flower, like a "turn again gentleman," only that it is very small. The musquitoes wer very bad indeed; they bit us horibly. There are hundreds of them. At Mr Steele's they have musquitoe blinds which keep them off. There *are* also black flies and sand flies — the latter are so small that we cannot sea them and they are the most irating. The black flies bit me so badly that my neck quite swelled up. . . . We were all delighted to get the stove. . . . We are very badly off for flower. . . . [Mr Steele] has sent down all his musty flower so [we think] he does not like to part with the good.

Grace can now talk a little and she runs about all day long. We

"Grace eating a bun"   **"Agnes carrying Grace"**   **"Grace with her saucepan"**

have had our barn and back kitchen [built], but they neither of them are roofed because we want lumber so badly. The *Willsons* have brought tow or three load but not half enough. . . .

My father went to Toronto and bought a great many things: he bougt a cow and calf, brown and white; we have named it Flora. . . . I have forgotten to say that the Drinkwaters have given us a very pretty little spaniele, which is very good for going after partridges. It is quite black exept a long white spot on his chest; we have named him Fido. . . .

We can't be sure why there are big gaps in Eleanora's journals — it's puzzling. Mrs. Drinkwater noted in her 1950s transcription that a volume from 1837 was missing — that of course would be the simplest explanation for the gaps. However, since Eleanora herself deliberately reviews big sections of time, there must have been additional factors. One which she herself gives is illness.

[July ?, 183?]   My father and George went up to a place that they are under brushing for the church. In the morning Sarah, Mary, Agnes and me went and bathed at their dam. We washed our heads well up at the house and then went down with our night gowns under our frocks; we ducked our heads well. In the evening we walked up to Mr Steele's to call for Mrs Steele to go on to sea the place were they have been under brushing; it is an acre. My father, Mother, George and I stayed at Mr Steele's [for] tea.

The reason why I have left off is because I have been ill.

Without a pause to explain why or when, though it seems to have been about ten days since her last entry, she goes on to say:

The musquitoes are still trouble some. We have the daisy in

blosom and the martin flower (which closes up in the midle of the day) crane bill, monkey flower, a little candy tuft, hudson flower, inglish columbine and a very preity red wild flower from ingland.

Maybe summertime, with all the gardening and outdoor tasks to attend to — let alone the clouds of insects to pester you if you sat down — was just too busy for journal writing. Or perhaps the opportunities for summer fun were just too tempting!

[June 14, 1837?] It is very cloudy and now and then rain. Maclean is gone to a bee for raising a house today. My father made a boat last week to go on the boys' dam; it hold three <u>very</u> well. Preston and Sceelar can go in it standing. We went down to it this evening. We were obliged to make little fires about to keep of the musquitoes.

[June 17] In the evening Laura came; she staid tea. We went to the dam. Laura wanted to get in the boat, but I was afraid to let her til her Mama was by. We had a game at prison bars and I spey.

But Eleanora didn't write much in the winter, either. Perhaps the conditions were too hard and cold — Eleanora's ink might even have frozen in the winter. Or perhaps, after their first year, things may not have seemed so new and interesting for daily reports. There are several entries that support this "boredom theory," but the best one is unreliable: "July 4 [1836 or 1837] Nothing ever happens, so I do not write." Unfortunately, the date is

"Romance of the woods in the summer"

unclear and it comes from Mrs. Drinkwater's transcript, so we simply do not know if Eleanora actually wrote these words!

Another explanation for the big spaces in her journal-keeping might be that all the older children were too busy with teaching or chores. The family had no governess, nor any servants until 1838.

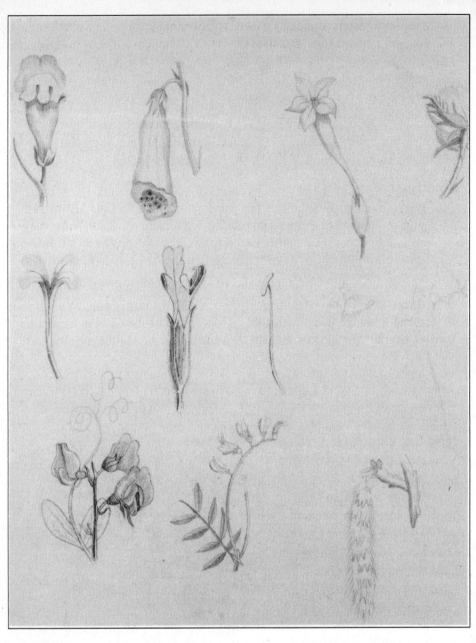

[June 13, 1837]   We each of us after every meal teach the little ones. I teach Richard the new way. He gets on very well. . . .

[June 15]   A very nice morning. We jenerally have dinner at 12 o'clock. Sarah churned — their is 6 pounds 6 oz very nicce butter indeed. . . .

Remember the two-week gap in July 1835? It probably meant that the work of settling in at Sandy Hill had interrupted the Hallens' writing schedule. Similar gaps occur at other busy times; December 1835, for instance.

As time passed Reverend Hallen probably became more occupied with church duties. If so, then perhaps the young Hallens had both to help him and do the jobs at home for which he had less time. Just visiting the sick and the needy wherever they lived in the backwoods was far more laborious than it had been in his English parish. And his new congregation was growing (which meant more baptisms, weddings and funerals):

> [June 3 , 1838]   We had service here has there is a sacriment. Livingstone and his wife . . . came to have their child baptized: its name is Dugan. There was a great mamy people came; there was hardly enough seats for them. . . .

Finally, we can tell that gaps also occur where Eleanora has been too sad to write, as we saw earlier in this book.

> [June 1, 1838]   I now again take up my [pen,] Never to lay it down again. I hope so. Since last I wrote a great many things have ocured both of pleasure and sorrow, but mostly of the latter. Dear little Grace is now no more living: on Cristmas day she died. She was three years old and the most engaging child I ever saw, so good tempered and very pretty. She was ill a little more than a week, of inflamation of the lungs. We never more shall hear her that laughing voice and see her run after the little chickens.
>
> Since the spring my father has had a log fence put round the place were she was buried. There are several very pretty trees in it, and we have planted a bed of flowers which will look very pretty. Mr. Drinkwater has given us a white lilly and a lilly of the valley which we have planted in a little border at the head of the grave. We intend to plant creepers up the logs this summer.

Sadly, death was an all too frequent visitor in the Hallen home. Little Grace was at a very similiar age to Edith, the little sister who died in England, and her death no doubt brought back memories which made it a doubly tragic third Christmas in Canada. What a painful way to grow roots in a new country — by burying a member of your family in its soil! Ironically, in settler days, many immigrants felt tied to their new land because of the graves they dug and the dear family members they honoured with grave markers and flowers.

No. 22. Buried 29th December 1837 Grace, daughter of
George and Sarah Hallen of Rushock eleventh
Lot of the eleventh Concession of the Township
of Medonte aged two years
George Hallen, Offg Minister

After setting down all the Hallens' sadness, Eleanora continues her
long catch-up entry with a great deal more news:

In September . . . [cousin] James Hooman came over and stayed
with us only little more than a day. We were delighted to see
him. He brought us a very long letter from my Aunt Dixon and
two more from my cousin Sarah and Mary. They sent us some
pictures of fashions — the [page torn] worn plated very low off
the shoulder and quite plaine above the elbow; some are quite
plain, but they do not look pretty. He thinks we are very much
grown. We sent some birch bark and a very pretty red bird
home by him.

In the winter the radicals under Mekeinze and Lount rose
but were soon put down. Every body went from this part of the
country. George was too young to go has it was such a long
march. We were very glad to see the people come home again,
[although] several of them stayed in Toronto in the volonture
[volunteer] companies, among which was Mr. Joseph Willson
and Mr. Rutherford. We have not seen them since.

There has been four acres and a half cleared off this winter
— it does not join this clearing, but we can see it. We have
heard that my uncle William is very ill and also my cousin
Annemaria. In the Autum my father shot a very large eagle; we
skinned it and stuffed it. The organ is come out but it is very
much damaged and I am afraid will never be put up.

In Feb[ruary] Miss
Steele was married; her
husband is a scotch man
named Mr. Henderson. My
Mother, Father, Sarah,
Mary, George and I were at
the weding, and Mr and
Mrs Drinkwater. This
spring Edgar has had a

very tedious illness, but he is now quite well; but George is still ill, [though] he is better. They have been [ill] for 7 weeks.

One day lately we saw a most beautifull meteorit[e]. A great many people seem to have seen it. The trees are very nearly quite out, and the three-leafed flowers are going. We are afraid there is going to be war with the States; they have behaved so badly.

After each big hiatus in writing, it looks as if exciting events inspired Eleanora to take up her journal once again. In the case of 1838, there was big news, apparent as soon as all the catching-up is noted!

[June 2]   Hebe hatched ten chickens, very pretty ones. In the evening Mr. John Drinkwater came; he is going to stay till monday. One day last week, I think, Mary told me that Sarah was engaged to Mr. John Drinkwater. I never was so surprised and sorry, for tho I like him, I do not like Sarah to be married. . . .

Well, here is the connection between Eleanora-long-ago and her family's descendants who preserved so many journals and drawings until today. In due course, Sarah and John Drinkwater were married and had three sons. Their eldest son had a son also named John (nicknamed Jack) Drinkwater. Jack was born in 1885, and lived until 1980. He was married twice; his second wife was *the* Mrs. Drinkwater who transcribed all Eleanora's journals in the 1950s!

Overall, John and Sarah's courtship was a lengthy one, during which Eleanora makes many sarcastic comments about Sarah's suitor.

[June 10 , 1838]   Still a very hot day. Sarah, Mary and Mr John Drinkwater walked to Livengstone's; it is a long walk. At dinner time Sarah's nose began to bleed and she was obliged to retire. I could not help laughing at Mr J D.r's concerned face: it soon gave over.

[June 16] . . . In the evening the dougty lover came.

[June 23] . . . it began to rain and continued for a great while. We thought Mr J-n D would not have been able to come, but did (and I dare say he would through fire or water). He had to change his coat; he brought a very pretty nosegay for Sarah. In it their was an Inglish honey sucle.

Given Eleanora's sarcastic tone about young Mr. Drinkwater, you might easily conclude that she was jealous. She was, but not about Sarah having a suitor. It's more likely she was unhappy that their close-knit family was breaking up. You'll see that they all were sad on the wedding day. But no matter what Eleanora thought about it, Sarah's engagement was another sign that the Hallens were truly settling in and putting down roots in Canada.

[June 28, 1838] Mr Drinkwater [senior] stayed all day. Today Qeen Victoria is crowned, so in the evening the men had so[me] whiskey tody and plum cake.

[June 29] In the morning Mr Drink went; Sarah as made him a coares white net vail to keep of the musquitoes. In the evening Capt Anderson came. He brought a great number of Inglish news papers from the post. Their as been one [unit] of lancers of Toronto cilled *by* a body of 2 or hundred rebells from America; they surounded the house were the lances were. Mrs Steele, Mrs Marey and Laura came down to call.

[June 30] In the morning the earthen ware from the Narrows came, which we are very proud of has we have not one large cup in the house, and only one jug without a handle. In the evening the hessian came; he said a good deel about his father's vail that we had made, so we said he was *hinting* for one.

Queen Victoria herself kept a diary from 1832 (when she was thirteen) until 1840. On June 20th, 1837, hearing that the king had died and she was to be queen, the young Victoria wrote, "Since it has pleased Providence to place me in this station, I shall do my utmost to fulfill my duty towards my country; I am very young, and perhaps in many, though not in all things, inexperienced, but I am sure, that very few have more real good will and more real desire to do what is fit and right than I have."

Her Most Gracious Majesty, Queen Victoria the First.

[July 14]   We did not expect the champion, but he came clothed in white. In the morning Mrs Steele and Laura walked down the [hill]; [they] brought a few strawberries for George.

[July 21]   The hay was carried and put in the barn. In the evening at dusk owh [who] should appear but Mr John Drinkwater. He as put most of is hay in cocks.

[Aug. 5]   There was a very heavy thunder storm, which deterred My father going to Livingstone's to a late hour. What was our surprise when about 1 o'clock Mr John D made his appearance! He said he had been kept up last night to 12 o'clock with his hay and doing nothing [last three words are circled].

[Aug. 11]   In the evening as usual Mr D came; he brought two Albions (we had seen one). One had the account of the Coronation in it.

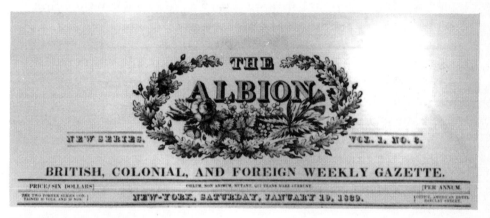

Masthead of the *Albion*.

It seems "Albion" was a popular name in the nineteenth century, and not just for ships! The word is derived from Latin, and means "Britain." The weekly newspaper carried news and views of life in the "old country" for North American readers, and printed serial stories. This issue had part of Chapter 28 of Charles Dickens' Nicholas Nickleby.

When did Sarah get married? What happened to all the others — did they marry? What about Eleanora?

To find out what happened to the Hallen children when they grew up, you'll have to turn to Part V. The picture is put together for you there — otherwise, this book would be far too long! But there's a neat little puzzle piece worth noting before going on, in two entries for August

1838. They mention George's future bride, although it will be twelve more years until he marries Arabella St. John!

> [Aug. 18]   ... In the evening Mary and and I went to bathe. Mary and I floated! Mary as done it once before — it was delightful. In the evening Mr J [Drinkwater — the son] came; he brought a newspaper, an Albion. It was fixed the last time he was here that Mrs. St John and her daughter should come next Monday, but it is again put [of]f till next Friday, as Mr D. [the father] is not returned from Toronto.

> [Aug. 24] In the morning Edgar and Preston set out to meet Mrs St John. They did not go in time, for Mr and Miss Drinkwater had to walk to Mr Steele's road in the burning heat of the sun. They were all very hot and tired when they arrived. Arabella is a very nice little girl.

We don't know how old the "nice little girl" was, though she must have been younger than Eleanora, who was fifteen when they first met. We do know that the Hallens who greet the latest visitors are seasoned settlers, who know how to enjoy the special delights of their Canadian home (like floating in their own pond) and, despite all the necessary work, have time for leisure and the genteel activities of their old, English middle-class life. A lovely drawing survives, which may be the one Eleanora refers to here, though the date of the caption does not quite fit:

"For my sister Eleanora, sketch by Mary Hallen with my love 4th Sept. 1837."

> [Aug. 25, 183?]   I have been a great while without writing my journal. We were very fond of sitting in the avenue; Mary as drawn the house from it.

The new Rushock looks well established, indeed — although undeniably rustic.

Perhaps the mismatch of journal and picture dates here is appropriate, for what true story is ever really complete? As much as we can assemble the pieces and try to make a good picture of times gone by, we can never be sure we have recreated the past absolutely accurately. . . . For now, let's just imagine the Hallen sisters, fondly "sitting in the avenue," drawing together.

Part V

Epilogue

. . . In Which We Say Goodbye to Eleanora, Her Family and Their Story; and in Which We Say Hello to History!

[Oct. 20, 1840]   Mr Drinkwater [the father] and Elizabeth [John's sister] came to breakfast. When we were all dressed we went into the hall, where my Father married poor Sarah and John Drinkwater; we all felt very badly. Mary and I wore white muslin dresses and Sarah a light brown silk; when it was over the Steeles came. We dined at 2 o'clock and everyone seemed to cheer up. We had a very nice dinner and everyone was hungry, as we had been so upset had eaten hardly any breakfast. Sarah and John Drinkwater left on horseback. We were all very tired and when they had cleared up we went to bed.

When Eleanora's journal entries break off in August, 1838, the Hallens are comfortably ensconced in the now enlarged Rushock, the church is underway, Sarah is engaged, and everyone is growing up. However, even though there are no more original pages to read for several years, the family's story does not stand still. Much of it can be pieced together from what Mrs. Drinkwater transcribed — the entry above is an example — and from a number of other family diaries, drawings, letters and documents such as church records.
  One of the first big events that happened, even before Sarah's

"Penetanguishene, 1836" by Eleanora Hallen. This may have been dated later, and incorrectly.

wedding, is that Reverend Hallen found a new job. He was appointed chaplain for the soldiers and sailors stationed at the British Army and Navy Establishments at Penetanguishene, a village west of Rushock.

St. James-on-the-Lines Anglican Church, Penetanguishene.

At the barracks, Mr. Hallen had the usual church duties — weddings, funerals, and baptisms. As well, he became involved in the finishing of a church for the Establishments, "St.James-on-the- Lines." Mr. Hallen was installed as its resident minister in May, 1840, and stayed until he retired, in 1872.

Although the new job meant a bigger house and more money, the move to Pene, as the Hallens called it, split the family. George and Edgar stayed at Rushock to continue farming, and family activity subsequently moved back and forth between the two residences.

> [Oct. 4, 1840] We have been here a long time now, my father is chaplain to the barracks, has also another church; I find it sometimes lonely as the boys are mostly at Rushock, George is farming with their help.

> [Oct.5] Sarah has decided to be married at Rushock as the others very much wish it.

> [Oct. 6] My mother has made three wedding cakes, look very good and should last Sarah a good while.

> [Oct. 30] We returned to Penetang, Mary stayed with the boys, they are getting another servant, so should be more comfortable.

After Sarah married John Drinkwater, the couple set up housekeeping in a little log house called Northbrook, six miles east of Rushock, toward the Narrows (later Orillia). In her adult journal, Sarah writes:

> [Dec. 20, 1840] ...We began with nothing but the farm which consists of between 40 and 50 acres cleared, some cows, steers

and heifers and oxen, a barn and cattle shed. Our house is square, a kitchen, parlour, a bedroom: no rooms upstairs are finished as yet. Our furniture consists of a table and two chairs borrowed from Mr. Drinkwater. . .

Eventually Mr. Hallen designed a bigger house for John and Sarah, which was built during the late 1840s (and became the Northbrook that still stands today). From that time on, the Hallens, and Drinkwaters, departed from the usual settler pattern of expansion — from shanty, to cabin, to frame house, to brick or stone — and merely added on to or renovated the homes they had.

"Rushock, Canada." This unsigned painting was probably done in the 1840s. Expanded, with "virandos" all around, the house looks quite handsome.

Given all the children in the Hallen family, you might expect there were many weddings after Sarah's. But few of the young Hallens seemed to find a replacement in marriage for their happy, close-knit childhood. Sarah herself recorded many complaints, much unhappiness and illness throughout her married life, and she was always grateful for a visit from one of her parents or siblings.

The sadness evident in Eleanora's description of Sarah's wedding day turns into distaste for married life in general in later accounts of her visits to Sarah's home, found in Mrs. Drinkwater's transcriptions:

[Dec. 3, 1840]   On Friday, Mary, Edgar and I went to Rushock to see how they were coming along. On Sunday Sarah and John came for dinner and I returned to Northbrook with them and stayed all night, very dull, poor Sarah misses us all very much, John is no fun.

In 1841, after a four day visit, she comments, " . . . I don't know about Mary, but I am glad [to leave]; married people are very tiresome." (Sept. 20) A year later she says:

> [Sept. 7, 1842]   . . . we were very jolly, much to Drinkwater's disgust, he does not like us to enjoy ourselves; he tried to sleep on the sofa and I made a great noise and sang and clapped my hands right in his ear; the others laughed a lot, but he was very angry and said we were very ill mannered.

Two days after this she writes, "We returned to Rushock and very glad to get there; I think married people are very gloomy." (Sept. 9, 1842)

Despite Eleanora's opinions, there was a lot of travelling back and forth by all the members of the family, to keep Sarah company and to help with her children and farm chores. Northbrook became almost a third household, and the Hallen's Canadian lifestyle became more and more like their old

Unsigned, undated Hallen sketch of writing and reading in the drawing room in England . . .

life as part of a large extended family in England. But possibly because of her opinions, Eleanora never mentions any desire to be married herself. Her journals rarely reveal romantic yearnings of any kind. Even as a grown woman, she consistently teases or makes sarcastic remarks about the various young men who befriend the Hallen family. For instance, in 1845 she writes about a Mr. Bush dancing very nervously, "as if [he] was afraid of his mustachios falling off." (Jan. 21, 1845, Kate Drinkwater's transcription.) And, on New Year's Day she says one male caller "having joined the temperance society, would not take a glass of wine, but [ate] a piece of rich cake, although I kindly informed him there was brandy in it." (Jan. 1, 1845, Kate Drinkwater's transcription.)

Unfortunately, before anyone special enough arrived to change her

... and a sketch by Mary Hallen of writing and drawing on the veranda at "Pene," 1845.

mind about marriage, Eleanora became terribly sick and died. She was twenty-three years old and she appears to have contracted a type of tuberculosis. We cannot actually say how Eleanora's long final illness began, but as you must have noticed, throughout her childhood she repeatedly writes about having colds and stomach problems. Perhaps she had what used to be called "a weak constitution" and just succumbed more easily than some other people to passing germs.

When Eleanora was very ill, she couldn't write, and so we have to rely on Sarah's adult diaries to fill in the picture. In early February, 1846, Eleanora says Mary has the mumps and ". . . I found I had a most wretched cold." By the 26th of February, a good while after the cold, Sarah notes ". . . Nora not well," and the following day says it is "her old bilious trouble." She continues to report on her sister's poor health over the next weeks, and finally writes at the end of April: "I hope one of my brothers will return with John from church when we shall hear how poor Nora is."

In fact, the news was bad, and Sarah was asked to go and nurse Eleanora. All the siblings were staying at Rushock while their parents were in England — first Mr. Hallen had gone on medical leave, and then he sent for his wife to nurse him, and they were sorely missed. Sarah was so busy looking after her own children and helping Mary look after Eleanora that there is a gap in her journals of about six weeks.

[June 14, 1846]   How little I thought when I last wrote in my journal that the next time the death of my poor sister Nora should have taken place; very great has been our trouble, it seemed too much for me to bear, my dear parents being in England e so soon to re-turn not even knowing The dear girl was ill, seems very dreadful. I will write in as short a manner as I can what I can remember.

After this entry, Sarah goes back to May 1st and recounts what happened and how she felt at different times while she was nursing Eleanora. She speaks so vividly of her feelings that it's hard to believe she wrote them down so much later:

[May 25, 1846] Dr. Ardagh came this morning — Poor Nora better though very very weak; we always have to turn her in bed e she dear soul was mere skin e bone. . . .

[May 26] . . . she at intervals made a moaning noise, her eyes were fixed and she took no notice when I asked her where she was in pain: When turning her I asked her she said "it hurts" e these were the last words she spoke dear soul — I sent for George (who was with his Brothers going to bathe) when she became worse, e Preston rode off for Dr. Ardagh. . . . Mary bathed her head continually, e I rubbed her dear hands, a white spot came near her mouth e a noise in her throat, oh! never never shall I forget the agony of my heart, her breathing became quiet, e one hand *hung* by her face; for one moment I hoped, but the breathing stopped oh, how agonising was the sight. . . . The dear girl died about 20 m. to 2 o'clock. . . . This ends the most miserable day I ever spent, may God of his infinite goodness grant it may be an everlasting benefit to my soul — How much have I neglected e how much to mend —

[May 27] Dear Nora looks so happy, not a vestage of misery

The Psalms marked by my poor dear sister Eleanora are 146 to verse 11 e 139. Dear Nora's favorite Chapter 12 Hebrews. The last Psalms I think I read to her here 102 e 103.

From Mary Hallen's journal.

appears in her face. . .poor Mary what a severe loss to her, it is sad sad to think of — Sat in dear Nora's room all day, we never leave it. Mary sketched dear Nora's face e colored it. . . .

[May 28] Tonight my brothers brought the coffin in, e we all helped to put my very dear sister into that melancholly place; my grief is very great —

[May 29] . . . It is always my dear father's particular wish to have funerals as quiet as possible, with no show e — We each put flowers on dear Nora, and then the last kiss, oh! agonizing thought: we all helped to put the lid on and now all is done by us for my very very dear e good sister. . . . Mary, Agnes and I walked up to the church, my brothers followed the coffin. . .[and] covered the grave. . . . Mary gathered some flowers to be put on the grave when finished. We all again sat down to tea together my heart felt very sad. My poor dear parents, how little you think what troubles await you. . . .

[May 30] — how gloomy does everything seem now. . . .

[May 31] My Brothers e John went to Medonte church. This evening Mary Agnes e I walked to dear Nora's grave to put some water to the /// flowers. My nights are very wretched; my heart does indeed ache.

After enduring a period of illness herself, Sarah returned to Northbrook with her children. Naturally, she and all her siblings were very anxious about how their parents would take the news of Eleanora's death. Sarah notes in her journal that George wrote a letter for them to receive in New York, warning them that their daughter was dangerously ill, but not telling them the truth: that she was already dead. Then we hear of the sad reunion:

This unsigned drawing is probably by Mary, and might be Eleanora — but we don't know for sure.

[June 22, 1846] John went this evening to the Narrows to see whether my Father and Mother had arrived at the Narrows by the boat He returned about 10 o'clock with the good news that they had. . . .

[June 23] About 1 o'clock Skeeler came with Jack [horse] for me; had a side saddle that they had brought from England — found it a great comfort, took the children, one behind e one before, Flora [the servant] walked — I almost dreaded seeing my dear Parents, Oh, what pleasure would it have been had dear Nora lived — We arrived about sunset. I bore the meeting better than I expected. It is very melancholy to think of, e often causes me great agony of mind. Every thing has such a damp put on it that we thought would be of so much pleasure to hear e see.

The family made mourning clothes and talked of their grief. Often, they walked up to take flowers to Eleanora's grave at the church, just as they had done for their Grandmama Hallen and little Edith, in England, and then for little Grace, buried at Rushock before there was a churchyard. Slowly, time softened their loss. In later years there are frequent references to "dear Nora," especially on the anniversary of her death. This is Mary's 1852 journal entry:

[May 26] This day always brings back very melancholy recolections. Dear Nora died this day 6 years. She was indeed a loss to me in <u>every</u> way. No one will ever fill the place in my affection she did. She was good in every way how different to me though we always agreed in everything & I think I should have been very different if she had lived to what I am now. I never remember having <u>one</u> uncomfortable word with her she always tried to please me & I did her. We were "two hearts in unity that only death unbound."

When Eleanora died, she was survived by her parents and eight siblings: Sarah, Mary, George, Edgar, Preston, Skeeler, Richard and Agnes, not to mention all those relatives in England, and friends and neighbours in Canada. For each of them, there's a story to tell . . . however, Eleanora cannot tell it! Again, the Hallen story must be pieced together, primarily from Sarah's journals and a number of family letters.

Let's start with Eleanora's mother. In one letter written in England in February, 1846, Mrs. Hallen says ". . . It will be a great pleasure to return again to Canada where I trust I shall be perfectly contented to remain for the remainder of my life. . . ." Sometimes over the years that followed, Sarah complained in her journal that her mother was too busy to visit her as much as she would like! Evidently Mrs. Hallen continued to be her active, but fairly invisible self until her death in 1864.

Mr. Hallen was grief-stricken when his wife died, and had a memorial plaque made. It described her as "... Dear to her neighbours, dearer to her own and dear indeed beyond measure was she to me." Despite his sorrow, he carried on as rector at St. James' until 1872. And as he travelled about on church business, he was often able to stop at Northbrook to see Sarah and his Drinkwater grandchildren. In 1881 he moved to Toronto and died there a year later, aged 88. The Anglican Church Journal (1883) called the Reverend Hallen a "venerable servant of God, the oldest clergyman in this Diocese."

The Reverend George Hallen, date unknown.

Sarah Hallen Drinkwater had one role outside that of daughter, sister, wife, mother, and farm worker. In 1864 she explains, "I wrote an article or two for the Orillia Examiner, which I do from time to time; it is the only way I can get money." (April 9th) She also kept writing in her journals until she was 60, though she seems to use them mostly to complain:

> [Sept. 6, 1845] ... Feel very dull, mine is a miserable life of work, work, though I suppose I should not grumble.

In her final entries she mentions going to visit her father in Toronto, on Ontario Street, and attending "... a

Sarah Hallen Drinkwater, date unknown.

Dr. W.R. Gilmour, Mary's husband, date unknown.

John Drinkwater, date unknown.

'conversatione' at Trinity College, saw all the youth and beauty of Toronto." (June 7-9, 1879)

And, despite all her ills, Sarah lived to be 70 years old! Her own death did not occur until 1888, 7 years after her husband's. They were survived by two of their three sons — their middle son, George, had died at age 18.

Mary outlived her eldest sister by almost 20 years. She, too, got married, but late in her life, and it didn't last very long. In 1875, at age 55, she married a Dr. Gilmour who was a widower with seven children; one year later, she was back in Pene! We can't be sure what about Mary's life with him made it impossible for her to stay. Sarah only comments, ". . . Mary has returned to my Father, as no longer living with Dr. Gilmour." (Sept 9th 1876) Perhaps it was simply too hard, moving in with a family of eight and probably being expected to take on a terrific load of household "women's work." We just don't know.

In any case, Mary kept the doctor's name, and her surviving artwork is all signed M.H. Gilmour. After her mother died, she was her father's housekeeper and companion. She produced many more sketches and watercolours before her death around 1905. Her adult journals also survive, and have not yet been transcribed.

George found a wife at a more usual age, after at least one false start. A journal entry by Eleanora (and a similar one by Sarah) in January 1844 mentions, "George is almost engaged to Laura Steele" — but nothing came of it. In fact Laura eloped with another man, not long after that! Eleanora noted, ". . . My Mother and sisters think it is a good thing, she was indeed a weak and stupid creature and he would have had an awful life." (date uncertain)

Agnes Hallen Cole, date unknown.

In the end, George married Arabella St. John, the young woman from Orillia who was mentioned as a visitor in 1838; he seemed more happily wed than his sisters. After their wedding in 1850, George and Arabella continued living at Rushock. They had one son (named George!) and eventually moved to Hamilton, Ontario, where our George became a piano teacher and organist.

Edgar and Richard never married and, in their later life, lived in Orillia with Mary. Skeeler married a woman from another Orillia family in 1864 (he was 38), and they returned to England to live. As for Agnes, in her forties she married yet another widower, a clergyman with, this time, *nine* children! She moved to Whitby, Ontario, in 1874, and apparently coped with all the housework. Perhaps the familiarity of a clergyman's lifestyle made it easier for her than it had been for Mary. Preston married last, in 1883 (in his fifties!), and lived next door to his single siblings; he also died last, in 1912 at the age of 86.

There's one more marriage that needs to be mentioned. Remember that Eleanora once wrote longingly about John Steele? Well, like his sister Laura, he made a scandalous marriage — by running away with the Steele family maid! The puzzle of *this* family story would be quite interesting to put together. . . . Eleanora writes:

[Dec. 17, 1845] . . .Just at dusk George Wil[son] came puffing up from the road where he had left Aunty in the sleigh to tell us the news that John Steele had run away with his father's servant girl and that they had been married beyond New Market. We can hardly believe he can be guilty of such conduct when his mother is now dying on her bed from where she is never expected to rise.

[Dec. 19] . . .He had pretended to his Father and Mother that he was going to see Miss Mairs to whom he is engaged, and has been for a year; and as the girl had asked leave to go home, he was to take her part of her way. Capt Steele had no idea of anything wrong . . .until the cutter was returned yesterday with a note from him. . . .

And what became of John Steele's father, or other neighbours of the Hallens? Captain Steele later remarried, and his son Samuel, by his second wife, actually became a Somebody in Canadian history. (He was a Mountie, among other things.) Joseph Wilson went to Sault Ste. Marie and became Collector of Customs,

From left to right, the men in the picture are Edgar, Skeeler and Richard Hallen, c. 1890.

with his Aunt (Miss March) as housekeeper. For years, they were well known in that area for their hospitality; which, of course, the Hallens had sampled much earlier! Good, patient puzzling would turn up many more pieces like these, fitting names Eleanora mentions into the history of Simcoe County. But those are other stories, for someone else to tell.

Instead, let's think about what might have become of Eleanora if she had lived, rather than dying at such a young age. Would she have married, after all, or found a career, or both?

— Consider the fact that she lived in an era of lady writers and journal keepers such as Susanna Moodie and Catharine Parr Traill, who would become very well known in Canada and England in the 1850s.

— Also remember that we know she copied out some of her own journals for some unspoken reason (the January to March section of 1835 is the surviving example). Presumably, Eleanora was thinking about other people reading them, but who?

— There are her paintings, too. Were they just for relatives in England? She and Mary were skilled though amateur artists. Once she almost gloats over the roughness of someone else's artwork, saying "... we raised Mr. B['s] spirits by telling him we could beat him hollow." (Sept. 2, 1845) How many more pictures might there have been, had she lived!

Eleanora herself never even hints that she dreamed of making her mark on the world, as an artist or as a writer. Yet she is taking a little place in history, and you are helping to create that place, by reading this book — fame of a kind.

The Hallens, although prominent in their area, were never very well known. Like the vast majority of us, they were pretty ordinary people in their time and place. None of them was important enough to their nineteenth-century world to be named in more than local history books. In a sense, however, although the Hallens were anonymous, the roles they played are well-known and celebrated. For instance, the great wave of British emigration of which they were a part is now well-documented. Eleanora's written record of her family's transplanting is just one of hundreds of journals kept in the nineteenth century, mostly by women. Also, the spread of the Anglican church in Upper Canada owes its success to stalwart clergymen like the George Hallen, though most of them are unacknowledged except in church annals, like the thousands of hardworking settlers who first cleared the land that is now called Ontario.

If Eleanora's family had not kept her journals safe for over 150 years, she, too, would have been forgotten. Suppose you were to search

The Hallens playing croquet, c. 1890: Edgar (playing), Preston and his wife May (seated), Richard and Agnes (standing), with Joe and Bristles, the dogs.

for other signs of that large family which still exist today. Here's all that you would find:

— In England, the village of Rushock is much as it was, with its old Anglican church looking across the gentle valley towards Hartlebury. There is nary a Hallen headstone in the graveyard, but Eleanora's grandmother Hallen and little sister Edith are buried in a vault inside the church. Across the lane, the old Rectory looks very well preserved, and sheep still graze on the field below it.

— Several farms in the area still bear the same names, though the ownership may have changed: "The Court," "Perry" and "Torton" all stand. Various town and village names also echo with Eleanora's words. But these are only traces of the places and people in that part of Worcestershire that once were important to the Hallens.

— In the United States, where the family sojourned for only four months, the traces are fainter. Some place names are the same (Glens Falls, for instance, is an interchange on the highway and a city of 16,000 people), other places, such as Sandy Hill, have disappeared: that original village is now part of the town of Fort Edward. Saratoga Springs, sections of the Erie Canal and the port of Oswego still stand, though they do not have the same functions they once did.

— In Canada, the most obvious memorial to the Hallens — apart from their gravestones — is St. James'-on-the-Lines Anglican Church in Penetanguishene. Inside, you can see the engraved brass plaque Mr. Hallen wrote, in Latin, in memory of his wife and of the three daughters who died too early.

(Incidentally, that plaque holds the most peculiar puzzle piece in all the Hallen's history! Where it mentions Edith, it says, "The body is in England . . . her heart in this cemetery, her soul with the sanctified." Does this mean the Hallens carried Edith's *actual* heart with them from England? No one knows, and nowhere else is there any reference to it. Eleanora certainly never speaks of it.)

Behind the altar at St. James' you can count the small Gothic arches on the carved reredos (an ornamental screen): there are eleven, one for each of the Hallen children, with six of them painted red (for the girls) and five painted blue (for the boys). The red and blue, with gold trim, are also exactly the colours of the old brass-buttoned regimental uniforms worn by the soldiers who attended service at St. James.

Down the road from the church in the Ontario provincial park

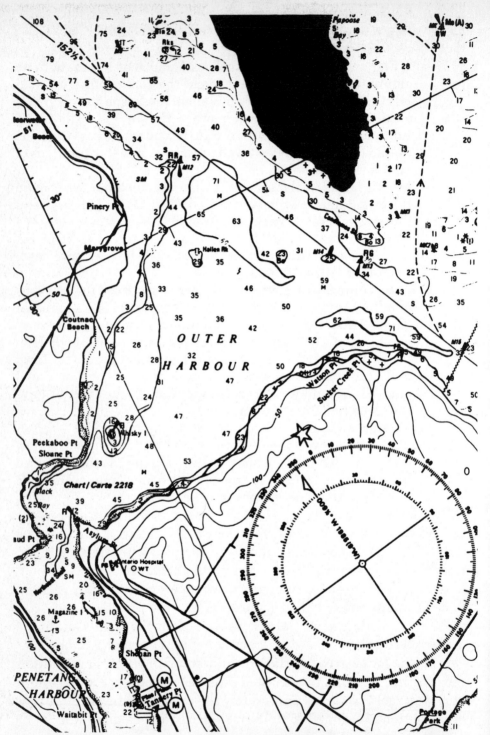

Eleven feet under water there's another memento of Eleanora's family — Hallen Rock. You can see it on this marine map of part of Pene Bay, to the left and above the centre.

The Hallen Chair, now given a place of honour right by the front door of St. James' Church.

Eleanora's gravestone (not the original) is on the right, with Preston's (d. 1912) on the left, in the graveyard of St. George's, Fairvalley.

Albion **wrecked at Richibucto, by E. J. Russell.**

While owned by Thomas Hunter Holderness of Liverpool, the Albion *was wrecked at Richibucto, New Brunswick, in 1853.*

called the "Historic Naval & Military Establishments," you can find evidence of the soldiers' barracks. You won't find the house the Hallens lived in, high on the hill above the Establishments, but if you go back to St. James', you can sit in the stone chair that once was outside that Hallen home. Apparently it was a wonderful hilltop perch

St. George's Fairvalley, c. 1890. The wooden building on the right is the original church (that they were "underbrushing" for in 1837).

from which to paint! Today it is called "the Hallen chair"; at one time, perhaps Eleanora sat there, and certainly her siblings did.

There are Hallen gravestones in the churchyards at Pene and Orillia, and Eleanora is buried at St. George's, Fairvalley, in Medonte Township. But where is little Grace's grave? It has been lost in the woods around Lot 11, Concession 11. The Canadian Rushock, that log house originally lived in by the Bywater family, has also long since disappeared. The name remains, along with dim outlines in the grass of its stone foundations.

As for the Drinkwater name, it too is part of local history. In fact, today in Simcoe County, "Drinkwater" is probably a more recognized name than "Hallen." All around Simcoe County there are other echoes of the Hallens, their friends and earlier times — the Huronia Museum, Ste -Marie among the Hurons, the historic mill at Coldwater, the County Archives and Museum, and various historic markers. If you are ever in the area, try exploring. . . .

The site of what used to be the Hallens' log cabin. You can still see the outline of the stone foundations, buried under the lawn of the present-day residents, the Hewetsons.

Afterword

Once, on a misty, moisty summer's morning, my family drove off the main highway, away from four lanes of cement, speeding trucks and smelly exhaust, into a grassy park on the banks of the St. Lawrence. The small road we had taken wound away from its source unhurriedly, and damp green fields surrounded us. We stopped the car and walked on.

It was so foggy we could not see the river, and we barely what we were looking for — the ticket booth of Upper Canada Village, for that was where we were. A bugle sounded, and the clip-clop of horses' hooves and the creak of carriage leather heralded the arrival of a not-yet-visible stagecoach. There was no time to even think ourselves away from the twentieth century before the coach emerged, looming out of the fog, with an old-fashioned driver so "real" we felt embarrassed to be wearing tee shirts and holding cameras.

Did we get on that stagecoach? I can't remember, but I do know that whole day was magical, and we felt literally transported into the mid-nineteenth century. From the shanty on the riverbank to majestic Chrysler Hall, the entire village seemed alive in the past, and the costumed staff truly might have been the settler folk of the 1860s. Thanks to the weather enveloping the park, we felt we were in another time and place, quite completely.

Such a rich experience as we had that day is rare, although many historic sites do an excellent job of recreating "how things used to be." The arts in general, and the theatre in particular, repeatedly try to create such illusions. And of course books have always transported their readers to faraway realms on ships of words. There are many books for young people today which involve a magical kind of time-or-place-travel; books where holding a special doll or wearing an old pair of glasses takes you back in time; stories where stepping though a wardrobe or falling down a rabbit hole puts you in a different world.

This book is not magic; there is no mystery here — unless it is that *Eleanora's Diary* cuts through the mists of time. Eleanora's words are not fictional; everything that is written between the covers of this book really did occur over 150 years ago. And yet I hope you have finished with a feeling that as you read, something mysterious *did* happen . . . that without quite noticing it happening, you got inside Eleanora's family, inside her house, even into her clothes or head, so that you really know in your bones what it was like to be her: a young girl crossing the Atlantic Ocean to grow up and be part of a new country, leaving behind a culture only partially re-created in Upper Canada, weaving a different world on the edge of the wilderness. . . .

The wilderness has long been cleared around the church at St. George's, Fairvalley, and the spacious cemetery is always deserted when I stop to visit Eleanora's grave. Yet the very air seems full, crowded with the memories of her words and images of her time that I now carry with me. As I prepared to share her story with you, I not only read and reread her journals myself, but also steeped myself in the history of the period and details of her family life. To me, she is real and almost alive, this English-turned-Canadian girl whose very lifeblood has long since changed into Ontario soil and whose name has only been remembered by only a few. Now that you have read so much of her writing, and puzzled together so much of her family story, I hope she seems just as vivid to you. I hope you are glad you got to know her here. And I hope Eleanora herself finds this book "very exeptable."

Appendix

. . . Enter Mrs. Drinkwater

In the nineteenth century it was common literary practice to keep a
journal or notes about one's travels, and perhaps copy it all out
afterwards. Many such efforts also served as letters home; others
eventually became books. Some famous Canadian examples are those
of the emigrant sisters Susanna Moodie and Catharine Parr Traill,
and their brother James Strickland. We don't know if any of the
Hallens hoped to be published, like those Strickland siblings, but we
do know that Eleanora herself re-copied at least one of her childhood
journals when she was a young woman: in 1845 she combined and
wrote out her own and Sarah's journals for the first two months of
1835. It's possible she copied more, as well. In any case, she herself
was the first person to transcribe her early writing.

Three generations later, a woman named Kathleen Nuthall married
Sarah Hallen Drinkwater's grandson Jack Drinkwater. She was his
second wife and got very interested in her husband's family history
and all the old papers. Bravely, Kate began copying out Eleanora's
diaries in longhand, as well as those of Eleanora's father and older
sister Sarah; apparently this was her winter evenings' project during
the 1950s, which she continued for a number of years — until
television interfered! After Kate Drinkwater's death in 1969, her
daughter Anne had someone type Kate's writing out, making a set of

carbon copies. It is wonderful that any one of those involved attempted such a huge task!

Jack Drinkwater lived to be 95. In his old age, perhaps just because he was very proud of his interesting family, he showed many of Eleanora's original volumes to friends and relatives, and we guess some of them got misplaced or were not returned. Thirty years later, as far as we know, only seven volumes of Eleanora's diaries survive, as well as numerous loose and handbound sheets. All that remains of the first year-and-a-bit of Eleanora's journal-keeping (April 1, 1833 to mid-May, 1834) is Mrs. Drinkwater's transcription. Unfortunately, from comparisons made between her work and the original journals that do exist, it appears Mrs. Drinkwater's transcription is often flawed by unexplained alterations, additions or omissions.

If you wonder what reading the original diaries is like, the opposite page shows a sample: a double page spread from the first volume of 1835, at the point where Eleanora herself, in 1845, stopped copying. You can see both her adult and her childish (age 12) handwriting. Try using a magnifying glass to help you decipher, and remember to rest your eyes if you need to. Mrs. Drinkwater and all the subsequent transcribers read pages and pages of journal entries, and no doubt needed many a break themselves! The copybooks the Hallens used for their journal-writing measure 6 1/2 by 7 1/2 inches (about 16 by 19.5 cm).

On the next few pages, you can see some of the typewritten copy of Mrs. Drinkwater's longhand transcription of roughly the same passage. But before that, it may interest you to see how transcriptions are done today. Great care is taken to show *exactly* what appears on the original page, so that future historians studying the transcription can do their own guesswork.

Finally, if you look back at pages 56–57 in this book, you can see how we corrected and cut — always with the intention of making Eleanora's words and meaning clearer, if briefer. We decided not to correct the original misspellings too much, because they're fun to decipher! Nor did we want to change her grammar and turns of phrase, unless it was really necessary. Have fun puzzling through these pages.

out of "Kennilworth". We think she is
a little better this morning. Grace is still
ill but the other children almost
well. About 5 Oclock this evening Mr. Wat[son]
came he says poor Edith cannot re[-]
main long in the state she is in. In
the evening dear Edith started very much
in her sleep; and as Sarah who was sat
by her felt her hands were cold my Mother
got her out of bed and nursed her
by the fire, which she seemed to like
before she was put in bed again [her]
bed was moved near the fire [place]
but although warmed flannel [was]
put to her feet, she did not seem
to get warm. When the others went to
tea I remained with her sitting close
by the side of her bed; she started
every now and then very much and
said "Oh dea, dea" as if she was not so
well: I therefore went to the head of the
stairs and called my Mother who
came directly and thinking she [did]
not seem so well I called my Father;
They thought she could not live till morning Sarah, Mary, George, Edgar & I therefore
remained in the room: sitting round
her little bed: My Father and Mother
on each side her pillow. She went to
sleep for a short time; when she was a-
-wake she would ask for mink (milk)
which she drank. She still continued
cold, so that we had a screen drawn
round. She seemed to have a difficulty
in breathing. She first looked up a/n/o/t/
at my Father and then at my Mother
after which she closed her eyes and
appeared to be dozing breathing quite
comfortably. She was quite sensible to
the last; after once more opening her
eyes she again seemed to doze from which
she never awoke: her breath stopping
so quietly that we hardly perceived it
W/e/a/l/l/ We were all very very sorry particular-

These two pages show a literal, line by line transcription of the two facing pages in an 1835 journal that bridge the adult/child handwriting. The right edge of the page is torn and quite ragged and several words are unclear — our best guess is in [brackets]. Crossed-out words are shown t/h/u/s/.

The adult handwriting, transcribed on the previous page, breaks off at "particular-" (it looks as if something has been torn out). The childish writing resumes with "she does not suck hardly at all", which Mrs. Drinkwater gives as March 3rd.

she does not suck, hardly at all.
my Mother sent to ask my Aunt
Chilingworth to come [here? because?] Little Edith
will be buried tonight we asked iff
we might carry her my father said
we might, iff itt was not too
heavy. my father and Mother, said
we [may] We carried it all the little
ones folowed the six eldest w/e/r/
carried itt, their was 7 candles in
the church, only John and John Jakson
and my uncle, were their. their were cross
peices of iron on the top of my grnd
mamas coffin i/t/ w/a/s/ p/u/t/ a/t/ t/h/e/ t/o/p/
their was a candle in the vault
John Jakson carried the coffin
in is harms into the vault John
received it. Joh Jakson tolled
the bell for an hour after my Uncle
stayed in the church till it had
done. When we came home my
Aunt had just arrived she
thinks the baby very ill I/ s/l/e
Mary slept in a little bed in
the room so that if my Aunt
wanted any thing Mary would
tell my Mother.

The typed copy of Mrs. Drinkwater's transcription looks like this:

1835 March

2nd   Mary sat up half the night with Edith, we think she is a little better;
Grace is still ill, but the other five are better. Edith started very much
in her sleep and Sarah who was sitting by her felt her hands very cold, my
Mother got her out of bed and nursed her by the fire which she seemed to like.
We wrapped her up in warm blankets, but she did not seem to get warm, while
the others went to tea I sat with her, she started several times and said,
"Oh! dea, dea." I called my Father and Mother who thought she seemed much
worse, so Sarah, Mary, George, Edgar and I remained in the room, my Mother and
Father sat by the pillow, she seemed to have difficulty in breathing, she
opened her eyes and looked at my Father and Mother, she was quite sensible
to the last, she again seemed to doze from which she never awoke, her breath
just stopped, we hardly noticed it, we were all very sorry.

3rd   Our baby Grace does not suck, hardly at all, my Mother sent to ask my Aunt
Chillingsworth to come.

5th   Little Edith is to be buried tonight, we asked if we might carry her, our
Father said we might if it was not too heavy for us. We carried it, with all
the little ones following; the six eldest did the carrying. Only John our
servant and John Jackson were there and my Uncle William. There were cross
pieces of iron on the top of my Grandmama's coffin and it was put on that,
there was a candle in the vault, John Jackson carried it and John received
it. John Jackson tolled the bell for an hour and my Uncle stayed in the
church until it was done.When we came home my Aunt had arrived, she thinks
the baby very ill. Mary slept on a little bed in the room with my Aunt and
baby so that she could fetch my Mother if she were needed.

7th   My Aunt is still here, the baby about the same, very ill. The mason closed
the vault in the church. Mr.Watson came.

8th   The buns came that my Mother had ordered for the school children and servants.
We went to church and my Father preached, my Mother did not go, my Aunt went

Glossary

&c
A symbol or abbreviation for "etc.", short for the Latin words *et cetera,* meaning "and so forth."

affected
Artificial or pretended, or "stuck up."

against
In preparation for, getting ready for.

allowance
A certain, measured amount.

antimonial
Fortified with antimony, a mineral which, when added to liquor, works as an **emetic**. A medicine.

archivist
A worker in an archive or archives, a place similar to a library, but dealing with public records and papers, rather than just books.

astern
At the stern, or the back, of a ship or a boat; behind the ship.

aucshanier [auctioneer]
A person who directs public sales,

or auctions, where items are sold to the highest bidder.

auger
A hand tool used to bore holes in wood, or a bigger tool to bore holes in the ground.

axes to grind
To grind an axe is to sharpen it on a rotating stone wheel, or grindstone.

banns
The public announcement of a couple's intention to marry.

beat him hollow
Easily beat (or bettered) him.

bereaved
Robbed or deprived of, usually by death; implies you are left sad and desolate.

berths
Sleeping places in a ship; probably means their beds were built into the walls of their cabins.

bilious
Having to do with the stomach and intestines; from **bile**, the

bitter-tasting fluid secreted by the liver to digest food.

bilious attack
Any upset of the digestive system, probably including nausea and vomiting.

binding
Fastening together; the Hallens bound their journals by sewing them into sets, and then gluing them into cardboard covers (to make them last longer).

blazes
Marks on trees made by chipping off the bark with an axe; they probably defined the limits of the Hallens' property. Blazes are also used to mark a trail.

blister
An irritating substance put on the skin; the resulting blister was thought to pull out sickness; thus helping cure you.

bough (currant bough)
A branch, as in "when the bough breaks, the baby will fall. . . ."

bowls
A very old outdoor game in which a wooden ball, or a "bowl," is rolled at other balls on the ground; bowling at standing wooden pins is related to the English game of "skittles" or "ninepins."

brig
Short for "brigantine," or two-masted ship, with square rather than triangular sails. The *Albion* was not a brig, because she had three masts.

burgeoning
Growing, flourishing.

bustle
To bestir yourself, be very active or hurried, with a certain amount of excitement or fuss; to be in a tumult.

bustles
Stuffed pads or cushions, or a small wire framework, worn beneath women's skirts at the back to puff them out.

by degrees
Gradually, inch by inch or piece by piece.

c.
Short for *circa*, the Latin word for about or around, usually used with dates to indicate an approximate time period.

cabin class
The better accomodation on board an **emigrant** ship, where you had a private cabin or room with berths, rather than a bunk in the **steerage** section, with little privacy.

calico
Cotton cloth, usually plain white and unprinted.

callers
Visitors; people who come to pay a call.

calomile [calomel] and jalap
Purgative medicines.

cant
Peculiar language or jargon; slang. Sometimes just a fashionable phrase with no real meaning.

catalogue
Complete list, often alphabetically arranged or under headings, such as "kitchen equipment" or "dining room furniture."

chapel
A place of Christian worship other than the main church or cathedral; here, specifically indicating a non-Anglican church.

cheese mongers
Dealers or traders in cheese; also

fish mongers or iron mongers.

choakcherries [chokecherries]
The fruit of a North American shrub of the rose family; it is dark red and astringent (it makes your mouth pucker up).

cholera
A disease which people succumb to very quickly and often die from; symptoms include diarrhea and vomiting.

cilt [kilt]
A pleated knee-length skirt, usually made from plaid cloth; part of Highland Scottish male dress.

clerical
Church-related; a cleric is a clergyman.

clergy
All persons trained and officially appointed, or ordained, to religious service; a clergyman is an ordained minister, especially in the Church of England.

coach
Big, horse-drawn carriage, with seats inside and outside, used for public transport.

cob nuts
Large kind of hazelnut.

cocked up (tail)
Erect, sticking up jauntily.

cocks
Roosters, or male chickens. Also, standing bundles of hay or grain.

collect
A nineteenth-century use of this word means to deduce or conclude; the closest we come to this meaning today is recollect, to remember.

comely
Pleasant to look at; attractive.

comforter
A piece of knitted fabric worn for warmth; usually a long scarf, but in this case small woolen cuffs.

communion
The Christian ceremony of sharing holy bread and wine in a church ritual, often called "the Lord's Supper."

Communion rails
A railing around the altar area, where people kneel to receive communion.

confined
An old expression meaning "gave birth"; to be confined in this sense is not to be imprisoned, but to keep to bed before, during and after the birth of a baby.

congregation
All the members of a religious group or a church, especially when assembled for worship.

consternation
Dismay; state of being upset, astonished or amazed.

consumption
Generally, the wasting of the body by disease — losing weight, getting thinner and thinner, etc.; the common nineteenth-century name for tuberculosis.

conversatione
Italian; a social gathering for intellectual and literary discussion.

coppice
Small trees and underbrush in a thicket, or small woods; often grown especially for cutting and selling.

copse
The underbrush of a wood or forest; more or less the same as **coppice**.

cordoroy [corduroy]
A thick, ribbed and bumpy cotton material. Thus, a corduroy road:

made by laying tree trunks tightly together widthwise across swampy areas of a roadway.

cosmorama
A device that shows scenes from all over the world, or cosmos. A slightly different view of the same object or scene is pictured on either side of a cardboard slide; held to both eyes, it creates a three-dimensional effect.

crackers
Firecrackers, or fireworks.

crown piece
A British coin worth five shillings; originally gold, later silver.

cubs
An out-of-use form of "coops" or pigeon houses.

curacy
The job of or responsibilities involved in being a **curate**.

curate
The assistant to the parish priest or rector; Mr. Hallen was officially only second-in-command in the parish of Rushock, Worcestershire, but his **rector** worked nearby and gave Mr. Hallen full responsibility at Rushock.

cut
A slash with a whip to urge a horse onward; also, to deliberately ignore or refuse to recognize an acquaintance.

cutter
Like a sleigh; a vehicle with curved runners instead of wheels, pulled by horses over the snow; also a small, single-masted vessel like a yacht.

cutting some teeth
Getting first teeth during babyhood — the new sharp edges "cut" through the gums.

delf
china dishes, particularly the blue-painted kind made in Delft, Holland.

denominations
Subgroups of a particular religion; Methodists, Anglicans and Presbyterians are all (Protestant) Christians.

descry
To see or catch sight of.

diabolical
Cruel.

dicky
A built-in seat for the driver (sometimes a dicky-box) at the front of a horse-drawn carriage, or for the servant or guard at the back.

dinner
Chief meal of the day; in the Hallens' time, eaten in the early afternoon.

divinity
Theology, or the science of religion, especially of Christianity.

doughty
Valiant or formidable; sometimes also means stout. Eleanora is simply being sarcastic about Mr. Drinkwater!

draggate [druggate or drugget]
A coarse woolen material used for floor coverings, table cloths, etc.

e
A shortened form of the Latin word *et*; Sarah's abbreviation for "and."

eat [et/ate]
The past tense of the verb to eat, pronounced "et."

eau paulettes [epaulettes]
Ornamental shoulder-pieces on a uniform, usually only worn by officers in the armed forces; from the French word for shoulder.

Wings are a kind of epaulette which stand out from the seams at the top of the shoulder.

emetic
Any substance that causes vomiting; used as medicine.

emigrant
Someone who leaves his or her own country to settle in another.

emigrate
To leave your own country and settle in another; the Hallens emigrated from England to Canada.

engraving
Cutting lines in wood or metal plates for printing.

episcopal
Literally, governed by bishops; the Episcopal Church in the United States is a denomination whose teachings and organization resemble the Church of England, the parent body to the Anglican Church in Canada.

espied
Past tense of espy, an old-fashioned version of today's spy; to catch sight of, as in "I spy with my little eye . . . "

et cetera
Latin for "and so forth"; see **&c.** and **e** above.

exercising
Soldiers going through their daily, formal military drill or athletic routine; Eleanora's use of this word is narrower than its general meaning.

familiar
In this lesser-known sense, "familiar" implies over-free, too intimate, impolite, or disrespectful of someone's higher standing on the social scale; if the Hallens considered themselves socially superior to the Willsons, this is another example of the Hallens' consciousness of social class.

fix on
To decide on, choose or select.

fly
A covered carriage drawn by one horse, usually for hire like a taxi. With readers of the future in mind, Mr. Hallen actually explains a fly on the opening page of his journal as ". . . a kind of small coach capable of holding four persons and drawn by one horse . . . " (Jan. 22, 1835).

folio
The largest size in the way printed material was measured in the nineteenth century and before; usually any book more than 11 inches (about 24 cm) in height.

forms
Long seats without backs, similar to benches.

fowl
Any large birds raised for meat and eggs, such as chickens, geese or turkeys.

frame house
A house made of boards over a wooden frame; more "civilized" than a log cabin, which was simply walls and a roof.

frock
A gown or dress; the word is dated and not often used today.

Gaelic
A language of the Gaels, a people largely from the Scottish Highlands; a Celtic language related to Welsh.

generation
A period of about thirty years; a step in the history of a family. Your parents are the generation before you.

gig
A two-wheeled carriage pulled by one horse; in contrast to a fly, a gig was open and lightweight.

Good Friday
The Friday before Easter, observed by Christians in solemn remembrance of the crucifixion of Jesus Christ.

grampus
Several different types of large dolphin or small whale, all of which blow (spout) and are blunt-headed.

gruel
Like porridge, but thinner, almost liquid; made by boiling oatmeal or barley in water or milk; a food often given to sick people, or to the very young or old.

Guy Fawkes
A Catholic who was hanged in 1605 for his role in an unsuccessful attempt to blow up the (Protestant) British parliament (part of the religious struggles of the period). The custom developed of burning a dummy "Guy" on November 5th each year.

haunch (of venison)
Cut of meat consisting of the leg and loin (from the ribs to the hip) of a deer or other large animal.

heartsease
Wild pansy flowers.

hoisted colours
Raised the coloured signal flags which identify the place of origin, owners, etc., of a ship. In the pictures of the *Albion*, the flag with the "H" on it indicates her owners, the Hammonds of New Brunswick.

homely
Plain, either in manner (unpretentious, "home-like") or looks (not very good-looking).

hooping [whooping] cough
A very infectious childhood disease characterized by uncontrollable fits of coughing followed by loud gasping (for breath).

hurse [hearse]
A special funeral carriage (or car, today) to carry a body in its coffin from the place where the funeral service is held to the graveyard for burial.

i.e.
Abbreviation for a Latin term, *id est*, meaning "that is"; in other words.

imbellishment [embellishment]
A decoration or an ornament.

immigrant
Someone who has come into a country to live; the Hallens were immigrants *in* Upper Canada who had emigrated *from* England.

impertinant [impertinent]
Saucy, cheeky or rude in general; in particular, children who talked back to their elders were thought impertinent.

Industrial Revolution
The major social change which took place in England from approximately 1750 to 1850, as new technology created new industries. As the economy changed from agricultural to industrial, thousands of labourers moved from the countryside into rapidly growing cities.

infilicum me [*infelicem me*]
From Latin, related to the word *felix*, "happy"; Eleanora's phrase "Oh infelicem me" means "O, wretch that I am!" — or "Oh, how unlucky!"

inflamation [inflammation]
Generally, a diseased, painful condition of some part of the body, sometimes marked by redness or swelling; that it was "on her lung" probably means Edith's chest was very congested, and breathing difficult. Perhaps she had pneumonia.

islands of ice
Icebergs.

kid
The fine, soft leather made from the skin of young goats ("kids"); used for gloves and shoes.

lancers
Soldiers armed with lances, long wooden spears with sharp iron or steel points.

larboard
Facing front, the left side of a ship; because the word sounds so similar to "starboard" (right) it has been replaced with the term "port" today.

lear [leer]
To give a sly, sidelong look or an evil glance at someone.

lunar caustic
Silver nitrate; used to help heal minor cuts.

lunch
In Eleanora's day, a light meal eaten at any time; a snack.

mantila [mantilla]
A short, loose cape.

marry
An expression of surprise or indignation.

mason
A man who cuts or builds with stone and brick; stonemason.

MDCCCXXXV
"1835" in Roman numerals; M = 1000, D = 500, C = 100, X = 10 and V = 5.

medical man
Eleanora's phrase for the family doctor, although he may not have been as thoroughly trained as today's M.D.; medical means having to do with healing or the science and art of medicine.

merchantman
A ship used in commerce and trade; Eleanora labelling the *Albion* a merchantman tells us that this ship's primary business was the cargo it carried from America to Britain for sale. Emigrants made the return trip profitable as well.

mizzen mast
The mast next behind the main mast on a sailing ship, or the third mast back on a three-masted ship.

mokuk
An Ojibwa word for a birchbark container made for storing maple sugar.

muslin
Cotton cloth in a plain weave, available in a variety of weights; book muslin was one of the most delicate varieties, gauzy and stiff, almost always used for girls, rather than women. A white dress of book muslin, with a wide coloured sash, was typical party wear in Eleanora's time.

mustles [mussels]
Shellfish like small clams, with dark-coloured, hinged shells; can be found in fresh and salt water.

mutiny
An open revolt against established authority; used especially to refer to sailors or soldiers resisting their officers.

nosegay
A little bunch of sweet-scented flowers to hold under your nose and enjoy.

nurse
To hold (a baby) close and give comfort; to care for or try to cure someone who is sick.

oat rick
A stack of oat straw, similar to a haystack, especially one made so that the rain will run off it instead of soaking in.

ordinance survey
A ordinance is a public rule, such as a city or county might make — in this case, a public decree was made to survey the land, measuring boundaries, positions of rivers, roads and buildings, contours, etc. to produce standard maps for public use.

packet
A ship that transported mail, goods and passengers on a fixed route and schedule.

palisadoes [palisades]
Fences made of pales (pointed wooden stakes) or of iron railings.

parish
In Britain, a civil district, or part of a county that has its own church and clergyman.

parishioners
The people who live in a parish, or the members of the congregation of a particular church.

parlour
A sitting room or living room, often the "best" room, used for receiving and entertaining guests.

paticas [hepaticas]
Any of a group of closely related small plants in the buttercup family.

petition
A formal request for some privilege, right or benefit, made to a superior or to someone in authority. The Hallen children writing a petition to their father about not going to church is an unusual, but perfectly correct, example!

petrifications
Objects that have been turned into stone, or petrified. Eleanora may have meant either fossils or pieces of petrified wood, or both.

philosophic
Wise, patient and calm, like a philosopher, especially in the face of trouble.

pinafore, pinbefore
Something to "pin in front of"; a garment like a full apron worn over other clothes to protect them, particularly by women and children.

plaited
Braided; three or more strands of hair, ribbon, straw, etc. are interlaced to make a plait or braid.

plate
Dishes or cutlery covered ("plated") with a thin layer of silver or gold.

playing at romping
Roughhousing; chasing or wrestling; physical play.

plumes
Feathers, especially large ornamental ones.

poaching
Trespassing; in the sense that Eleanora uses this word, Mrs. Parry is simply being too nosy, and investigating the Hallen's home and family in an invasive way.

pool
In card games, all the players' fines and bets collected together. Also, a

small body of still water; a pond.

poop
The stern, or back, of a ship; the aftermost and highest deck, above the ordinary deck and often forming the roof of the best cabin.

Prison Bars
A complex, fast-moving outdoor game involving two teams and four bases; sometimes known as "Prisoners' Base."

proceshion [procession]
Parade of people, especially on religious, festive or important occasions — such as the funerals and wedding Eleanora describes.

prolific
Producing a lot; for example, a writer who publishes many books.

purgative
Any substance that causes excessive urination and/or diarrhea.

quadrille
A dance for four couples standing in a quadrant, or square formation. Today's square dances are derived from the quadrille.

quarantine
A period of isolation imposed on sick people to protect others from infection, or on travellers to prevent the spread of any disease they might carry.

radicals
Generally, people who favour extreme changes or reforms, especially in politics. Specifically, Eleanora is referring to those who opposed the government in Upper Canada in 1837 and its leader, Lieutenant Governor Sir Francis Bond Head; a violent opposition that lead to what is known today as the Rebellion of 1837 or the Mackenzie Rebellion.

rector
In the Church of England or the Anglican Church of Canada, a rector is a **clergyman** in charge of a parish; in the Catholic Church the rector is the priest in charge of a religious house.

rectory
The rector's house.

regiment
A unit of soldiers, larger than a battalion and smaller than a brigade; usually consists of several companies of soldiers commanded by a colonel.

regimentals
Military uniform.

rigging
The ropes, chains and other equipment used to support the masts and sails on a ship.

rod
A stick used to beat or punish someone.

roman candle
A kind of fireworks, made of a tube that shoots out successive balls of fire etc.

routed out
Dug or searched out; found.

rusticity
Having to do with country life; a state of being unsophisticated, unpolished, a little rude or rough.

sacrament
The holy bread and wine used in the Christian ceremony of Communion; or, a holy ceremony.

saddles or sandals
On low shoes, fastening straps that pass over the instep or around the ankle.

sallied out
Went out, set out briskly; went on an excursion.

salt meat
Any meat that has been cured or preserved in salt, whether pork, beef or fish.

schooner-rigged sails
Triangular sails, fastened (or rigged) from front to back, rather than square sails attached on crosspieces to the main masts; also called fore-and-aft-rigged sails.

schooner
Fore-and-aft-rigged ship with two or more masts.

senna tea
A laxative tea made from the dried leaves of several cassia-family plants; a **purgative**.

serpents
Fireworks shaped like small cones, which, when lit at the tip, burn slowly, producing a long, coiling, snake-like ash formation.

settled
Finished, disposed of, got rid of; spilled, in the case of Eleanora's "nice cup of tea."

shanty
A roughly built log hut or cabin, usually with the roof slanting in just one direction rather than peaked and two-sided.

shoots
New growth of a plant; buds, roots and small stems.

siblings
Children of the same parents, both brothers and sisters.

sight trees
A "sight" is a device on a surveying instrument, used in the same way a sight on a gun helps you take aim; these sight trees must have been trees in positions that were useful in land surveys, and so were marked accordingly.

sill
A horizontal piece or wood or block of stone that forms the bottom of a door frame; a main-entryway sill might be a stone big enough to form the top step, as well.

skib [squib]
A firecracker; firework thrown by hand that explodes with a bang or burns with a hissing sound.

sleighing time
Wintertime; snow makes roads smoother and freezes lakes and streams, which makes for easy passage in sleighs.

sloop
A sailboat with one mast, generally rigged fore-and-aft, like a **schooner**.

slops
Dirty water or other liquid; the waste from kitchen or bedroom containers.

speak a vessel
To speak or exchange information with another ship.

speaking trumpet
An old-fashioned megaphone; ships' captains used speaking trumpets to make their voices carry over the distance between them and a vessel they were "speaking."

stalking
Taking the stalks or stems off something; in this case, currants, berries about the size of blueberries.

stalwart
A loyal supporter who is strong, brave or steadfast.

stays
A corset; a close-fitting women's

undergarment worn to shape and support the torso. A stay (singular) is one of the many thin flat strips of bone — frequently whalebone, in Eleanora's time — used to stiffen a corset.

stone
A unit of measurement, still common in Britain, equal to 14 pounds (a little more than 6 kg).

stearidge [steerage]
The part of a ship occupied by passengers travelling at the cheapest rate, usually in the bow (front) and below deck.

steerage class
The cheapest accomodation in shipboard travel.

subscribe
To support or contribute to a group purpose; the young men of Baker's Falls had each a contributed a sum of money to the cost of a community swing.

swatches
Samples cut off a whole.

tabered
It seems Eleanora made up this word to describe the sound of rain on their cabin roof. There is a kind of drum called a tambour — perhaps that is what she was thinking of.

tablet
A small slab of stone (or ivory or wood) especially meant to be written on, or inscribed.

tack
Food or fare, especially bread; foodstuff not very highly thought of. Hardtack was a food more endured than enjoyed.

tea
In Britain, the meal taken in the late afternoon or early evening, at which tea is commonly served.

terra firma
Latin for "solid ground."

tippet
A cape or muffler, sometimes of fur, coming down some distance in front; worn by women and girls.

tipsy
Somewhat intoxicated, but not thoroughly drunk.

toddy
A brewed drink, usually hot, made of whiskey or other alcoholic liquor mixed with sugar, spices, and water.

toll
To sound a bell with slow, single strokes.

transcribe
To decipher and copy, by hand or keyboard. Mrs. Drinkwater transcribed by hand, and then someone else transcribed her writing into type with a typewriter. The second 1835 journal, plus many of Eleanora's Canadian journals, were transcribed directly onto a computer.

transcripts, transcriptions
The result of **transcribing**; written or typed copies.

traverse
To pass or to travel across, over or through something.

tuberculosis
An infectious disease affecting humans and some other mammals. Small hard lumps, caused by the "tubercle bacillius," form in body tissues, usually the lungs.

turned (bonnets)
Reversed the material from which something was made, so that it looked fresher or newer.

turnpike gate
The gate at which a toll (a small amount of money) is paid for the use of the road (called a turnpike).

underbrushing
Taking out the underbrush, or young trees and bushes that grow under large trees in a forest; getting ready by making room to cut down the larger trees.

unpalittable [unpalatable]
Unpleasant, not nice to the taste, disagreeable to eat.

vault
A place for burial, often underground, with an arched roof; the Hallen vault was underneath the pulpit area inside Rushock church.

vignettes
Decorative designs or small drawings.

virando [veranda or verandah]
A large covered porch along one or more sides of a building.

waiter
A small tray used to serve someone something ("wait" on someone).

weighed anchor
Lifted up the anchor, so as to be free to sail off.

whiskey tody [toddy]
A **toddy** made with whiskey.

whist
A card game similar to bridge, for two pairs of players; said to have been so named because the players demanded "whist!" ("silence!") so that they could concentrate on the game.

whitewash
To whiten walls or woodwork with a kind of paint made of lime mixed in water.

wild beasts show
From Eleanora's description, this was a combination travelling zoo and circus.

Credits

Back cover: Portraits probably by Elizabeth Watkins, c. 1820 (George Hallen born 1794). Wayside inn scene and children dancing a quadrille, unsigned, from a Hallen sketchbook dated 1833.

Front cover: Photo by Susan Ashukian.

Model: Amy Sedgwick. Costume courtesy Black Creek Pioneer Village.

Title page: Photo by Paul Heersink.

2, 36, 47, 86, 106, 107, 179, 193, 194: Photos by Caroline Parry.

4, 23, 39, 53, 64, 90, 125, 140, 150, 153, 159, 166, 178, 181, 182, 184: Courtesy Norah Bastedo.

9: English country cottage, c. 1833 by Eleanora Hallen; courtesy Norah Bastedo.

11: Material by Mary Hallen, used throughout, is taken from her journal covers, 1834, and are courtesy David Bohme.

12: Doodles and small sketches throughout are by Eleanora Hallen, unless otherwise noted. For use of her journals, from which the doodles were taken, we thank Norah Bastedo and David Bohme.

14: Courtesy the McCord Museum of Canadian History, Montreal.

17 (toyshop), 28 (cuckoo), 61, 74, 97: Courtesy The Osborne Collection of Early Children's Books, Toronto Public Library.

17 (cosmorama), 156: Courtesy the Museum of Science and Technology, Ottawa.

20: Photo courtesy Dorothy Yardley.

22: The truth about the "Latin" poem with thanks to Philip Martin.

28, 63, 180: Courtesy Gary French.

37: Ships on Georgian Bay by Eleanora Hallen; courtesy Norah Bastedo.

41: Ordinance survey from Her Majesty's Stationery Office, England.

42: M. Hussingtree church and Watkins painting courtesy Katherine Drinkwater.

45, 170, 171: Courtesy the National Library of Canada.

50: "Planting and digging" from *Mrs. Hurst Dancing and More Scenes of Regency Life 1818-1823* reproduced with permission of the publisher, Victor Gollancz, London, England.

51: "Regimentals" with thanks to Chester Gryski.

52: Photo courtesy the Canadian Museum of Health and Medicine; with thanks to Peter Honour.

54: From *Gleanings from the "Graphic"*, (London, etc.; George Routledge & Sons) 1889; courtesy The Osborne Collection of Early Children's Books, Toronto Public Library.

62: Pigeon house sketch by Mary Hallen.

65: Church interior by Yüksel Hassan.

66: *Albion* advertisement courtesy Liverpool Public Library.

68, 168: Parish register excerpts courtesy the Archives, Diocese of Toronto, the Anglican Church of Canada.

71: Portrait by Thomas Dove: oil on canvas, 102.0 X 71.0 cm; #986.10; courtesy the New Brunswick Museum. Unsigned portrait: 82.0 X 61.5 cm; #985.19; courtesy the New Bunswick Museum; purchased with a grant approved by the Minister of Communications under the terms of the Cultural Export and Import Act.

73: Information regarding Marryat and Marryat's Universal Code with thanks to Mystic Seaport.

75: Man in rigging from the Mansell Collection, London.

78: Sailor by C.J.B. Ellice; courtesy the National Archives of Canada (C13374). Hoisting anchor vignette with thanks to Chester Gryski.

81: "Sentry, will there be a sunrise?" by C.J.B. Ellice; courtesy the National Archives of Canada (C13376). "Tina in her cot" by C.J.B. Ellice; courtesy the National Archives of Canada (C13379).

82, 92, 109, 117: Maps drawn by Paul Heersink.

82: Statistics from *External Migration*, Carrier and Geoffry, 1953.

83: "New York From Brooklyn Heights" after a work by J.W. Hill; "South Street From Maiden Lane" from *Megarey's Street Views of New-York*, c. 1834; courtesy The New York Public Library.

84: "Broadway from the Park" from *Views in New-York and Its Environs...* [The Peabody Views], 1831-34; courtesy The New York Public Library.

85: "Hudson River from Hoboken" from *Views in New-York and Its Environs...* [The Peabody Views], 1831-34; courtesy The New York Public Library.

86: "Table d'hote" by C.J.B. Ellice; courtesy the National Archives of Canada (C13388). Mansion House from *Troy's One Hundred Years* by A.J. Weise. Used with permission of the reprint publisher, Higgins Book Company (Salem, Mass.). St. Paul's Church from *Troy and Vicinity* by A.J. Weise, 1886; courtesy the Rensselaer Historical Society.

92: New York statistics from *History of Immigration to the United States*, W.J. Bromwell (Arno Press/The New York Times) 1961.

94: "Broadway, New York" by C.J.B. Ellice; courtesy the National Archives of Canada (C013389).

95: Harriet Pettit House and George Weston portraits from *History of Washington County, New York*, 1878; courtesy Washington County Historical Society.

95 (map), 98 (McCrea tree), 102: Courtesy the James R. Cronkhite Collection of the Fort Edward Historical Society, New York.

97: Dame School pictures with thanks to Chester Gryski.

98: English robin from an EH journal cover. American robin courtesy Chester Gryski.

99, 121 ("skipping"): Reprinted from *Girl's Own Book* by Lydia Maria Child (Applewood Books, Bedford, MA).

100: Remedies from *Death in Early America* by Margaret M. Coffin (Thomas Nelson Inc., NY) 1926.

103: Circus courtesy Black Creek Pioneer Village Printing Shop.

104: Advertisement courtesy Ringling Bros/Barnum and Bailey Circus World Museum, Baraboo, Wisconsin.

107: Saratoga Springs pictures reproduced from *Gleason's Pictorial Drawing Room Companion*, 1852; courtesy the Metropolitan Toronto Reference Library.

108: Low bridge picture from *Marco Paul's Travels on the Erie Canal* by John Abbott, 1840. Boats passing illustration courtesy the Erie Canal Boat Museum, Syracuse, NY.

111, 113, 115 *(Peter Robinson)*, 118, 162: Courtesy Metropolitan Toronto Reference Library.

112: St. George advertisement from *Chronicle & Gazette and Kingston Commercial Advertiser*, July 1, 1836; courtesy the National Library of Canada. "Enigmas" and the "'Tis in the..." riddle from *The Girl's Book of Diversions*, 1835; courtesy The Osborne Collection of Early Children's Books, Toronto Public Library.

114: Distances table from the F.A. Mackenzie Fraser manuscripts; courtesy the Metropolitan Toronto Reference Library. Stagecoach from *Pioneers of Old Ontario*, William L. Smith (George N. Morong, Toronto) 1923.

115: "Ladies' Cabin" by C.J.B. Ellice; courtesy the National Archives of Canada (C13390).

116: Trinity Church from The Livingstone Album, courtesy the Simcoe County Archives. "The Woods" courtesy the Archives of Ontario, MU 868, "O'Brien Journal", 1828-1838, in F 592, Mary S. O'Brien Papers.

119: Cassin-Haugh House courtesy the Ontario Agricultural Museum.

121: "A bush road, Upper Canada" by P.J. Bainbrigge; courtesy the National Archives of Canada (C11818).

123: Roots vignette with thanks to Chester Gryski.

129: Snowstorm painting by Mary Hallen; courtesy Gary French.

133, 186-190: Courtesy Simcoe County Archives.

143: "Gentleman on their travels on the Lake Simcoe" by H.B. Martin; courtesy the National Archives of Canada (C113035).

162: "Corduroy Road over a swamp in Orillia Township, Upper Canada" by T.H. Ware; courtesy the Metropolitan Toronto Reference Library.

163: "The Backwoodsman" courtesy the Committee for the Preservation of the Anne Langton Collection, Fenelon Falls.

172: "Rushock, 1838" line-enhanced by Russ Hewetson, from the original owned by Gary French.

175: "The Hallen home, 1880" by Mary Hallen Gilmour; courtesy the Huronia Museum Collection.

183: Courtesy David Bohmy.

192: Portion ot marine map reproduced with the permission of the Canadian Hydrographic Service.

193: Portrait by Edward John Russell: charcoal, 33.0 X 46.0 cm; #989.72.2; courtesy the New Bunswick Museum.

194: St. George's Fairvalley courtesy Mildred Walker and the Medonte Historical Society.

Born in Philadelphia, Caroline Parry moved to Canada in 1973 and has since become fascinated by the rich history of Eleanora territory. A singer, performer, writer and teacher by trade, Ms Parry has travelled almost the world over, experiencing folklore first hand. She credits her love of books and folktales to her kindergarten teacher — who happened also to be her grandmother. Ms Parry lives in Ottawa, Ontario with her husband, two grown children, a cat and a dog. Her first book, *Let's Celebrate!* (Kids Can Press) was the winner of the Children's Literature Roundtable of Canada 1988 Information Book Award.